P9-DII-664

Also by Joe Shine

I Become Shadow

bobby sky
BOY BAND OR DIE

JOE SHINE

This is a work of fiction. Names, characters, places, and incidents either are the product of the author's imagination or are used fictitiously, and any resemblance to actual persons, living or dead, businesses, companies, events or locales is entirely coincidental.

Published in the United States by Soho Teen
an imprint of
Soho Press, Inc.
853 Broadway
New York, NY 10003

Library of Congress Cataloging-in-Publication Data

Shine, Joe, 1980–
Bobby Sky : boy band or die / Joe Shine.

ISBN 978-1-61695-841-1
eISBN 978-1-61695-842-8

1. Bodyguards—Fiction. 2. Adventure and adventurers—Fiction.
3. Singers—Fiction. 4. Bands (Music)—Fiction. 5. Popular music—Fiction.
PZ7.S55683 Boy 2018 DDC [Fic]—dc23 2017034703

Interior design by Janine Agro, Soho Press, Inc.

Printed in the United States of America

10 9 8 7 6 5 4 3 2 1

To Lincoln and Kit. My very own FIPs.

bobby sky

BOY BAND OR DIE

"Jingle bells,
Jingle bells,
Jingle all the way . . ."

Oh, I get how weird it is to be quietly singing Christmas songs to myself right now. Believe you me, I do. But I dare you, no, I challenge you to think about Christmas and not have a carol or seven pop into your head. It's impossible. Christmas songs are like potato chips—you're gonna need more than one.

"—in a one-horse open sleigh . . . HEY!"

Funny thing is, it's not even the holidays right now. I had a random thought about what Christmas might be like here, and the dang things popped into my head. That's how powerful those songs are. Right now it's April, I think, and I'm straitjacketed up in a padded room, pretending to be crazy. Bonus, though, quietly singing carols to myself only adds to this stellar performance. There should be Oscars for acting in real life. I would totally be nominated for this.

Why am I pretending to be crazy? Why am I so nonchalant about being locked up against my will? Why am I laughing inside through daily beatings? Why am I not at all worried that I haven't had anything to eat or drink in days and am slowly dying? It's because I did it; I fulfilled the sole purpose of my life. Death? Cool with me.

It's okay if my story ends here—heck, maybe it's supposed to. It has been a ride, I'll give you that. I was betrayed, heartbroken, shot, stabbed, and run over. And that was just during my first year in the program. That's not even the good stuff. How do plane crashes, death squads, car chases, and the Yakuza sound? Are you interested? If not, you need to seriously reevaluate what you're looking for in your entertainment needs, because that stuff should raise the eyebrow of a hairless cat. It's a pretty long story and, if I had to guess, it'll take a good . . . I don't know, ten hours or so to tell? I'm not going anywhere, obviously. You got the spare time? Fair enough. Let's do this.

I guess we could start with the first time I heard "Jingle Bells," since that would sort of bring this rambling introduction full circle. But I have no idea when that was. I was four, maybe? Who knows? Doesn't matter. No, we'll start with the last time I was arrested, which, ironically, *was* during the holiday. (Take that, random "Jingle Bells" intro!) I was barely fourteen. I thought it would be like every other time I'd been cuffed, booked, and sent off to juvie.

It wasn't. Oh boy, it wasn't.

So, are you ready for a trip down memory lane? Good, because singing to myself and drooling on the plastic mats in here gets old pretty quick. Speaking of which, I should probably let out a good stream of craziness. I can't let my captors realize I'm faking it. That would really screw everything up.

"JINGLE BELLS! JINGLE BELLS! JINGLE BELLS! JINGLE BELLS!"

Okay, that should buy us some time. I don't think I'm due for any more torture sessions for a while.

chapter 2

TIME TO PAY THE FIDDLER

"Just open up, okay?"

The voice was friendly but commanding. A cop's voice usually is. At least the cops I knew. This particular voice belonged to Officer Willis.

I'd put all my weight and strength into keeping the door shut. I was pretty big for a fourteen-year-old, already close to six feet. My muscles were getting thicker by the day, thanks to weights and the demands of Texas football. I knew I couldn't stop them from coming in, but doing nothing seemed like giving up, which I'd never been good at. Like my dad always said: "Give it all you got until you can't give anymore, and then try again to make sure you're really done." He'd drilled that into my head since birth.

"I'm not coming out," I yelled. My trademark shoulder-length hair had fallen over my eyes, so I shoved a greasy clump behind my ears.

"Open the damn door, Hutch."

A different voice, this time: Officer Ramirez. The other voice. They were a team.

I'd decided when I was five that "Bobby" was a stupid kid's name and "Robert" was an old man's name. I'd wanted no part of either. With my last name being Hutchinson, I had insisted on being called Hutch. It had stuck. One of the few victories in my life.

"Never!" I yelled back playfully, but totally serious, too. Opening the door wasn't going to happen. They'd have to kick it in. Keeping my shoulder pressed hard into the door, I took a look through the peephole. No surprise, Officers Willis and Ramirez were smirking at each other. They shook their heads, as if they had better things to do than hang out on the rotting deck outside the small apartment I shared with my mother. I agreed that they probably did. The home, if you can even call it that, sat above the landlord's garage, and this door was the only way in or out.

The two officers had been dealing with me off and on since I was a little kid. It was mostly petty crimes, fights, that sort of thing. So we all knew each other pretty well. They were pretty relaxed.

"You got nothing on me," I yelled, still watching.

Officer Ramirez pulled out a notepad. "Grand theft auto."

"The keys were in the car and I brought it back when I was done. If anything, that's just Grand Borrowing. Oh, and ungrateful, I changed the oil for them."

The officers shared a grin. They were on one side of the game, and I was on the other. We both enjoyed playing it to its fullest.

"Armed robbery."

I smiled and joked, "Can you be more specific?"

"Russ's Convenience Store."

"That? Come on. He wouldn't sell me beer."

"'Cause you're only fourteen."

"I'm almost fifteen!" I corrected them. "But anyway I paid for it, so it's not robbery."

"You were brandishing a weapon."

"That's just armed shopping, then. I never pointed it at

him. He just assumed I was going to. I have the right to bear arms. Are you trying to deny me my constitutional rights?"

Still keeping my weight up against the door, I kept watching through the peephole as the officers exchanged a glance. Officer Willis nodded to Ramirez.

"Aggravated assault."

I paused. I didn't have a smart-ass answer to that one. "He was hitting his four-year-old with a baseball bat. I took it and hit him back with it . . ."

"Not saying we disagree, but it's not your place, Hutch, you know that. You nearly killed the guy. It's time to man up. Now, open the door."

I liked Officers Willis and Ramirez. They were actually pretty cool guys. None of it was personal and they tried to help me out of jams when they could. You couldn't call them friends—they were the fuzz—but they were nice to me when they could be. I put my back to the door again.

From the stereo I could hear the faint singing of Christmas music. My mother was a nutter for holiday tunes. She'd bought one of those Monster Christmas Song Collections you see on the infomercials at two in the morning. I knew every carol and song upward and backward. Publicly I'd say I hated them all, but privately I loved 'em. Who doesn't, really? It gave me an idea. We all knew how this ended, but they were gonna have to earn it and I was gonna have some fun with them while they did.

"Guys, come on. This isn't very festive of you. It's the holidays," I called out.

"It's December first," Officer Willis responded.

"Our lights are up."

"Your lights haven't been taken down in years, Hutch."

"December's the holidays!" I sorta yelled, before calming down and adding, "Which is why I have a proposal."

"Hutch, we don't have time for this," Officer Ramirez groaned.

"Hear me out and yes, you do. You join me in a festive carol and I'll come out."

I waited for a response, but when I didn't get one, I decided to go for it and began to sing:

"Deck the halls with bells of holly . . ."

I waited for them to join in. Seriously, who can resist a *falala-la-la-la-la-la-laaaaa!* People will run in from the street to yell that one out. Apparently these coppers were the minority since I got nada. I tried again.

"Deck the halls with bells of holly . . ."

I waited again for them to join in but still got only crickets. I was about to try a third time when I heard . . .

"Falala-la-la-la-la-la-laaaaa!"

I peeked out the peephole and saw Officer Ramirez shaking his head at Officer Willis, who shrugged.

"Yeah!" I couldn't help but yell out. "Willie-boy's a bass. Didn't see that coming. Not bad, man. Okay, okay. You ready? Ram-Jam, you gotta join in, too. That's the deal. Come on." I cleared my throat before going on: *"'Tis the season to be jolly . . ."*

"Falala-la-la-la-la-la-laaaaa!" they both sang out loudly and then together . . .

"Don we now our gay apparel,
Falala-lalala-la-la-laaa,
Troll the ancient Yuletide carol,
Fa la la la laaaaaaaa la la . . . la . . . laaaaaaaaaaaa."

I peeked through the hole and saw them both smiling.

"That's the spirit, boys!" I yelled.

"You do realize it's 'boughs of holly' not 'bells of holly,' right?" Officer Ramirez called out.

Best to end this Christmas sing-along.

I bolted toward the living room window.

I was halfway out when Officer Willis's size twelves kicked the door open. I smiled and gave them a mocking "Merry Christmas, boys," before swinging my other leg over and going into free fall, then landing in the thick shrubs one story below. It hurt, but I'd done it before. I rolled out and sprinted across the yard.

They'd never be able to catch me in a footrace. I was younger, in better shape, and this was my home, so I knew every back alley and shortcut for blocks in every direction. I would lose them easily. I hopped over my back fence into the neighbor's yard, jetted out to their front yard, and crossed the street toward the next house. I kept on cutting through lawns and hopping over fences as I went. A few streets away a massive, eight-foot wooden fence was staring me down, separating whatever house I was currently in the backyard of from the next. I scaled it easily, but only when I reached the top did I see the row of rosebushes on the other side. I tried to stop, but my momentum was too much and I fell headfirst into them.

I popped up out of the shrubs, my entire body cut and stinging from the nasty thorns. A shocked housewife stared openmouthed ten feet away with her pruning shears.

"Ma'am," I said as I pulled a thorn out of my forehead. I ran across her backyard and out onto the front lawn. There were some sirens in the distance, but everything around here looked quiet. I stopped running, covered my face with my hair, and casually started to cross the street to the train tracks like any normal guy out for a walk. The plan was to get on the tracks and use them to avoid the roads for a bit.

I'd made it halfway down a back alley when the jarring, terrified shriek of a child stopped me dead in my tracks.

"Jesse! No! Help!" the voice screamed out.

I didn't have time for this. I tried to convince myself it was nothing. This lull in the chase wouldn't last much longer, so I had to keep going. Kids screamed all the time about stupid stuff, right? I didn't need to worry about it. Or it was a crazy person who sounded like a kid; this area was full of them. Yeah, that's all it was. I began to step forward when . . .

"Help! Help! Someone help!" the kid screamed again. The panic sounded genuine.

Something bad had happened.

I growled in frustration. Hating myself, I turned and sprinted toward the cries. A small girl appeared out of a backyard and flagged me down.

"Is everything okay?" I asked her.

"It's Jesse. He's hurt real bad!" She turned and ran back into her backyard.

I knew I shouldn't do this. But I followed her into the backyard, where she fell to her knees in front of a flower bed and started sobbing, "No, no, no."

Once I slid to the ground next to her, I saw her clutching a small dead frog in her tiny hands. *You kidding me?*

"I . . . I stepped on him," she admitted. "I think he's . . . hurt," she said, sniffling.

Hurt? Oh, he's dead, kiddo. I was ready to get up and walk away when she held the sad, limp body of the little frog up to me and stuttered out, "Can you p-p-please help?"

Ugh, why did she have to be so damn adorable?

"Um, uh, yeah, let me see," I said, reaching out for the frog and taking it from her. What the heck was I supposed to do with this slimy thing? "You know, uh, let me take it to my, uh . . . vet friend, yeah, and I'll see what he can do."

Through her tears the girl suddenly had a sliver of hope and asked, "Really?"

"Yeah, he saves frogs all the time," I lied. "I'm sure he'll be able to save little Jesse here."

"You think?"

"Yeah, totally. But you might not see Jesse again," I added as I got an idea.

"Why not?"

"Well, my vet friend, you see, lives in a swamp and Jesse may want to stay there 'cause it's awesome. It'll be up to him, and I'll bet he'll want to stay and play around with all the other frogs that live there. You do want him to be happy, right?"

She nodded. The squawk of a patrol car in the distance brought me back to the reality at hand.

"Okay, well, I gotta get Jesse here to the vet now before it's too late, okay?"

"Okay. Goodbye, Jesse, enjoy the swamp," she called out to me as I walked away.

ONCE I'D DITCHED THE dead frog, I headed to Zilker Park, my go-to hideout from the po-po, which was only a mile or so away. I would wait there until a plan emerged, take a dip in Barton Creek, maybe . . .

My phone rang.

Mom.

I ignored it. I was supposed to be in school and answering your phone there was a big no-no. If I answered, she'd know I wasn't there. The call was immediately followed up by a text that simply read: Know you're not in school. Call me NOW!

Crap.

"Hey, Ma, what's up?" I said, whispering like I was in class.

"Where are you?" she asked flatly.

So she knew I wasn't in school, didn't she? Or was this a test? You never know with parents.

"School," I lied.

"School," she repeated coldly.

"Yep. Fillin' my head with some book learnin'," I added lightly. "Math is awesome."

"Come home, right now." The line went dead.

I most definitely didn't want to do that. In fact, it was so far down my list of things to do you could say it wasn't even on the list. I wanted to run and hide, but disobey a direct command from Mom? I had fifty pounds and nearly a foot on her, but do I dare go against the supreme commander like that? I was stupid, yes. Reckless, of course. But I wasn't crazy. I had no choice. Home it was.

The walk home was awful. Nothing quite like knowingly walking toward impending doom. And the adrenaline had worn off long ago, so I felt miserable in the winter cold in only my T-shirt and jeans. When I rounded the corner onto my road and saw the police cruiser parked out in front of my house, I paused. For a moment I considered turning around, but where would I go? I mean, what was my long-term plan here, really? Be a hobo in Zilker Park? Yes, I was a bad kid on paper and played the part well. But that wasn't really me.

As I passed the neighbor's crumbling redbrick house, I could hear voices talking, voices I recognized. I felt sick with guilt. Waiting for me in the driveway, right next to the rickety wooden stairs that led up to our tiny apartment, was my mother. Officers Ramirez and Willis were there, too.

They stopped talking when they saw me. I tried to look as defeated as I felt. My mother teared up, shook her head, and went upstairs without so much as a hello.

"Mom?" I called after her. She didn't look back. Not once. It hurt, worse than I could have imagined. And had I known that was the last time I'd ever see her, I would have forced her to turn right around and race back to me, to hug me, to

itae,

Do these 2 math work sheets <u>with</u> London. Do not do them <u>for</u> her.

say something. That moment—and the look of my mother, wholly disappointed in her son—still haunts me to this day . . .

There I go, getting ahead of myself again. You'll understand soon enough.

Officer Ramirez held out a pair of handcuffs for me. "Nothing personal, Hutch."

"I know, Ram-Jam," I replied, holding out my hands without protest.

His face was grim. As soon as the cuffs were on, he steered me to the car. "Let's get this over with," he said.

AFTER BOOKING THEY BROUGHT me to the juvenile detention section of the building. It was an area I knew all too well. It was practically a second home. I reckon I'd spent more time in juvie than school at this point. I'd stayed silent the whole ride there and throughout the booking process—not to exercise my right to remain silent, but to keep my emotions in check. It sorta worked until now.

"You take care of yourself," Officer Willis told me once he dropped me off in my personal holding cell. He gave me a friendly nod before walking off.

I grunted in response.

A few minutes later, Officer Ramirez stopped in to check on me. I know he believed in me and had higher expectations of me than I did. He and Officer Willis commonly referred to me as the dumbest smart kid they knew. They'd tried to convince me that I could probably get a full academic ride to most colleges if I only applied myself.

It had never occurred to either of them that I didn't have the money to take SAT prep classes. I was out in the real world, where my experiences happened to be sharpening my skills as a baby criminal. A life of crime wasn't my first choice, but it was what this life seemed to have in store for me.

Hell, maybe I'd get to see my dad.

No doubt *he* was on the officers' minds, too. With me in here he was definitely on my mom's.

When I was eight, my dad had been sentenced to twenty years at the Huntsville State Pen for drug smuggling. It was a raw deal. A friend of his had been trying to pay off a loan my dad had given him for a car with two hundred pounds of pot instead of cash, when the cops showed up and busted both of them. My dad had been labeled a drug kingpin, and his arrest had been the cornerstone of a local sheriff's re-election. The shock and humiliation of it all had destroyed my mother. I'd had to grow up in a hurry after that and do what I could to help make ends meet. A long and winding road had led me here.

Now I was fully alone with my thoughts and wished my brain had a sleep mode. Depending on what they charged me with, I was looking at anything from a slap on the wrist to, who knows, years? I had managed to hold my emotions back and fight them off, but I finally lost the battle and teared up. I may have acted and seemed older, but I was still only fourteen.

Alone, I allowed myself to drop my guard and loosen my armor. I'd dreamed of getting out of this town, of making something for myself. Now I was trapped in a cage. I wish I could say it was a metaphor, but it wasn't, and I'm also not entirely sure what metaphor is.

So I sang.

"Deck my cell with bars so gnarly,
Falala-la-la-la-laaaaa,
It's my life, come join the party,
Falala-la-la-la-laaaaa . . ."

This sucks.

chapter 3
PEACE OUT

The judge I got had zero sense of humor, absolutely none, and sentenced me to nine months in juvie.

It would have been the longest stretch of time I'd ever seen. *Would* have seen.

A few weeks into my stay, while in Biology—yes, you still have to go to school in juvie—the clicking of heels coming down the hallway announced the arrival of an unknown guest.

"Do you have Robert Hutchinson back there?"

A woman was talking to the guard outside the classroom door. Her voice was crisp, authoritative. Hearing my name woke me up a bit. I had zoned out since the teacher had started talking about genetics. I didn't get it and I didn't understand how it would help me in life, given I wasn't going to be a scientist. Look at who you're talking to, dude. Do we look like the future-doctor types?

"Maybe," the guard responded. By the tone of his voice, I could tell she wasn't someone he knew. Yes, this was a prison, but this was *our* prison. We were sort of a dysfunctional family, in that we all distrusted outsiders.

"Bring him to interview room D, please," the woman replied.

There was a pause. Suddenly the officer stammered, "Oh, uh, yes, ma'am. Right away, ma'am. Room D."

Officer Limpy, overweight and limping, appeared at the door. Yeah, we called him Limpy because he had a bad hip. We were uncreative, terrible, horrible, no-good delinquents, remember? He didn't know we called him that, of course.

"Let's go, Hutch. On your feet," he commanded.

I stayed in my chair. "Who wants to see me?"

"On your feet, Hutch, let's go," Limpy ordered seriously.

I looked around the room. All eyes were on me. For the briefest of moments I thought about refusing to move, but all that would do was buy me a good manhandling. If I'd needed to up my cred, it would have been worth it. But I had plenty of cred here. The long-termers knew me and we were cool, and any fish looking to make a name for themselves took one look at my size and thought otherwise. No, if I cooperated, it might help me later on. This place ran on favors.

I got up and followed him out into the dull, gray hallway.

I knew it wasn't my mother. Was it my lawyer maybe? Seemed out of character for a court-appointed lawyer to come visit. They represent you, get the verdict, and move on. This was not my first rodeo; I knew the routine.

Then the panic hit. Oh no. They had found out about . . . no, no way. Never. But . . .

"Who wants to see me?" I tried asking as Limpy led me down the hallway.

"Does it matter?" Limpy responded.

"I think so. Am I in trouble?"

"You're here, aren't you?"

"Who wants to see me?" I repeated.

"No more questions."

"Come on, man, who—"

"Silence, inmate," Limpy said with menacing finality. He even went so far as to reach for his baton.

"Okay, chill out." I waited a few moments before saying, "You know, I've been working on a new one. Wanna hear it?"

A faint smile crossed his face. He rolled his eyes, and his hand dropped away from the baton. "Sure, kid."

"Still a little rough, work in progress, so, you know . . . Okay." I took a deep breath. *"On the first day of Christmas the po-po gave to me, nine months of life in juvie."*

Limpy's smile reappeared.

"On the second day of Christmas the po-po gave to me, two pairs of slip-ons and nine months of life in juvie. On the third day of Christmas the po-po gave to me, three squares a day, two pairs of slip-ons, and nine months of life in juvie . . ." I stopped singing and shrugged. "That's where I'm stuck. Got any ideas for four?" I asked him.

"I'm not that creative, kid. That's your department." He turned and led me around a corner to a blue metal door painted with a white block letter D.

Limpy knocked. There wasn't an answer. He pushed the door open. The room was empty.

"In," he instructed. Then he slammed the door behind me.

The room was sad and barren except for a rectangular table. It was lit by a single gloomy light in the middle of the ceiling. Two chairs sat on either side of the table—one normal, the other with places to shackle someone. Pretty obvious where I was supposed to sit, but I just paced and worked on my newest jingle.

"On the fourth day of Christmas the po-po gave to me, four daily beatings . . ."

No . . .

"Four-minute showers . . ."

No . . .

"Four . . . four . . . four . . ."

"Four hours' yard time . . .

Fiiiiiiive BATHROOM BREAKS!!!!"

I started laughing. I used to crack myself up. Sometimes.

The laughter stopped when the door opened. In walked a stocky, thirtysomething woman. She had on a snug, off-the-rack navy pantsuit and her thick, curly black hair was pulled back into a loose ponytail. Strands of it had come free and poked up around her head.

"Please, have a seat," the woman said politely, shutting the door again.

I sat across from her, confused. She had a sparkle in her eye. Maybe even a small smile. It was a bit off-putting, to be honest. I hadn't seen a look like that since I'd been inside.

"Robert Hutchinson?"

I nodded.

"And you like to sing?"

I shrugged. "Helps pass the time as good as anything."

"You're not bad."

I shrugged again. "Okay." What was the point of all this?

"You only do goofy holiday songs, or you take requests?"

"Both. Whatever."

"It embarrasses you?"

"No."

She reached into her pocket and pulled out what looked like a small tape recorder.

"Watch this," she said, nodding at the camera in the upper corner of the ceiling. A red power light was glowing underneath it. She pushed a button on the side of the small tape recorder device. The device began to hum quietly, and at the same time the red light on the camera flipped off.

"Scrambler," she said with a wink. She pocketed it as she continued, "Just in case. Don't want anyone watching or listening."

"Because . . . ?" I began. But really my mind was more

focused on how I could steal that scrambler from her and sell it.

"Because the people in charge here don't need to know what we're going to talk about."

"What are we going to talk about?"

"What indeed," she replied playfully.

"Are you my lawyer?"

"Heavens, no. Do I look like a lawyer?"

I shrugged. The cheap suit, the hair—I didn't want to offend her. "Yeah, sorta."

The woman waved me off.

"Leslie Tanner," she said, standing up to shake my hand.

I stood up and took it. She had a grip like a vise. I winced and she let go. Having completed the formal, adult-style introductions, Leslie sat back down. I did, too.

"If you're not my lawyer, then why are you here?" I asked, massaging my fingers under the table.

"I'm here on behalf of the government."

"City?"

"The secret kind."

There was a hefty silence.

"Ooooookay, so is this like where you tell me I was genetically made in a CIA lab and I'm sorta like a super spy?" I asked snidely.

"No, and I'm not with the CIA," she said. "I'm from an agency you've never heard of, and I'm here because you die tomorrow."

She didn't even blink. Her smile was gone. I wasn't sure how to react.

"Uh," was all I could muster as I stared at her for a few seconds, waiting for her to break character and laugh.

"Is this a joke? It is, isn't it?" I asked, grinning. "They put you up to this?" I fully expected Limpy or another officer to burst in. Like I said, we had our differences in here, but we could still have some fun with each other. Something like this was pretty elaborate . . . but I wouldn't have put it past them.

"I promise you this is not a joke." Not a hint of a smirk, smile, or grin. Helluva poker face on this one.

"Riiiiiiiight," I answered.

"What if I told you that tomorrow a young boy, trying to prove his toughness to a gang, will stab and kill you."

"Bummer? Oh, but then I'd remember that no one can see the future and ask if you'd forgotten to take your anti-crazy pills this morning."

Again, no response. This wasn't even a good lie. How much longer would they keep this going?

"If you can see the future, what am I about to do next?" I asked.

She shook her head. "I can't see the future, not like that."

"'Not like that'? So you're admitting you can in some other way?"

She sighed and shrugged. Then she muttered, as if to someone else, "This is why I don't have kids."

"Hey, you'd be lucky to have a kid like me."

"Really?"

"I'm an acquired taste," I admitted.

"Riiiiight," she said, mimicking me from earlier.

Now I was pissed. "Look, no offense, *Leslie,* but I don't know you. I've had more realistic conversations with drunk hobos at two in the morning than I'm having with you."

She shrugged again and said, "I told them this wouldn't work, and that they should just do the extraction like always, but no . . ."

"Them? Extraction?"

She either didn't hear me or ignored me. "Look, I read your file. I know you have trust issues." She pulled out a light blue folder from a leather carrier bag on the floor, then flipped it open. Lo and behold, my picture was looking up. "But generally I liked what I saw in here, trust issues aside, of course."

"Of course," I echoed.

"You're rebellious, but not without cause. You're intelligent, charming, athletic, but above all else when you see something wrong, you try to stop it. You don't look around for someone else to do it, or simply move on, shaking your head. You act, which very, very few do. It's a trait we hold in high regard, and we want you to come work for us."

The file was an interesting development, but I still didn't buy this story. If it was a prank, though, it was pretty damn elaborate.

"Work for you . . . at . . . the . . . crazy . . . farm?" I asked.

"All right, kid," she snapped. She shoved the file back into her bag. "I'm tired, I'm hungry, I'm sweaty, and this is going nowhere fast. I'm leaving. You coming with me or what?"

"Or *what*," I snapped back. I was tired, too.

"The alternative is that I beat the piss out of you for being a stubborn, stupid child, and drag you out of here by your disgusting, greasy hair."

Now *that* was a threat and the way she stared at me made me believe she was serious about doing it.

"Try me," she added menacingly.

Um, where had fun Leslie gone? I wanted to call her bluff, but something about her made me rethink that. Gone was the cheery, I-can-see-the-future crazy lady. Now a suddenly dangerous woman sat across from me.

"Come with me right now and all of this goes away."

She flashed a badge of some kind, but the motion was too quick for me to read it. "This means no one will stop us."

"Then I'm in," I said. At least I'd get an answer.

"You don't think I'm crazy anymore?"

"Oh, you're certifiable. But I'd follow the Hamburglar out of here if he could set me free." I stood up and asked, "So we're just gonna walk out of here and into the sunset now?"

"Like Butch and Sundance."

"Butch and who?"

She stood, too, and shook her head. "Your generation depresses me," she said sadly. "Come on." She moved past me and walked out of the room.

I followed but hesitated at the door. Limpy was long gone. The hall was deserted. Was this really happening? Was I actually buying into this? When Leslie reached the intersection down the hall, she paused and looked back at me.

"Let's move, Hutch," she barked.

My heart began to pound as I followed her. We strode through the prison like we owned the place. Or she did. I only followed her lead. Around every corner I fully expected to run into a group of guards laughing hysterically, but never did. We never even slowed down. Every locked door buzzed and swung open for us in advance. All eyes turned away as we passed. Nobody tried to stop us.

When I passed my prison-appointed therapist, he waved at me.

I had to ask.

"Is this a joke?"

He exhaled. "Hutch, whoever that lady is, become her friend. She's got some serious connections."

"For real?"

"Hutch!" Leslie cried out before my therapist could answer. "Move it!"

"I would get moving," my therapist offered.

"That your professional opinion?" I joked.

"Stay out of trouble, Hutch," he said with a wry smile, knowing full well that would never happen.

Before I knew it, we were through the visitors' area and headed straight for the exit. I paused. This *was* really happening. What was going on?

"What about my stuff?" I asked, remembering my clothes, wallet, keys, and phone that they'd tossed in a bag when I got here. You were supposed to get those things back when you left.

"Won't need them," she called from outside.

I hurried through the final door.

The prison had a yard, and I got to spend a couple hours out there every day, but there's something about free air that tastes better. I took a deep breath.

"Now what?" I asked. Out of the corner of my eyes, I saw something rapidly approaching down the driveway. A van with darkened windows screeched to a halt in front of us. The door swung open.

"Now comes the fun part," she said, grinning.

In a move faster than I thought possible, Leslie reached out and used that crazy strong viselike grip of hers to snag my right wrist. I jerked my arm. I was big enough and strong enough that I should have been able to shake myself free, but her grip didn't give; it somehow got tighter. She took a quick step toward me. An instant later I was soaring through the air over her hip. I landed hard on the concrete sidewalk. Before I could even say "Ow," her knee jabbed right into my rib cage, knocking the wind out of my lungs. Leslie grabbed my wrist again, folding it in half like origami. The pain was excruciating.

"Up," she instructed.

My wrist felt like it would snap in half if I didn't obey. I looked around for help as she dragged me to my feet, but none was offered from the guards in the parking lot. *What the hell, prison family?!*

She shoved me into the van and the door was closed before I'd even crumpled to the floorboards, clutching my wrist. While I tried to catch my breath, I barely heard her shout out, "Deputy US Marshals, we're all good here."

US Marshals? Was I being transferred? Seemed like a pretty rough way to do it. This was not protocol; this was not how the Marshals worked. I'd watched *Justified,* so I knew. This was something new and different. It was also pitch black. And weirdly silent. When the van suddenly accelerated forward, I fell backward. When I regained my balance, I felt my way forward until I reached a solid metal wall. I banged on it as hard as I could.

"Hey! What's going on?! Let me out of here!"

Okay, I'll admit it. I was afraid now. My imagination wasn't too shabby and I'd seen too many movies to believe this would end well. Look, I talked a big game, but I was still only fourteen and this had gotten scary in a hurry. Luckily, before I could really panic, I heard a *hiss* and the air unexpectedly smelled sweet like honey. My eyelids felt heavy and my thoughts became slow.

Mmmmm, honey. Drizzle it on toast . . . it's stickeeeee . . .

"Hu-neeeee," I said with a smile.

After that, I was out cold.

Allergy pills. That's how I felt. You know, like how you feel super sleepy after you take one of those allergy pills at night but then have to wake up way too early the next day?

I wanted to go back to sleep, but there was some annoying, repetitive beeping. It was accompanied by a definite cold breeze on my junk. I forced my eyes open. I was in (best I could guess) the middle of some kind of hospital-patient-room-type place, strapped firmly to a chair by my arms and wrists, wearing only a hospital gown. That explained the breeze. Super. The smell of bleach was so strong it burned my nose. I knew better than to try to fight my bindings. I'd been in these before, after a scuffle at juvie a couple years ago. I'd given those things hell back then and had gotten zilch out of it except really sore wrists.

No matter what you see in the movies, you ain't chewing, rocking, or pulling yourself out of true prison-issued restraints. No, I was stuck here until whatever was going to happen happened. Might as well save my energy. I was scared (who wouldn't be?) but I was more curious than anything. This day, if it was even the same one, had taken one helluva turn for the bizarre. If Leslie had wanted me dead, I would be, so that was comforting, I guess. She could have let me die in juvie, like she claimed I would have, or killed me in the van.

Why keep me alive if the plan was to kill me anyway? Made no sense. Right? But there were some messed-up people in this world. Like Leslie. Any moment now I'd pass the threshold between keeping my cool and really freaking out.

I was about to scream for answers when the door slid open. An old dude in a white lab coat came in. He totally looked like a real doctor and for some reason that calmed my nerves. Maybe it was the glasses.

"Good morning, Mister . . ." He peered down at a thin, paper-size piece of square glass in his hand and tapped it. Instantly the glass came to life and a picture of me was staring up at him from it. I could see it from behind. My eyes widened, but he tapped the screen blank after he got my name and continued, ". . . Hutchinson. How are we feeling?"

It was a pretty stupid first question. Didn't he know I had just been busted out of prison, gassed, and then woken up here?

"Tired?" I answered.

"That will wear off soon enough," he told me. He took a seat on the round rolling stool next to me. I hadn't even noticed it until now.

The door slid open again. In walked a petite, pretty cute, red-headed girl. I was suddenly very aware of how near-naked I was.

"Get lost?" the man asked her.

She was super pale. I mention this because when she went red with embarrassment, it looked almost fake.

"Sorry," she answered, eyes down.

"Don't be. Confusing place. We don't have the convenience of the lights to guide *us* around. Prepare the shot please," he instructed. He turned back to me and rolled his eyes, adding under his breath, "New interns, right?"

Interns? What the hell was this place?

"Where am I?" I asked.

"I guess you could call it home?" he answered. "I never understood why they insist on doing this before explaining everything to you. Seems a bit cruel, like they get off on the fear or something, but I just work here."

"I'm not afraid," I lied.

"Good, you shouldn't be."

"What's about to happen to me?" I asked, swallowing. I knew I couldn't move, but I struggled anyway. A reflex. Instinct.

"I'm not going to kill you," he assured me.

"Thanks?"

The intern appeared at his side, holding a metal tray with the biggest syringe I'd ever seen. Needles didn't bother me, but this—this thing was almost as big as a turkey baster. All my veins quivered in fear.

"I'm all up to date on my vaccines, Doc." It was worth a try.

The doctor smiled. "Cute."

The syringe was filled with what looked like black paint. The doctor took it from the tray and held it up but then scrunched up his face.

"You know what?" He put the syringe back on the tray and looked at the intern. "Why don't you do it?"

He got up and patted his old seat.

"I've never . . ." she began.

"Given anyone fire? First time for everything."

". . . never given someone a shot before," the intern finished.

He waved her off. "He's a tough kid. You're a tough kid, right?"

What was the right answer here?

"Look at those muscles. He can handle it," he told her, patting his empty seat again.

She sat down. For the first time she looked at me. She'd been avoiding eye contact this whole time. She had pretty green eyes. Yes, they were worried and scared eyes, which concerned me, but they were pretty. The old man took a call and left the room without a word. It was just the two of us now.

Now, I pride myself on being a tough guy. I can fake it, even when things get crazy. But if I have one weakness, it's a sad girl. It's the kryptonite to my Superman. I can't handle it. I'll do anything to cheer that girl up. Tears? Forget about it. I'll run through a brick wall to make them stop.

The intern took the needle from the tray. I couldn't help but gulp as she looked down at my arm.

"Hey," I said quietly. When she didn't look up, I repeated, "Hey."

Her eyes flashed to mine. She was nervous.

"Just do it. I'll be fine. You're not trying to kill me, right?"

She shook her head.

"Then do it. No grudges, promise. You know, assuming I live."

A smile flitted across her face. Her hand was still shaking, and she noticed I was staring at it.

"Sorry," she said. She took a deep breath.

"I have an idea I think will help." I closed my eyes and sang slowly . . .

"Silent night
Holy night
All is calm
All is bright . . ."

I opened my eyes. She was speechless. Worked like a charm.

"Weren't expecting that, were you? And check it out," I said, nodding at her hand, which had stopped shaking. "Now, hurry up before you think about it too much and go all Norman Bates in the shower on my arm."

She laughed. "Ha, okay. Thanks. Interesting song choice, though."

"It's December," I said. *Interesting?* I wondered as she tapped at the bubbles in the syringe. What was it with everyone these days? I mean, yeah, *early* December but . . .

"No, it's January. You've been out a while."

I blinked. Her words made no sense.

With a sigh, she used her free hand to pull out her phone. She showed me the date on the blank screen: January 10. "You've been out for a few weeks."

"What do you mean, 'out'?" I had to ask, but I was figuring it out. Not the sharpest spoon in the drawer, folks . . .

"You should feel lucky. Recruits are gathered throughout the year—"

The door opened, silencing her. The doctor (again, assuming he *was* a doctor) popped his head into the room. "How are you not done yet? You stick it in, push the plunger, chop-chop. They need us in C3-11Y. We've got our first fry of the year. Come on!"

She looked at the shot and then again at me. I wanted answers. I deserved them. I turned back to the old guy, but he was gone.

That was the moment she chose to plunge the needle in my arm.

The initial pain was indescribable. The moment the black liquid entered my bloodstream, I let out every curse word I knew. Trust me, I know a lot. I might have called the intern a few choice words that I'm not proud of, but it felt as if she'd stabbed me with a fiery piece of metal, not given an injection. And if that wasn't bad enough, the pain was spreading like a snakebite. *Why in the hell had I been so helpful?!*

The girl stood. I tried to scream, but it was all so intense, so awful, that I felt paralyzed. I closed my eyes to try to fight the pain. It was an agony like no other. I was going to lose this battle if it didn't let up soon. When I felt hands unstrapping me, my eyes popped open. Two men—they looked like soldiers—were taking off my restraints. The moment my right hand was free, I tried to punch the one on my left, but even the slightest motion made the throbbing worse. It ended up looking more like I'd reached over to scratch my other arm.

It felt like someone had put a fire demon in my body and it was trying to burn its way out. The hurt washed over me in waves.

The two men plunked me down into a wheelchair.

I'd hoped that the cool metal frame of the chair would be soothing to my flaming skin, but the torture worsened. As we rolled through a maze of hallways, I tried to follow the route to remember it for a later escape, but I blacked out.

Screaming coming from all over woke me up. Still in excruciating pain. Still in the wheelchair. We rolled past door after door. Each seemed to house a unique scream. Girl. Guy. Could be either. Girl. Girl. Girl. Guy. There were so many it was like listening to hell's choir. I closed my eyes. Darkness was coming again. I needed relief.

The wheelchair jerked to a stop. I dry-heaved. The guards grabbed me, their hands like hot razors. They dragged me into a dark room and dropped me down on a bed before leaving. I dry-heaved again. The screaming was coming from all over, and after a few seconds I couldn't help but join in. One more singer for the devil's choir.

I HAD BEEN REFUSING to wake up for a few minutes now, but there was this really annoying, high-pitched noise coming from somewhere in the room.

"Uhhhhhh," I moaned as I forced my eyes open. The noise stopped.

An all-too-familiar cinder block wall looked back at me. So it *had* all been a dream. Wow, that had been awful. Maybe I was going crazy. I closed my eyes. The annoying noise came back the nanosecond my lids fell shut. It stopped again when they opened. Seriously? Of course, there was no way I could resist playing with this. I spent the next minute or so opening and closing my eyes to make the noise stop and start.

"Okay, I get it," I shouted at the empty room.

Wait.

The cinder block wall in my juvie cell was white; this one was gray. And this one was a lot cleaner, too. *Mine* had doodles and carvings from detainees of yesteryear all over it. This was not my cell. So . . . the van, the supersized shot, the torture . . . it was . . . real? It all sort of hit me at once and I sat up on the bed in shock. Big mistake. Everything hurt. No part of me felt okay. I was the most sore I'd ever been—*ever.*

Moving was not an option, so I examined my room from the bed. Looked like a prison cell. Prison-issued toilet-sink combo kit. Tiny desk and simple stool chair. If this wasn't prison, someone was trying really hard to make it look like one.

On the desk was a stack of yellow clothes. All yellow. As in no other color but. It reminded me of the time my grandma got a "great deal at the flea market" on some blue fabric with hot dogs printed all over it. She made me an entire week's worth of clothes out of it. Shirts, shorts, and even boxers—all made out of the same fabric. It did make choosing an outfit really easy. I called that summer "the dog days" . . . get it? Not coincidentally, it was the summer I got into the most fights. At least the yellow clothes were better than my drafty hospital gown. Gingerly, I swung my sore legs over the edge of the bed. I put them on the cold linoleum floor. Tracksuit, shorts, shirt, yep, all yellow down to boxer briefs, socks, and even shoes. Where do you find yellow shoes? It was very clear that unless I was naked someone wanted to be damn sure I would be wearing yellow. Or maybe they'd just gotten a good deal like my gram.

I winced as I eased into the various items. Now, normally I was a jeans and T-shirt kinda guy, but the clothes were made from that "athletic wear" moisture-wicking stuff, so I had to admit they were pretty comfy.

With nothing to do, I decided to do what always must be done in a new prison cell—tag it. Make sure whoever comes after you knows you were there. It's tradition. All prisoners do it. Using the zipper from my tracksuit I carved my initials into the wall. *R.H.* A crude tag, but a tag nonetheless. I'd do better later if could get my hands on a Sharpie.

After that I snooped around. Bed was a bed. Sink and toilet ran and flushed—boring. The desk was interesting. It looked lame and prefab, but the top of it was shiny black glass. It felt out of place. Honestly, given that doctor's device, I wondered if it was a screen, a giant tablet, or something else. But no matter how many times I poked, swiped, or pinched the surface, nothing happened.

"On!" I even tried yelling at it. It didn't respond.

"Good morning. I hope you slept well," came a calm man's voice behind me.

I instinctively spun away from the desk and raised my fist. It was no one, of course. The place was empty. I'd gone over every inch of it, so there was no way someone was in there with me.

"I see the clothes fit well."

The voice reminded me of those hilarious "breathe in, breathe out," "you can do it" motivational recordings that old people listen to in the car to convince themselves their life doesn't suck. It does, by the way. Life, I mean. Just accept that it sucks, and you'll be happier. I tried to remind myself of that now. I *was* alive, wasn't I?

"Looking good," the voice added.

I looked over my right shoulder—and yep, there it was: a small speaker above the door. Oh, and a small camera, too.

"Hope you enjoyed the show," I commented, remembering how naked I'd been while changing.

"I am sure you are bursting with questions, my dear, most of which will be answered now," the voice replied.

I was going to comment on his use of "my dear," but before I could, a cinder block slid out from the wall like a dresser drawer and stopped. Inside was a pair of clear, plastic-looking glasses—a much, much cooler version of the ones I'd worn in Biology class when we dissected a frog.

"Put those on," the voice commanded.

Hey, I'm no genius, I can admit that, but I didn't need that last part, dude. A little faith, please. Had someone actually not known what to do with the glasses before? Had they thought they were a toothbrush?

"We'll speak again once you are finished. Hurry along, now. There's no time to waste."

Bull. You're a recording. We both know this, so from here on out I'm calling you Pre-taped.

I picked up the glasses, which were beyond light, and used them as a toothbrush.

Kidding.

IT'S A LITTLE HARD to explain what the glasses did.

Say you decide to watch a movie, but turn fast-forward as high as it can go. Then you put your face an inch from the screen. Lots of flashing images. No sound. Nothing really to focus on. Total confusion. But then somehow when it ends, you totally remember the whole movie like you'd watched it at normal speed. Only, this movie explains everything that happened to you until now and why.

Long story short, the people who now owned me could see into the future. Well, sort of. They could see glimpses of it, like pictures, so they knew who was important and they knew who wasn't. Not only was I *not* important, but I was dead at fourteen. That was the "why" of why I was here. Leslie, crazy, I-can-see-the-future Leslie, wasn't so crazy after all. I saw my tombstone. I saw my mom standing over my coffin. I even saw a freeze-frame image from the video of the kid stabbing me. Really exoskeletal. No, that's not right. Exo . . . sential. No. Existential! Whew, that would have eaten at me. It was really existential to watch.

How could they see the future? I could go into it, but do I have to? You either believe me, or you don't. Accept it, and let's move on. It's a lot cooler if you do. Since I was dead, and a rotting corpse is useless, I was brought here along with a bunch of other teens my age who would have died, too—though probably not from being stabbed, but in more normal ways like car crashes and stuff.

Today was the first day of our training.

From here on out, we were alive for one thing and one thing only: to become "Shadows." That was their word for us. We were each chosen to protect a Future Important Person, FIP for short—to make sure nothing or no one got in the way of their doing the miraculous, world-changing thing that they would apparently do.

First we had to learn a lot, of course. But after four years of brutal training, my fellow dead teens and I would graduate as certifiable badasses. It was like high school in that way. Every year, seniors would finally achieve their title of Shadow and get linked to a FIP. Once you're linked, you're linked for life. Here—at the official headquarters of the Shadow Program, a highly classified facility known as the FATE Center, which stood for Future Affairs Training and Education—I'd learn to fight, spy, shoot everything, drive everything, become a ninja at evasion, you name it.

The strange thing? I wasn't scared anymore. Now, I wasn't sure exactly what the right emotional response to all this was—the norm would probably be terror, depression, anger—but I was excited as hell, actually. It sounded fun. Not that it would be all sunshine and daisies. My life, as I knew it, was *over.* Totally. No going back. No phone calls to my mom, and no apologizing. Not even a goodbye hug. This was my new home. There were only three ways out of here: die, go insane, or graduate. Zero other options. Die from training (the most common outcome); go insane, thanks to a steady regimen of those nasty shots (sadly pretty common, too); survive it all, become a super stud who feels no pain, and graduate.

Apparently only around 5 percent graduated, so odds were I'd never leave this place. Bonus! Then again, my mother had always told me I was exceptional . . .

"FEELING BETTER?" PRE-TAPED ASKED. "Now please sit up and listen carefully to what I am about to say."

I hadn't been sitting at all, so there was my proof the voice was pre-recorded. I had no clue how long I'd been standing there like a statue, though. Could have been five minutes, could have been fifty.

Pre-taped continued, "Please exit and follow the markers toward the Echo room. The correct path will be obvious. Do not stray off course or attempt to escape. Any deviation from the path will result in severe punishment. Chin up, back straight. You have nothing to fear here if you behave."

"So can I go now?" I asked a bit sarcastically.

As if on cue, the door slid open.

One thing I'd learned in all my stints in juvie is when

you're given the chance to not be in your cell, you take it. I took a few steps to the door and poked my head out into the hallway. I spotted a few others doing the same and caught the eye of a cute girl. I smiled and gave her a nod. Always braver when there's a girl around, I stepped out into the hallway.

The door to my room slid shut behind me the moment I was clear of it.

MORE JOINED US, DOORS sliding shut behind them one by one, but I kept my eyes on the girl. She had plain, dark brown hair, which was pulled into a ponytail, and wore all yellow about as well as you could hope. Then my gaze shifted. From down the hall I saw a huge guard in full-on riot gear forcing the noncompliant out of their rooms.

Flashing green lights began guiding us all to the left. I'd been so busy staring at the monster in the riot gear I hadn't noticed that the girl was suddenly standing next to me.

"You coming?" she whispered.

"Oh, uh," I stammered, "yeah."

We walked in awkward silence, side by side.

"Hutch," I said, introducing myself. "I'm Hutch."

"Sam," she replied.

We shook hands.

"Like short for Samantha?"

"No, like short for Sam. My dad wanted a boy." I could tell by the way she said it she'd been explaining it her whole life and was tired of it. "Hutch can't be your real name."

"Robert Hutchinson," I told her.

"Hutch is much better," she admitted with a smile.

I smiled back. "Right?"

As our eyes met, her smile vanished. She stared at the floor. I straightened and craned my neck. A sea of yellow filled the hallway. Who knew how many kids there were? From what I could see I was one of the biggest guys here, but that was pretty normal. There were a few who were taller or wider, but I was near the top. It was good to know. It's always good to know how you stack up against potential enemies.

chapter 5

FOLLOWING THE RULES: LESSON 1 . . . AND 2, 3, 4, OH, YOU GET THE IDEA

Getting to the Echo room was a hike. I filled the minutes by making hushed small talk with Sam. The other kids were whispering amongst themselves, too, so apparently it wasn't against the rules. She was from Canada, eh? And played soccer and hockey, eh? By the time we reached the massive double doors that led to the Echo room, I was officially crushing hard. No doubt about it. Maybe the FATE Center *would* be all sunshine and daisies.

The Echo room was more than a room. It was the biggest, most massive indoor open space I'd ever seen. It reminded me of the situation rooms that you'd see in the movies. You know, the ones with TVs on all the walls flashing what are supposed to be really important images and information, but if you pause and zoom in, it's just nonsense. Only, the stuff on the walls in here didn't look like nonsense.

Aside from the light that came from the screens along the edges, the middle of the room was bathed in black. Small bubble-like things, perfectly spaced out, hovered in the air around ten feet off the ground. They projected circles of white light onto the ground. In the middle of the circles were names.

"Walk you to yours?" I asked Sam.

"Sure. Last name starts with *W*."

The names were alphabetically listed, so it wasn't hard to find *W* and finally, *Sam Whiskers.*

"Wait, your last name is Whiskers?" I asked, trying not to laugh.

"Ha-ha," she said, playing back.

"So your dad is Mr. Whiskers?"

She smirked. "Original. You're only the millionth person who's asked."

I swallowed a laugh. "Meet up after whatever this is ends?" I asked. "Assuming we're alive, of course."

"Sure. Bet you a loonie we'll make it."

"A loonie?"

"A Canadian dollar."

"Oh, cool. Yeah, see you in a bit." I walked back toward the H section, wondering where I could scare up a Canadian dollar at this place. Every prison had *some* kind of barter system, guys who were good at getting contraband. How different could this place really be underneath the sleek shine?

I started noticing that as kids stepped into their lights, the color switched from hot white to a relaxing blue. By the time I reached my own bubble, I was one of only a handful of white lights left. I quickly stepped into the light and onto my name.

"Well done, Hutch," said Pre-taped. "I told you there was nothing to fear."

It sounded like his voice was coming from every direction. Then I remembered the cool bubble above me. Everyone was looking up, of course. *Ha. Guilty as charged, Pre-taped. I knew you weren't a real person.*

"Please wait patiently while the others find their places. You're doing very well."

If I was going to be fed compliments for standing in the

right place, this whole thing was going to be a piece of cake—other than the shots, of course.

Then some stupid a few rows away tried to leave his bubble. The light turned red. The short kid froze, his face all scrunched up and grimacing from some unseen or unheard pain. After a few seconds he was allowed to move back into his bubble. The light went back to blue, but from the way he clutched his heaving chest, it was obvious he was pretty shaken up by whatever had happened.

Okay then. Stay put. Got it.

We were all facing the same direction—I'm sure some psychology experiment could explain why—when a spotlight, a big legit one, lit up a man in front. Had he been there this whole time? He was dressed in all-black fatigues like a SWAT commander and had the thousand-yard stare down pat. He looked around the room at us.

"Have a seat," he said. He sounded like nice dude, actually.

Only, ain't nowhere to sit, buddy. I almost added, *Burn.* But a block rose up from the floor behind me and stopped at the perfect height for sitting.

SWAT Commander Dude: 1

Me: 0

"I first want to apologize for what you've been put through," he said. "I understand it has been, and probably still is, the most frightening experience of your life. And I'm not foolish enough to think that a glorified slide show has earned your trust. But please believe me when I say you have nothing to fear here. You are the special ones, and we are only here for you. I am Lieutenant Colonel Shane, and I will be overseeing your training here at FATE." He started walking around among us. "You will be tested here beyond the limits of your mental and physical abilities, challenged like never before. You *will* hate us.

You *will* want nothing more than to hurt us, maybe even kill us. We don't take it personally."

He paused next to a tall Indian kid. He touched him all buddy-buddy on the shoulder.

The kid didn't move. Smart.

"We understand none of this has, or will be, easy for any of you," Lt. Col. Shane went on. "But you have been chosen for something noble, something beyond all of us. In time you will understand this and accept it." He stopped by the stupid who'd tried to leave his bubble earlier and asked, "Are you all right, son?"

The boy nodded and Shane responded by giving him a bro-style, attaboy slap on the shoulder. The kid smiled.

I felt sick for a second. No way would he make it.

"A lot of you are probably thinking there's been a mistake. There hasn't been. You will leave here a Shadow, or die here in the shadows."

I resisted the urge to groan. Really? *Waaa-waaaa.*

"You will now begin your formal training and it comes down to one simple philosophy: or die. Listen to your instructors or die. Learn from your mistakes or die. Be vigilant or die. Kill or die. The only enemy you don't have to worry about is a dead one. That is all the time we have today," he concluded. "Thank you for your patience. Thank you for your sacrifice. Good luck."

A leathery, old, war-movie, drill-instructor type suddenly appeared next to Lt. Col. Shane.

He yelled, "Do not move until directed!"

Pre-taped followed up with, "When your light turns off, you are to exit through the designated door. Do not attempt to leave before then. Best of luck over the next four years, Robert Hutchinson. I'm rooting for you."

Sure you are. And I'm rooting for your hard drive to be corrupted by a virus.

A door on the other side of the room opened. Fifteen random lights went off. The fifteen kids made their way to the exit. And so it went until it was my turn. Sam's was still on, though, and I could see the weight of all of this was getting the better of her, so I whispered, "Psst! Sam!"

She was too far away to hear me, so I round-abouted my route in her direction, planning on cracking a joke to help her relax a bit. Not the best idea I've had.

"And what in the hell do you think you're doing?" the drill instructor called out.

He was on me with a baton before I could reply, cracking me in the middle of my back. When he took another swing, well, that's when my street instincts kicked in.

I ducked it and jammed my shoulder into his chest. I wrapped my arms around his legs, drove my feet into the ground, and football-tackle-slammed him to the ground. Normally, that did the job and the scuffle was over. But this guy had latched himself on to me like a snake, and in a move I'd only ever seen while watching MMA on TV, he flipped me over onto my back. He was on top of me in a flash, raining down haymakers. He busted open my lip, bloodied my nose, and finished by popping me nice and hard in the left eye. It would be black by morning. Satisfied I wasn't going to fight back anymore, he got off me.

"Move," he commanded, pointing toward the only open door.

I rolled gingerly to my feet and chanced a glance at Sam. With sad eyes, she mouthed, *Obey or die.* The glance did not go unnoticed. My leg got a good crack from the baton.

"I said move!"

I didn't lose many fights, but I'd lost a few. I knew when not to push it. Embarrassed, pissed, and aching, I walked through the door. It closed behind me. Not everyone in the hall had seen me take the beatdown from the drill instructor, so my bloody appearance was met with a few gasps.

"You okay?" a petite blonde girl asked me.

"What, this?" I joked. My lip was already swollen, so the words sounded funny. "It's nothing. Disagreement between friends." The adrenaline was wearing off. It was all beginning to hurt, *a lot.* But I would never show them that.

The familiar flashing lights guided us down a few hallways. We were led into a white room with thick, padded wrestling mats on the ground and up against the walls. No sooner had we entered from the main door than a hidden door slid up and opened on the other side. Out walked . . .

"Leslie?" I cried.

Everyone shot me a *who-the-hell-is-this-guy* look.

"Making friends already, I see," she said with a smile.

"What can I say? I'm a popular guy." I winced a little. It hurt to smile.

"You ever finish your little Christmas ditty?" she asked.

I shook my head. "Apparently I've been unconscious for a few weeks, so no."

"Who told you that?"

I shrugged cockily. "My file says I'm charming, remember?"

"Feel like singing a little something for the group?" she asked.

"Doesn't really feel like a singing-type place."

"I knew you were smarter than you look," she said, her smile fading.

"Don't count on it."

With an enigmatic shrug, she turned to address the class. "Line up against the wall over there," she ordered, pointing across the room.

We obeyed and lined up in no particular order. I used the

chance to lean back against the wall. My leg was killing me where the drill instructor guy had whacked me.

"As you may have guessed, thanks to Hutch, my name is Leslie. I will be your instructor." As she spoke she walked back and forth in front of us, drinking us in. "As you already know, the chances of making it out of here are slim. I'll try my best to give you the greatest shot of surviving, that much I promise. Since it will inevitably come up, yes, I'm the one who kidnapped you, all of you. Every instructor is responsible for obtaining the kids on his or her list. Get it?"

We all nodded. But no, we didn't get it.

"You got me, so I got you. Bruisy McBruise face over here"—she pointed at me—"was a failed attempt at trying something new, which is why he knows me, or thinks he does. The rest of you, just like countless others before, never saw me coming. You woke up here terrified and lost. Won't be the first time and won't be the last time. And yes, some of you have been waiting in cryostasis for quite some time. Now that you're here, it's my job to test you to your limits and then beyond. I will break you. Then I will rebuild you. The sooner we get started the sooner the worst will be over, so let's begin, shall we?"

When she finished, a block like the one that rose out from the ground in the Echo room slid up from the ground over by the far corner. She took a seat on it.

"Darlington Kanu and Renata Mitic, please step forward," she called out.

A tall, slender black girl off to my left took a step forward, as did a short, stocky brunette even farther down.

"Face each other," Leslie ordered.

They turned and looked at each other.

"Bow."

They were confused, but they obeyed like good little Minions.

Minions! That's what we looked like. A giant army of Gru's Minions! Whew, that had been bugging me for a while.

"Now fight until one of you is unconscious," Leslie commanded, her voice calm.

Neither girl moved.

"Absolutely serious, ladies. Fight. I'm not picking on you. This is day one stuff for everyone. Get to it."

Still, neither moved. I mean, it looked like Renata at least clenched her fists, but that could have been from nerves.

In a flash, Leslie whipped out a gun from behind her back and shot Darlington in the chest. It was so loud and so surreal it all seemed to happen in slow motion. Darlington fell to the ground lifeless, blood slowly pooling across the floor. Tendrils of smoke from the barrel of the gun rose up into the air in front of Leslie's emotionless face.

Renata stiffened. She stood frozen in shock.

As the surprise of it wore off and everything went back to real time, a few people along the line lost it. One or two even started to scream.

Leslie fired the gun twice more into the ceiling as she barked, "Silence!"

That seemed to work. My eyes never left Darlington. I'd never seen anyone get shot before. The hidden door opened and two men in all-black combat fatigues—dressed exactly like Shane—entered. They took Darlington by the arms and dragged her lifeless body out as if she were a bag of trash. The door closed behind them. My ears were still ringing, but it wasn't enough to drown out the sounds of quiet sobbing coming from some of the others. I blinked, I think for the first time since the gunshot.

"Failure to obey commands will not be tolerated," Leslie said flatly.

I couldn't help myself. I blurted out, "What about the 'you'll try your best to help us survive' crap? If you—"

"Mind yourself, Hutch," Leslie interrupted. She eyed me coldly. "Your survival hinges on your absolute obedience and ability to follow orders. Do we understand each other now?"

Everyone nodded. A few even whispered a quiet "Yes."

"Obey or die," I clarified.

"Straightforward and easy to remember, no?" she said. She straightened, her eyes sweeping the room.

"So if we all refuse to obey you right now, you'll kill us all?" I tried to say coolly.

She nodded as she said, "Yes, and then I'll get the year off, or maybe get assigned to the armory like I want, so don't think I'll lose any sleep over it. I have zero feelings for any of you and plenty of bullets left if you want to try me. Renata, step back in line. Robert Hutchinson, please step forward."

We stared each other down for a few seconds before I stepped out. Now wasn't the time to test her.

"Jennifer Schwartz, please join him."

The little blonde girl—the one who'd foolishly asked me how I was earlier—stepped forward on the wobbliest of wobbly legs.

"No," I said instinctively, knowing what was coming.

"Oh, yes," Leslie responded.

"No," I repeated. I looked at Jennifer, who looked like she was about to puke. "Why?"

"Because you have a weakness," Leslie said. "And I will exploit it until it no longer is one. You know what to do. You know the consequences," she said. She sat back down and placed the gun on her lap.

Jennifer slowly walked toward me. Fear of death had trumped everything else.

"Just get it over with," I told her, shoving my hands in my pockets. No way I'd be touching her.

She didn't know how to react.

"I'm not going to hit you, so hit me. Come on, hit me. HIT ME!" I finally yelled.

She took a wild swing and caught me on the bicep. I'd been hit by Wiffle balls thrown by toddlers harder than that. If that was the best she had, this was going to take a long time. I guessed I could take a dive.

"Again," I instructed her.

Jennifer lined up for another shot, but it never came. Something out of the corner of her eye made her pause. She was looking at Leslie. I turned and looked, too. Leslie was on her feet, her gun pointed right at me. Not the first time I'd had a gun pointed at me, but it was the first time I actually thought I might be shot.

"Do it," I dared, in spite of the fear. "I'm not gonna hit her."

Leslie smiled and shifted her aim toward Jennifer.

"No!" I cried out, and jumped in front of her right as Leslie fired the gun.

A little something for the memory banks: getting shot sucks. It does. I won't sit here and sugarcoat it or glorify it to make it sound like a badge of honor. A piece of metal is traveling faster than the speed of sound and you've decided to use your body as the best way to stop it. It's a poor choice. The bullet tears through you, ripping up muscles and flesh, destroying nerve endings, and crushing whatever bones are in its way. It will feel like you just got hit by a sledgehammer and, if it doesn't instantly kill you, you'll wish it had. There is no toughing it out. Yeah, it sucks.

This particular bullet slammed into my left shoulder and spun me around like a top. I nearly lost my balance but threw the hand from my good arm down on the ground to keep me upright. Staggering, but still standing, I saw Leslie striding toward me and assumed it was to put the finishing touches on her "murdering Hutch" masterpiece.

I want to say my life flashed before my eyes, or I got a burst of clarity about the meaning of life, or even that I was so filled with rage I reached out to strangle her. But in reality, my jaw just fell open. Real proud of that moment. When Leslie was close enough, instead of dealing some death, she slammed the butt of her pistol down hard on my forehead.

Ouch! And out.

chapter 6
BACKSTAGE PASS

I woke up in a hospital bed who knows how many hours later with a hard, plastic-like patch over where I'd been shot. (I say "plastic-like" because . . . well, that's the best I can describe it, okay?) Holy hell, my shoulder hurt, though. It felt like someone had tried to rip my arm clean off. Painkillers, anyone? *Anyone?*

There was a curtain draped loosely around my bed in a semicircle, but I knew I wasn't alone. I could hear people all around me. There was some chitchat and the sound of padded footsteps. I sat up, careful to keep my left arm as still as I could, and then gingerly got to my bare feet. (Oh, great, I was in a hospital gown again. I was starting to get used to having a breeze down below.) Using my good arm, I grabbed the curtain.

As I pulled the thin fabric aside I caught a glimpse of an infirmary of some kind. It was simple, sort of like the ones you'd see in old war or prison movies. Beds with wounded people in them. Not much else. Some were hidden by a curtain like mine, but most weren't. The beds were full of kids. Some were sitting up chatting with friends. Others, well, they didn't look like they'd make it.

One nearby conversation made my ears perk up. I recognized that woman's voice. I regripped the curtain and gave one last tug to it, flinging it to the edge so that I could finally see . . . Darlington? She was sitting up happily in a bed two spots away from mine, chatting with Leslie.

"You!" I gasped at Leslie. "You shot me!"

They both turned.

"Hey, he's up!" Leslie said. She patted Darlington. "Glad you're okay, and congrats," she murmured before standing up. As she walked toward me, Darlington—smiling way too wide for someone who'd been shot in the chest—walked over to an excited group of kids, who, coincidentally, all had similar injuries.

"You shot me," I repeated for emphasis.

"Yeah, I did," she said. "You were being a world-class a-hole. I had to."

Okay, then. Another lesson learned: apparently here they could shoot you for being an a-hole.

"You *shot* me," I said for the third time, trying my best to make sure she understood how uncool that was. "Right here," I added, tapping my finger on the hard, plasticky thing that covered the wound. Terrible idea, because it still hurt like hell. "What is this crap, anyway?"

"It's a bandage that won't get in the way of your training," Leslie told me.

"What's going on? Why is *she* alive?" I jerked my aching head at Darlington. "Why didn't you kill me?"

"Getting shot was Darlington's final test. She'll be a Shadow now."

I blinked at her. "You people are insane."

"Or we know how to motivate people. Every class gets the same first-day show because we need them to believe that if they don't obey, they'll die. Or at least get shot like you."

She seemed to be waiting for me to say something. I didn't.

Leslie sighed. "Look, Hutch, I'm pretty sure you've figured

it out by now, but you're not like the other kids. You have everything it takes to make it through this, and only a freak accident or your body's inability to accept the fire shots will get in your way. The others aren't so lucky. They're weak and scared, and they still have hope that this is all a bad dream and they can go back to their families."

I bit my lip. "That's why you shot me?"

Her smile widened. "Yes, and because I was curious to see how you'd handle it. You've seen behind the curtain now, Hutch. Your classmates believe I killed Darlington. They also know I shot you, so they will do whatever I ask now. Which is in their best interests, and I think you know this. But you can tell them the truth. You've seen that she's alive and well. Will you tell them?"

It was twisted and sick, but she was right. They needed to believe. If this was real, they needed to believe to survive.

Leslie nodded, as if reading my mind. "You're wild and you're hotheaded, Hutch. But you understand the world better than I think even you know." She slapped her knees and stood up. "Hungry?"

I hadn't thought about it until now and my stomach growled as if on cue. "Starving," I admitted.

"Then get dressed and let's go," she said. "Your clothes are on that table."

I glanced at the pile of yellow, then back at Leslie. "So just to be clear," I said, "you're gonna shoot me again if I refuse to hit Jennifer, aren't you?"

"Over and over until you do," she replied.

"Hope you got a lot of bullets, 'cause it's never gonna happen. I don't hit girls."

"Your chivalry isn't as charming as you think it is, Hutch," Leslie said, her smile intact. "It's insulting and sexist. I've seen girls her size rip guys like you apart in seconds. But I'll make you a deal. If you obey me without question, without back talk—if you act like the perfect teacher's pet—then I won't pit you up against her or anyone, guy or girl, who's half your size for a while."

"Promise?"

Leslie nodded. "Promise. Trust me though, Hutch, after a bit of training and toughening up, you'd be surprised what some of them will be capable of. You won't *want* to fight them, if you catch my drift."

I threw on the last of my clothes and joked, "Looking into the future again?"

chapter 7a

TIME JUMP! THE TECHNICAL VERSION

What? I can't skip forward a bit? Why not? It's my story, and I can do whatever the heck I want. I need some control here.

You don't want to see how the video game is made; you just want to play it, right? But I get it. All you need to know is that while most of the others didn't really like it at FATE, I had a blast from day one. (Okay, day two—since being shot by Leslie sucked.) It was fun here. I was a street thug who was being trained to be like James Bond—only meaner. I drank the FATE Kool-Aid. It was awesomely refreshing. I admit it. Isn't that good enough?

Ugh, fine. Do you want to know what you missed? Here it goes:

Lots of fighting. Like every martial art you can imagine, all the way down to even learning "drunken boxing." Learned things like the monkey-death-claw, the Succubus, a spinning-kicking-flipping move called the Charybdis, and about a hundred other unique Shadow moves that could deal straight death.

Learned how to drive everything that drives, floats, and flies. Motorcycles, cars, busted up farm trucks, tanks, snowmobiles (okay, I get it, that's more skis, but you get the idea). I'd never really been a boat guy, but shooting a grenade launcher from a Jet Ski is something you can't help but enjoy. And flying is weird fun. You're in a hunk of metal, going three hundred miles per hour, that floats in the air. Think about it. We started on small Cessnas and then worked our way up to Gulfstreams, Apache helicopters, even old F-15s. I quickly learned I didn't have the patience for drawn-out dogfights.

Guns? Can shoot 'em all. Rocket launchers, pistols, crossbows, machine guns. You get it. The Glock 41 Gen4 was my favorite, though. Simple, small, and reliable. If I had to choose a second, any machine would do. AK-47, SR-3 Vikhr, M4—they're all good fun. Edged blades? . . . Yeah, never really got the hang of those, but I sure cut my hands a lot.

They taught us every method of surveillance in the book. Or, as I liked to call it, being super creepy. In under sixty seconds—the length of a bathroom break—I could have a room fully set up with mics, pinhole cameras, heat sensors—the works. I then got to watch everything unfold on my laptop screen from the comfort of my own chair like a dirty voyeur. I called it my Creepster Gear.

In one of the more odd moments, we took a creative writing class. No seriously, like a real class. Apparently we had to learn how to create believable cover stories for ourselves once we were out, in case someone saw something they shouldn't have. The CIA, NSA, and DoD were the go-to options. It was a very strange few weeks that we spent writing.

The fire worked like a charm on me, and I was pain-free in eleven months. It was awesome. Others were jealous.

I picked up everything really quickly (like ticks to a hound, one guy said) and within a few months moved up from my year to train with the older kids. Within two years I had made it all the way up to training with the oldest kids there. I rarely got to see my friends anymore.

chapter 7b

TIME JUMP! THE EMOTIONAL VERSION

Promise, this is the last time I'll mention sunshine and daisies. Because it wasn't all that. Learning to be a Shadow sucked sometimes. Yeah, just about every moment of the day was dedicated to training like machines, but we were still kids, you know? You can't help but be human.

In a sneaky-sneaky exercise, little Jennifer snuck up behind me with a shovel and beat the crap out of me. I had no issues fighting anyone after that, guy or girl.

A month or so after starting, a group of Hunters (they're the best of the best, like the SEAL Team of FATE) came and told us that if we could escape campus, we'd be free. As in *never-come-back, go-live-your-old-life* free. I didn't really want to—going back home was a downgrade, aside from being able to hug Mom one last time—so I played along. While most kids bolted for the stairs and went up (we assumed we were underground), I went down to explore areas we'd never been allowed to go to. Long story short, it ended in the most humiliating beating I received during my time there. Too humiliating to discuss. But I got to see and play with some cool stuff before they got me.

After my first year Leslie told me privately that she got her "promotion to the armory." I figured that meant she would be the new Lt. Col. Shane. But what the hell did I know? She snuck me a piece of cake, which I ate.

In one of those *no-bleeping-way* moments, I ran into a guy I knew. His name was Jurgen. He was a beefy football player from across town. I'd hated his guts; now I hugged him, and we hit it off instantly. We were like peas in a pod: Hall and Oates, Lewis and Clark, Franco and Rogen. Jurgen died nine months later in a torture exercise, thanks to some overzealous third year.

I got close to Sam. Too close . . .

They used the attraction against us so much that we had to stop seeing, talking, or even sitting together. They even promoted me—moved me up ahead to train with older classes—but that didn't mean I stopped stealing the odd glance or five. Didn't fool them one bit. Every time I did, I was clobbered. They hunt down, destroy, and torture attachment out of you. She was my one weakness, and it had to be beaten out of me.

Feel better? Good, because I'm sort of depressed now. Thanks for making me rehash all of that. Nothing like remembering lost love, abuse, or cold-blooded murder to start the day off right.

chapter 8
SERIOUSLY?

I was pretty sure I was sixteen. Our calendars didn't have numbers—only the days of the week with our schedules listed out. I lost track of actual days pretty quickly here. But I knew I was close-ish to being sixteen, give or take a few weeks.

Does that really matter? I guess not, but in the outside world sixteen was a big deal, so I figured I should at least acknowledge it.

Happy birthday to me. I'd take an extra portion of fruit at dinner or something.

Anyway, I'd been training with the fourth years for a couple months at this point and holding my own. I didn't have any attachments in that class, not like I had with Sam, or even (briefly) with Jurgen. Fourth years had a lot more free time to train on their own and fine-tune weaknesses. You can only train so much though before you burn out, so I had been in the armory, hanging out with Leslie. Sick as it was, she was probably my closest friend. She had become like my big sister. She seemed to need our relationship as much as I did. Yeah, she'd shot me, but we laughed about it now.

"YOU DON'T HAVE TO like it; you just have to do it," Leslie reminded me for the hundredth time.

I'd gotten the order to go to the driving simulation room—a place I never wanted any part of—and Leslie had tagged along to pester me like only a sister can.

"I know," I said. "Just seems cruel for cruelty's sake, you know?"

"It isn't and you know that."

"Do I?" I only half joked. We walked a bit in silence before she smiled and said, "Remember when you used to sing all the time?"

I gave a polite snort. "Yeah. Y'all broke me of that habit." I held up my arm. "In three places. I got it: stop singing or die."

"Do you still sing?" she asked.

I frowned at her. "Why?"

"You should know better than to ask 'why' around here, Hutch," she murmured.

"Fair enough." I shrugged and turned away. "Yeah. Sometimes when I'm alone and I know I won't get my arm broken again for it. So pretty much only in the shower, I guess."

When we reached the door to the driving simulation room, she stopped. "See you tomorrow," she said.

I raised my eyebrows. *Anything else you want to add? Like Happy birthday?*

"You don't have to like it," she reminded me.

Well, there was my answer. I saluted her. *Thanks, Big Sis. Happy birthday to you, too.*

THE REAL DRIVING ROOM housed every type of enhanced weaponized vehicle you could name—car, boat, tank, aircraft . . . whatever. I'd gotten to the real room quicker than most. First and second years stuck to the simulator. It was safer. It was also less costly, but I'm just guessing here since money didn't really appear to be an issue in these parts. I hadn't talked or thought about money in over two years, but it was basically all I thought about beforehand. Still, you lose control of a seventy-ton state-of-the-art tank and bad things happen, no matter where you are. Everyone got to use the cars, boats, and tanks at some point, but you *really* had to earn real flight time. There was the obvious, and understandable, hesitation about tossing the keys to a plane that can go Mach 5 to a homesick kid who might choose to bolt, and then there was the location of the FATE Center itself. Keeping its location secret was not something that was taken lightly. So all flight training outside the simulator took place at night. Hey, if you can fly at night, you should be able to fly in the day, right? Maybe a handful of kids in the driving simulator room I was going into would ever get the chance.

Waiting for me inside were Clayton and Elin. I'd known Clayton for a while now—ever since I'd gotten bumped up to the seniors. He was a short but super muscly guy from South Africa (loved hearing him talk), and Elin was a stunningly gorgeous and fit girl from Norway. Actually, to be fair, anyone who survived here was fit. Hard to be anything else.

They were sitting with a tech behind an array of monitors, which showed mostly excited first years scrambling into the driving simulation boxes.

"Who do you want, Hutch?" Clayton asked me.

I stared at the monitors and put off choosing for as long as I could, but in the end I had to point at someone.

Lessons had to be learned and limits had to be tested for all of us at all times.

A common one was forcing a first year to drive near his or her home—and ignore it. The strong kept to their mission; the weak did not. Most turned home and then needed to be reminded about the importance of following orders. The reminder came in the form of a beating. Did I think it was crude and caveman-ish? Some silly skullduggery? (Heard that word in a movie once, still not a hundred percent sure what it means—certain areas of one's education take a back seat here.) Orders are orders. You follow them or you die.

Right now, the painful part was having to choose someone to beat up, knowing that whoever it was had done nothing to me and had done nothing to deserve it. The FATE people liked me for tasks like this. (Thanks to Leslie, I'm guessing.) I'd never been one to pick a fight for the sake of it. I needed a good reason. When someone messes up by their own doing, you teach them a lesson: that seems fair. Stacking the deck against them like that? Not cool. This always seemed purely psychopathic. Not that it was any different from 90 percent of what else went on here.

I scanned the list of names and stopped on Box Six—a girl named Ren and a boy named Junie. Ren and Junie? What the hell kind of names were these? Were their middle names Apple and Moonbeam? I shook my head.

By the way, this was the sort of the mental exercise I went through to justify the beatdowns. I created imaginary grudges. *Hipster parents. No doubt about it. Showering baby Ren Apple and Junie Moonbeam with unearned praise and presents. Participation medals. No clue how cruel the real world is. These spoiled brats could use a lesson in negative reinforcement . . .*

"Box Six," I said.

I smiled. I remembered my first simulator. They're beyond real. The speed, the sound . . . There's even wind that smells like the air outside. It's easy to forget where you are.

The tech pulled up Box Six on the main screen.

As soon as I saw the girl, I figured it was over. She was weak and didn't even try to hide it behind a mask of wannabe badass. Small, skinny, with short black hair and freckles, she definitely wouldn't make it past year one. But holy hell, was that a big fourteen-year-old boy. Reminded me a lot of . . . me. He looked the part, but I could tell he had feelings for this girl. Could he be strong enough for the two of them? The moment he turned left when the car he was supposed to be following turned right, we all shook our heads and headed for their simulator. They were just exiting as we approached.

"Should have kept following the green car," Clayton told them.

Man, even his threats sounded cool.

"Ren, go. Run," the Junie boy whispered, placing himself between her and us.

He *was* a lot like me.

"I'm not leaving you," the girl said.

"Please, go," Junie begged her, not even trying to hide his feelings.

She should have listened to him. Zero chance of love lasting in this place. I knew that firsthand. Her attachment to this overgrown kid didn't make me feel any sorrier for her. If anything, it brought up old memories and made me angrier.

Like a coordinated pack of raptors, we attacked. Clayton took the girl, while Elin and I focused on the boy.

In a few years Junie might be something special, something to reckon with. Heck, sooner than that, but not today. No, now he was raw. Raw emotion, raw training, raw everything. He was ready to sacrifice himself for her. Rookie mistake. The same one I made my very first day of training. Sweet, but stupid. Like they tell you on airplanes: put your mask on first and then tend to your kids. Can't help anyone if you're unconscious.

Clayton tackled Ren to the ground like she was a bag of feathers. Instead of letting her fight her own battle, Junie took punches and kicks from Elin and me and forced his way toward Ren. Before either of us could land the knockout blow, Junie grabbed Clayton from behind and hurled him like a rag doll into the door of the driving box. It was a pretty impressive toss, I'll give it to him, but it was reckless and left him wide open. I swept out his legs while Elin slammed her foot across his chest. He flipped and landed on the floor with an awkward splat. We didn't let him get back up.

Ren tried to help, but Clayton welcomed her enthusiasm with a kick of his own, right to the temple. It knocked her out instantly. Actually coulda killed her, but I think she lived. Not that I checked. But we aren't supposed to kill people during driving room exercises, so chances are she lived. Let's just go with the odds on this one before I feel guilty.

After dragging the unconscious bodies of the two lovebirds back into the side room, we called the medics to come take them away.

"Who's next?" the tech asked me when we climbed back upstairs. He wasn't alone, though. Standing next to him was Cole. He was basically another version of Shane. A certain type of a-hole instructors existed here. They all seemed to have one-syllable names and were universally disliked. We'd run into each other here and there, but I didn't know him too well. I'd only heard what a world-class jerk he was. Like Shane.

"What are you doing here?" I asked him.

"Whatever I want," he snapped. He glared at me, as if daring me to ask anything else. "Choose who's next," he commanded.

Yeah, I had to choose more. In fact, I had to choose a lot more. The full simulation lasted two hours. Box Six had taken . . . what? Two minutes? I wasn't much of a fan of this to begin with, but after what we'd done to Ren and Junie, the whole process disgusted me all over again. This wasn't who we were. This wasn't what we were about, was it? Beating for the sake of beating? But orders are to be followed. The mission must be carried out. I knew this, of course, but that didn't mean I had to agree with it. I held my tongue.

"Now," Cole ordered.

I blindly pointed at Box Twelve.

The medics coming for Ren and Junie were still en route when the suckers in Box Twelve took the bait. With any luck, the medics would arrive right as we were finishing off the other two kids, saving them a double trip to the infirmary. It's the little things, you know?

Anyway, it was rinse and repeat after that.

"DINNER?" CLAYTON ASKED ME.

I shrugged. I was sweaty and hungry after beating the crap out of strangers for two hours. "Sure."

I got along with the older kids just fine, but I rarely ate with them. Mostly I ate alone. All they talked about was how close they were to graduating. Yeah, I was training with the fourth years, but I wasn't *really* one of them. I was only sixteen, so I still had two more years. Besides, talking always quickly turned to being linked, and that's where I shut them out, so eating alone was sometimes more peaceful. But Clayton had asked. That was a first.

As we exited the side room to head out to dinner, I saw that Cole was waiting for me.

"You, upstairs," he said.

I hesitated. "What'd I do?" I asked. Upstairs was never good.

"You know better than to ask," he said menacingly.

He was right, but I'd stopped being afraid of everyone and everything a long time ago. "See ya, I guess," I said to Clayton. I have to admit, both he and Elin looked a bit worried on my behalf. Creases on their foreheads. Twitching lips. Worry is not an emotion you generally see at the FATE Center except among those who don't make it.

Cole led me straight to an elevator. Bad sign. We didn't get to use the elevators. This was for real.

"Seriously, am I in trouble?" I asked as we got inside.

"Would it change anything?" he replied.

I shook my head.

"Then does it matter?"

"I'd like a heads-up if I'm facing my impending doom."

He sneered. Once inside the elevator, he pressed his finger to the print scanner and waited. When it was recognized, he hit the top-most button three times before hitting the bottom-most one twice. The elevator dinged happily at the random button pushing as if to acknowledge its acceptance.

"Enjoy the ride," Cole said.

He slid out before the doors closed.

chapter 9

CHEERS TO ME

Alone. All alone. *Great.* How long had it been since I was in an elevator? Were they always this slow? And no music?! The ride wasn't long, but I had no clue how far I'd traveled. Hundred feet? A thousand? No clue. All I know is when the doors opened, I was greeted by two men in suits. Like actual business suits. Not combat gear. I'd sorta forgotten real clothes existed.

I stepped into a small room. A single door on the other side was the only way out, aside from the elevator. Hanging on the wall was a black clothing bag, the kind for suits.

"Put those on," the bigger of the two ordered, pointing at the clothing bag. "And at least tuck your hair behind your ears." I figured he would say that. He had a crew cut.

I knew better than to question orders. But when I unzipped the bag and saw the clothes inside, I couldn't help but say, "You're joking, right?"

Inside the bag were a pair of pleated khakis, a blue button-up shirt with a dark navy tie, and a pair of brown leather boat shoes.

The men didn't answer. I put the clothes on. I looked like a preppy East Coast nerd, but at least everything fit well.

"If anyone asks, you're an intern," the other guard instructed.

"Uh, sure. Got it." I nodded. Anyone? Where was I?

As it turns out, we were in the middle of a busy office. A real one. Full of real-life functioning, working, taxpaying people. I couldn't say what they did, but they all looked really busy. I followed the guards down some hallways. If anyone gave me a second look, I never caught them. It wasn't until we passed the copy machine, where I saw a line of young kids all dressed pretty similar to me, that I got it. My costume was spot on. I could have slid right in with them and no one would have been any wiser. Well, except for my shaggy hair. Yeah, I'd tucked it behind my ears, but it didn't quite fit in with these side-parted business wannabes.

I was led outside through a pair of metal double doors. A golf cart was parked there. This was the first time I'd been outside and not training since I'd gotten to FATE—one of the harder things to adjust to. I paused to take a deep breath.

This was something I remembered from juvie: free air always tastes better.

"In," the smaller guard ordered, directing me toward the cart. He shoved me in the back.

I turned and glared down at him. His reaction was priceless.

"Sorry, uh, please," he stammered.

No wonder these soft, doughy guards looked unfamiliar. I'd never seen them before. *Ever.* They were normal, real-world, fake-badge types.

I climbed into the front seat, next to the other guard. The smaller one raised his hand to object but decided against it. He climbed into the back seat. I think I caught the bigger guy smirking.

Soon we were bouncing along a path through the woods. We emerged and passed a few more offices before stopping outside a building that looked pretty much exactly like the one we'd come from. Maybe it *was* the same one, and the joyride was only to fool me. Doubtful, but you couldn't put it past them. We went through another plain old side door, but the moment I was inside, I knew it wasn't the same building. As loud and active as the other building was, this one was the exact opposite: quiet and empty. As in silent. Deserted.

The guards led me to a bank of elevators, but instead of pushing a button to call one, they walked me right up to a blank wall. There was a *ding*, and the wall slid open to reveal a hidden elevator. Okay, this was more like it.

"In," the larger guard ordered.

I shouldn't have been surprised when they didn't follow, but I was anyway. The larger guard clicked the button for the top floor and stepped off the elevator.

As the doors slid closed I asked, "Where am I going?"

"To meet the boss," the smaller guard said.

The boss? The *boss*. Nobody got to meet the boss. What was going on? What had I done? I racked my brain for anything I could have done that would get me in trouble, but I couldn't think of anything major. But what if . . .

I *was* alone and had taken whole classes on disabling and escaping from elevators. It was easy. Should I? Or was this a test? Was I supposed to try to escape? I didn't have time to make a decision. Apparently this elevator was super fast because no sooner had the doors closed than they were sliding back open again.

I was totally unprepared for what I saw.

I'd expected another boring hallway. Or more guards. Or something normal. But what I was looking at felt so out of place I thought maybe I'd passed out somewhere and was dreaming. I was looking out across a field of beach grass, and sitting all cozy in the middle of it was a full-scale wood-shingled beach cottage. Beyond the cottage was a long beach that led down to the ocean. *What in the hell?*

A thin path cut through the beach grass that was lazily waving in the soft ocean breeze. Really, a breeze? A puff of smoke was even dancing its way out of the chimney. It was surprisingly cold in here now that I thought of it. And what was that? Waves? Was I hearing the ocean, too? Did a seagull just fly by?

It was all so real I forgot it was fake. I kept having to remind myself I was in a building. Wasn't I?

A man wearing jeans and a loose, faded sweater appeared on the porch. He waved happily at me and called out, "Oh, great, come on in, Hutch. We have business to discuss."

He turned and went back inside the cottage like all of this was normal. Business? I looked around for, I don't know, anything to clue me in on what was going on. *Who the—? What the—? Business?*

The man appeared again and called out, "Your tea is getting cold. Come on."

My tea?

I walked down the well-beaten path toward the cottage but paused when I reached the wooden stairs that led up to the porch. Whistling—carefree whistling—was coming from inside. My mind flashed back to the driving simulator. That Junie guy had been big. Had he killed me and this was my purgatory? Or heaven? At least that would make sense because *this* didn't. Then I had an idea. The simulator.

I picked up a small beach rock from a pile by the stairs and chucked it as hard as I could at the ocean. If it hit the water, I was dead or crazy. Luckily, it thudded against a wall forty or so yards away and a ripple of color rolled across the image. Nothing more than a simulator. Whew. But an awesome whew.

"I won't ask nicely a third time," the man called from inside, and I knew he meant it.

I climbed up the stairs and pushed through the half-open door. The inside was just as cozy as the outside. Old wood floors and comfy turn-of-the-century furniture. In front of me was a living space with a fire crackling in the fireplace, and off to the right was a small kitchenette, where my host was pouring tea.

The man turned to face me. He was good-looking, I'm not ashamed to admit it—talent recognizes talent—and he had one of those super-wide, friendly smiles we all wish we had. He had shaggy brown hair that was barely starting to go gray, but it looked good on him. Reminded me of Matthew McConaughey actually.

"Tea, Hutch?" he offered. "You don't mind if I call you that, do you?"

I shook my head. His voice sounded so familiar, but I couldn't place it.

"Good. Here," he said, handing me a cup. "With milk and sugar—the only way to drink it."

He took a sip and by his expression I could tell he wanted me to do the same. Never been a tea guy, but when in Rome . . . It wasn't that bad. Not my first choice but not terrible.

"Sit with me by the fire," he said, walking past me and sitting down in an old recliner next to the fire. An empty brown love seat seemed to have my name on it. Careful not to spill the tea, I sat down. I had nothing against the boring regulation furniture I was used to, but I found this couch to be comfy like a marshmallow. The fire, the ocean, and the hot tea—all made me feel instantly sleepy.

"Relaxing, huh? You like it?" the man asked me.

"Yeah, it's cool," I admitted. It was weird and out of place, but there was no denying it was one of the cooler things I'd ever seen—and at FATE, that's saying something.

"It was my grandparents' house. Well, not the exact house.

They sold it when I was in high school, so this is from memory, but I think I did a good job. Had to take some guesses, but it felt like they were steering me, rooting for me to get it right."

Finally! When he said the word "rooting," I recognized his voice and couldn't help but shout out, "Pre-taped?!"

"Excuse me?" he asked, genuinely confused.

"You're . . . the voice. The one who talks to us."

"Oh, yes, that's me. Pre-taped, huh?" he said, shaking his head playfully. "I do enjoy the nicknames you all come up with for me. But please, call me Blake."

He took a sip of his tea and stared off into the fire. I did the same but only because he did. What the heck else was I supposed to do? Where was this going?

"I am pleased you went through with today's task at the driving simulators without issue. There had been concerns, but those are now gone. I must admit, Hutch, you have surpassed every expectation we set for you and then surpassed the new ones we set after that. We—I am extremely impressed."

"Thanks?" I blushed, still not good with compliments.

"I think you'll agree that you have little left to learn here, correct?"

"I mean . . ."

He waved me off. "No need to be coy with me, not here. Are you not enjoying your tea?"

I hadn't touched the stuff since the first sip. No, I wasn't.

"Would you like something else? Coffee, Coke?"

"Dr Pepper?" I said it as a joke because I hadn't had one since before FATE. Water, milk, and juice were all we got.

"Okay," he said.

We sat in silence for maybe twenty seconds before there was a polite knock on the door.

"I think that's for you," Blake told me.

I got up, went to the door, and opened it. Standing in the doorway was, I guess, his assistant. She was professionally dressed, had her blonde hair in a perfect, tight ponytail, and was holding a Dr Pepper for me. Cute assistant who delivers Dr Pepper on command? This dude lived the life. I took the can from her, cracked it open, and took a sip for the ages. Man, I'd missed that. Sah-weeeeet-ness. When I sat back down with Blake, I couldn't stop smiling. He gave a friendly laugh.

"Better?" he asked.

"You have no idea."

"I bet you're right," he admitted. "Cheers to you," he said, raising his glass.

I raised my can.

"To the youngest graduate we've ever had," he said, clinking his teacup against my can.

"Youngest?"

"By two hundred fifteen days," he said, taking a sip before adding, "If you don't sip after a toast, it's bad luck."

I quickly took a sip. Then it really hit me.

"Wait, I'm graduating?"

He nodded like a proud, caring father.

"Like getting out of here?"

He smiled. "Not just yet. We have a very special assignment for you. It will take a bit more specialized training, but yes, soon you'll be out of here."

"Hunter?!" I asked, way too excited. "You're making me a Hunter?"

Being a Hunter was the best it got. We all dreamed of being one. Meant you were the best of the best of the best. And if what I was hearing was true, that sounded like me. Getting a cold Dr Pepper and being made a Hunter? This was turning into the best day *ever*.

"Oh, dear boy, no." He nearly laughed.

Well, you don't have to laugh about it.

"The Hunter ranks are full, and you're far too young. No, we have something much more important and special for you."

There is something more important, more special than being a Hunter? Go on.

"You're still going to be a Shadow, but the cover you will have to assume is truly unique and requires, as I said, some additional training that's not currently offered as part of our core curriculum. It also takes a little bit of natural talent, which . . ."

He polished off the last sip of this tea, put the empty cup on the table, picked up the tablet next to it, and pressed a few keys on it. A creepy video of me in my shower sprang to life on the screen, and even better, I was singing.

". . . you have."

"That is such an invasion of privacy," I whispered, totally disgusted as I stared at the screen. At least I sounded good. Wait, please tell me the natural talent he's talking about is my singing and not my, oh no, is this going where I think it's going? *Paging Dusty Spicewood, you're wanted on set.* (You know the game where you take the name of your first pet and combine it with the street you grew up on to get your porn name? My first pet was a mutt named Dusty and I grew up on Spicewood Drive. Yep, Dusty Spicewood.)

"And we know you can dance, too," he added, bringing up another video of me and a group of third years goofing off dancing to some music in one of the hangars. "But"—he paused—"can you do them at the same time?"

Whew, that had quickly been heading toward a very unwelcome direction. Yeah, Dusty Spicewood was a great name, but well, yuck. Still didn't mean I wasn't beyond confused by all of this, so all that came out of my mouth was, "Uh."

"Can you?" he asked again. "Sing and dance at the same time?"

Was he serious? How did this matter?

"I'm serious. This matters," he said as if reading my mind, which maybe he could. I don't know. This place was crazy.

"I mean, uh, I guess."

"Well?"

"Like, sure, why not?" I never had, but . . . "How hard could it be?" I added.

"Good, because"—and he looked at me with all seriousness as he spoke—"we need you to join a boy band."

Yeah, you heard that right.

chapter 10
INTRODUCING BOBBY SKY

"Uh . . ." was all my brain could muster. No way I heard that right, right? But I know I did. I mean, what the—

"Excited?" he asked, totally reading me wrong.

That was a word, but not one I'd have used to describe what I was feeling. Shocked? Disgusted? A little pissed? Yeah, those were the more PG-rated words I'd have used.

Look, once you realize that waking up from this nightmare or escaping aren't options, you don't get to have too many fantasies at the FATE Center. You sort of give them up. But there *was* the slim chance that your cover could be something super awesome when you became a Shadow.

For example, there was a rumor—and we all believed it, probably because we were all so desperate—that one guy's FIP was a billionaire recluse who lived on a lake in Italy. So the Shadow's cover was to be a fellow billionaire who lived next door. He had his own tennis court and helicopter! Now, *that* was a cover. Of all the possible scenarios I could come up with once I got out of this place, being in a boy band was definitely not one of them. How do you land on *that*? On *boy band*? And did they know me? As in, what I looked like? When you saw me, the last thing you thought was boy band. Rock band, yes. Eighties hair cover band, sure, why not? Metal band, maybe. But boy band?!

It was insulting. Or ignorant. Or both.

I knew this wasn't a joke. Nobody in this place had a sense of humor. Boss Man Blake was all serious. I'd just spent the better part of two years turning myself into a lethal killing machine so that I could . . . I couldn't even finish the thought. *Boy band?* These things don't just happen though, right? They're started in a Disney factory or something. Merchandise first, talent later. How would this even work?

"So," I began. Apparently I still wasn't ready to form sentences, so I only managed to follow that with, "How?"

Decent question, I thought.

"Excellent question. With training. You'll spend the next few months in this building learning to sing and dance at a professional level."

I sneered. Had this clown even heard me sing or seen me dance? I didn't need any training.

"Hutch, please. Don't overestimate yourself." Blake arched an eyebrow. "You're an amateur with talent. We're going to ensure you go pro, so to speak. In August you'll go to a nationwide casting call in Chicago, where you will try out like a normal person."

"But I'll be more talented than the competition," I said. "Right?"

Blake shook his head. "No, it will be rigged," he answered bluntly. "Thanks to some incriminating pictures we have of one of the producers, you'll get selected to be in the band." He smirked. "Bob's your uncle."

"What? Who?"

He waved me off. "Figure of speech. Forget about it." He fixed me with an intense stare.

"Why?" Apparently I could only form one-word questions now.

"So you can be linked to Ryo, one of the band members. Do you understand?"

I nodded.

"Good." Blake seemed to relax again. "What better way to keep him safe than to be at his side at all times?" He leaned back, grinning and crossing his arms as if he'd made the point of the century.

Now I was confused. "But we're not supposed to interact with them. Isn't that, like, rule number one . . . and two and three?" It was like the first and second rules of *Fight Club.*

"I told you this is a special case. Of course, I cannot tell you what makes Ryo special, or what he does, but what I can tell you is that no amount of interaction with you could stop him from doing what earned him a Shadow in the first place. Trust me on this."

I stopped trusting people a long time ago. It happens when you wake up strapped to a chair in a place you're afraid is going to kill you, and then said place spends the next two years actively trying to kill you. But, if you remember, I also drank the Kool-Aid. I'd fully accepted that I was in this for the long haul, with all the long-haul rules that had been drilled into my head. Now the rules were being ignored? *And* I'd have to be in a boy band. Would I have preferred a rock band? A solo act? Riverdancer? Yes, yes, and—okay, no—but boy band it was. They were cool in their own way, right? Don't answer that.

"Your presence will not be an issue, I promise," Blake said in the silence.

"So is it Rio like the city in Brazil?"

"No, it's with a 'y.' R-Y-O. Ryo Enomoto. A Japanese national around whom the band is being formed. He is the real talent. The rest of you will be fillers around him."

"So he's the Harry to One Direction."

"Sure," he said. He clearly had no clue what I was talking about.

"What will the band be called? No Direction?" I joked.

"I can't remember the name of it, but it is perfectly appropriate and eye-roll-inducing all at the same time."

I tried to smile. "So, when do we begin?"

"That's the spirit," he said. He sounded genuinely excited. I'm glad someone was.

There was a knock on the door. He seemed to be expecting it, because he stood and waved for me to follow.

"Come on," he said.

We went outside. Whoever had knocked had vanished. There were two wooden aardvark beach chairs set up for us in front of the simulated ocean. I know they're not actually called aardvark chairs, but I know that's close and can't remember the real name, so aardvark it is. Can you name all the different PPK pistol variations? Exactly. We each have our own wealth of useless knowledge. Sitting between the aardvark chairs was a table with two pizza boxes on it.

Pizza. My mouth began to water.

"Not every day do we have someone graduating two years early," he said, sitting down. "Let's celebrate."

I didn't move. My eyes were on the boxes and nothing else. I hadn't had pizza since I left home. I hoped there weren't any veggies on them. Time couldn't change how I felt about veggies on pizza. They ruin it. Blake flipped the top off the first one. Supreme. Disgusting. Then he flipped the top off the second.

Oh, dear pepperoni and cheese, how I've missed you . . .

I grabbed a slice of the good stuff and sat down next to Blake. He grabbed a slice of the supreme. We ate in silence while watching the "sunset" over the "horizon." By the time I'd KO'd the pepperoni single-handedly and moved on to flicking off the veggies from the pieces of the supreme, the "stars" had come out. Nice touch.

Blake slapped his hands on his knees and stood up. "Well, I think it's time for you to get some rest, Bobby."

Bobby? Nobody had called me that since kindergarten. I *hated* that name.

"Hutch, call me Hutch," I reminded him, but played it cool.

"Wrong. As of today, Hutch no longer exists. Hutch's life is officially over. From here on out, you will be Bobby Sky."

"Do I have a say in this?" I asked.

He smiled.

"Bobby Sky," I said, trying it out. It sounded just as terrible coming from my own mouth.

"The one and only," he chimed in. "Trust me, you'll get used to it, Bobby."

Bobby Sky? Was it too late to not be cool with all of this? Or had the pizza sealed it?

The pizza began to churn in my stomach. "So let me get this straight," I started. "After using every dirty trick in the book to stop me from singing for fun, like breaking my arm, breaking friends' arms, and torture while I could still feel it, you now need me to sing? You see the hilarity of that, right?"

"I see serendipity," he said.

"Seren . . . who?"

"Oh, you're funny," he said, looking past me.

I twisted in the chair to follow his gaze. I could see his assistant, the one who'd brought me the Dr Pepper earlier, heading my way down the path. I turned back to Blake, but he was gone, already halfway up the steps to his cottage.

"Did your meeting go well, Bobby?" the assistant asked.

"Bobby? News travels fast," I muttered. I stood up from the chair.

"It was going to be Bobby Blue, but I convinced him to change it to Sky."

Bobby Blue?!?!

"Thanks, I guess?"

"See, it's not as bad as you thought," she offered as we walked toward the exit.

"It's still pretty awful."

The door to the elevator slid open. While we rode it down, I had to ask, "So, you know what goes on here?"

"Yeah."

"And you're okay with it?"

She shrugged. "I try not to think about it too much. But whenever I do, I remind myself that you were all dead anyway, and that helps. This is better than being dead, right?"

"For some," I said, knowing what many of my friends went through before they *still* died. Or lost their minds. Had that been better than the wildcard death that had been in store for them out in the real world? Debatable.

We got off on the seventh floor, and she led me to my new apartment.

Yeah, you read that right. *Apartment.*

Not the prison cell they'd called my room for the past two years. It was . . . adult. It had rooms, like actual rooms. I had a bedroom, living room, and even a kitchen room. Kitchen-ette? Whatever. Wait, was I supposed to cook my own meals now? They skipped over that one in my training. Sure, I could still cook a mean cereal, but that's about it.

"Good luck, Bobby," the assistant told me. "If you need something, use this," she added, pointing at a small screen next to the door.

She was the first non-Shadow recruit I'd talked to since I got here and I wasn't about to waste the chance. Yeah, she was older, but she was cute—so there was that, too.

"So, uh, wanna hang out?" I asked.

"Oh no, I have work to do," she said politely. She headed for the exit.

"Where you from? How old are you?" I quickly blurted out.

She paused outside. "Why do you want to know?"

"Curious. What are you . . . what, twenty-four?"

"Oh, you're adorable," she said sweetly. She sounded as if she were talking about a kitten.

"Older?"

"Much. Is twenty-four your cutoff age?" she asked in the same syrupy voice.

"My cutoff age is however old you are, plus one day," I added smoothly.

She smirked. "Get some rest, Bobby. Take a cold shower."

"At least tell me your name."

"Claire."

"Well, there's space for two in that cold shower, Claire."

"You're incorrigible." But I heard her chuckle as she closed the door behind her.

A chink in the armor, I see. Victory.

I quickly explored my new place. The fridge and cabinets were stocked full of food. I had clothes—not just athletic ones but real ones, like jeans—in the closet. My bathroom was almost as big as my cell and it had a bathtub. I never took baths before all of this, but since I'd only had the option for a shower since I got to FATE, I was strangely excited by it. The best part by far though was the huge flat-screen TV. Were my favorite shows still on? Who'd won the Super Bowl?! The past two Super Bowls? So many questions! I plopped down on the couch and clicked the remote. I'd never had so many channel choices in my entire life, and it took me a good ten minutes just to find the sports options. While I was in a pizza coma, watching *SportsCenter*, there was a moment where it felt like the past two years hadn't happened. Like I was sitting at home watching TV like a normal teen.

It felt nice.

chapter 11

KILLER DANCE MOVES, BRO

Beepbeepbeep! Beepbeepbeep! Beepbeepbeep!

The sudden noise made me jump a little. I looked around. What time was it? And where was that dang noise coming from?! The small screen by the door was flashing in rhythm with the beeping that seemed to be coming from all over. As I stood up, I suddenly realized how tired I was. No sleep? I was an idiot. True, I didn't need much anymore, but I needed some. Ugh, that was stupid of me.

I lurched off the couch and jabbed the screen, a little harder than I'd meant to, and cracked it. There goes my deposit. The alarm shut off though, which was the goal. A message appeared.

Class—8:00 A.M.—Rm 1979

My bleary eyes flashed to the bottom of the screen. It was 7:50 A.M. I had class in ten minutes? *Ten minutes!?* What type of class? I poked at the cracked screen, but it stayed blank. Was it singing? Dancing? Both? What was this strange feeling? Was I . . . nervous?

I stopped getting nervous a long time ago. Pretty much the same day those injections finally made me incapable of feeling any pain. Was *this* what real nervousness felt like? Why? Why now? I could kill someone from across the room with a spiral notebook spring, so why in the hell would singing or dancing make me nervous?

AFTER THROWING ON SOME new (real) clothes, I hurried to the elevator and poked the call button. Second surprise of the morning: when the doors opened, the elevator wasn't empty. Elin was standing in it.

"Hutch?" Elin asked, seeming just as shocked. "What are you doing here?"

"What are *you* doing here?" I asked right back.

"They came and got Clayton and me right after you left. We're graduating." She reached out of the elevator and hugged me as she said, "I'm so glad you're alive. We weren't sure what was going on."

At first I didn't react. We didn't hug here. What had they done to Elin? But when in Rome . . .

"I'm fine, really," I said as I ended the weird hug. "So this is where they bring you to graduate?" I knew—well, rumor had it, anyway—that graduates spent time in an apartment complex before they got linked to their FIP to get acclimated to the real world. So this was it, huh?

"This is it," she confirmed.

I stepped inside the elevator and tapped for the nineteenth floor, hoping I was right about where room 1979 would be. There were apparently forty-two floors and I didn't have time to be wrong. It was 7:58 A.M.

"How long will you have to wait until you're linked?"

"No idea. Takes a while sometimes. They have to make it perfect, or time the match right, or something like that." She shrugged, like, *what can you do?*

The elevator stopped on the sixteenth floor. She hesitated before getting out. "What are *you* doing here?" she asked again.

"Oh, uh, graduated early," I admitted, which wasn't a total lie. I wasn't supposed to talk about my assignment to anyone. Not that I wanted to say the words "boy band" out loud if I didn't have to. The shame was still too recent.

"Wow. You must be the youngest ever." She stepped outside.

I shook my head. "Maybe, don't know."

"What's here?" I called after her. "I mean on this floor?"

"Gun range."

"Cool."

She spun as the doors began to close. "Wanna grab dinner?" she asked.

"Sure." Maybe I didn't have to cook for myself after all.

"Cafeteria, say around eight?" she called out as the doors closed tight.

"Okay."

Alone in an elevator . . . again. After two years of never being alone, except in my room, a new pattern was emerging.

The doors opened again, and I got out. The hallway on the nineteenth floor was deserted. A few lights here and there, but it was mostly dark. The first door was marked 1901. Whew. Yeah, I had a long way to go—but at least I was in the right place. I didn't hear anything as I walked. I didn't see anything either. No one used this floor as far as I could tell.

1925 . . . 1946 . . . 1972 . . . getting closer.

Was that music? Old-timey music that grandparents in movies listened to on record players? As I walked, the music got louder. I got more nervous with each step.

Room 1979.

I took a deep breath and composed myself before stepping inside. Okay, I admit it. I was fully expecting the cliché: wooden floors, walls of mirrors, and a stuffy, uppity instructor who may or may not have worn a unitard and a monocle. I hadn't prepared myself for bare concrete floors, no mirrors, and a young girl—hardly older than me—in baggy jeans, Adidas Sambas, and a tank top.

"Hey," she said with a crooked smile. She seemed cheery. Happy to see me, in fact. Her big eyes sparkled.

She had her brown hair in a loose ponytail, was dancer-fit, and had that crooked smile working for her. Do I have to say it? Yes, I was instantly crushing hard. What? I'm sixteen and for the past two years every girl I've known has worn yellow, blue, red, or black from head to toe, depending on their year, and was trained to kill. Seeing normal girls again was—this was only my second one. She was hot. Sue me. Like you'd be any different.

She walked over to me and said, "I'm Ariel, but you can call me Leggo."

We shook hands as I asked, "Lego? Like the toy?"

She shook her head playfully and explained, "No, as in Leggo my Eggo. My last name's Eggot. E-G-G-O-T, but the *T* is silent. It's a lot better than Waffle, which some people did call me."

I laughed, even though I didn't have any idea what the hell she was talking about. But yes, I was flirting. Bit out of practice, though.

"I'm—"

"Bobby," she said, cutting me off. "I know. And I know I'm not supposed to ask anything else either." She raised up her hands for effect.

"What do you mean?"

"Part of my deal. I train you up, don't ask why, keep my mouth shut forever, and they'll wipe my record and won't press charges for . . . never mind."

"You can't *not* explain now." Knowing she was in trouble with the law only upped the hotness level.

She mimed locking her mouth with a key.

I was curious, to say the least. I also hoped someone had given her a sideways warning that if she breached the agreement, she wouldn't see us in court, if you catch my drift. (Psssst, they'd kill her.)

Lovely awkward silence as we stared at each other.

"So, you wanna learn how to dance?" she asked me.

"That's the dream," I said flatly.

She just kept smiling. Didn't bat an eyelash. If she was judging me at all, I couldn't read it on her face. "Front and center," she said, snapping her fingers and pointing at the middle of the room.

I walked to the middle and looked at her.

"Since you have zero formal training, we'll start with the fundamentals: the box step."

I'd done that one before. You put a box in front of you and then stepped up on it. We did them in football. I didn't see any boxes in here, though.

"What are you looking for?" she asked me.

"A box."

"Oh, honey," she said sadly, and I didn't understand why until she showed me the simple, basic step. It did not require the use of a box.

"Feet together. And left foot up. Right foot diagonal. Left joins right. Right foot back. Left diagonal back to the beginning, and the right joins it." She did it three more times before asking, "Got it?"

Yeah, I'm not an idiot. But . . .

"Why is it called a box step?"

"Because it makes a box," she replied, like I was the dumb one, and showed me the move one more time for good measure. "A box," she said slowly, tracing the shape in the air when she was done.

"Uh, I'm no Will Hunting math genius, but boxes don't have diagonals. *That* was two triangles. *This* would be a box step."

I stepped forward, sideways, backward, and then sideways again.

"Box step," I added, pointing at myself with mock pride before pointing at her and adding, "Double-triangle step."

"I don't care if you call it the loosey-goosey," she argued. "Just show me you can do it."

I did it three times. It was easy, and I made sure I had the most bored look I could muster while I did it. When I was done, I raised my palms and said, "Happy? Don't you want to see what I've got in my arsenal of moves first so we don't waste time on this crap?"

"No," she answered flatly. "I don't need to see, and I don't care."

"But I'm, like, a dancing servant."

"You mean, savant?"

"Huh? I'm a dancing Rain Man."

I started to roll my shoulders and move around a bit. She quickly held up her hand for me to stop.

"At best, you can party dance. Works at a kegger but not at an audition. You need to memorize routines, learn timing, and respond to basic dance terms."

"Maybe down the road, but for an audition? I need to wow them. Can you teach me how to moonwalk?"

"You want to know how to moonwalk?"

"Yeah. I mean, I go into an audition and do a double-triangle step? Come on. But I go and nail a killer moonwalk? A make-MJ-proud kinda walk? They'll offer me the gig right then and there."

"Okay," she said, nodding, clearly thinking about something. "I mean, it's your call, but this was what I thought you should do."

She flipped on some techno and did a short but crazy awesome routine. There was flipping, popping, and some nasty cool stuff on the ground I didn't even know was dancing.

"That was awesome!" I yelled when she finished.

"You want to be able to do all that at an audition?" she asked, cutely flipping a loose strand of hair behind her ear. It was adorable.

I nodded.

"Starts with mastering the box step." She smiled, then corrected herself when I raised my eyebrows. "Sorry, double-triangle step."

I groaned.

"But I get it. We should have some fun and warm up first." She pulled out her phone and turned on some kind of dance music. She bounced for a few seconds before starting to dance. "Come on, Bobby, let's go. Get out here."

Dance on command for real in front of a cute girl like this? Uh, no.

"What, you're embarrassed?" she called out in the middle of her handstand.

"No!" *Yes.*

She did some sexy slide-walking thing toward me until her face was inches from mine. Dang, she was cute! She kept rocking back and forth to the beat. Our bodies brushed up against each other. Ripples of attraction pulsed through me.

"It's just dancing. It's supposed to be fun," she whispered flirtatiously.

She slowly backed away, motioning seductively with her fingers to follow her.

Reluctantly I joined in, feeling pretty stupid at first, but before I knew it, I wasn't nervous anymore and being embarrassed wasn't even on my radar. This was fun! I started with some old classics, but to try to impress my new crush, I worked in some more elaborate spin flips and kicks I'd learned in my martial arts training. It worked. Leggo was impressed.

For the first time in over two years of being under the lock and key of the Man, I finally felt free.

chapter 12
BECOMING BOBBY SKY

Mornings were for dancing with Leggo and my afternoons, for singing with a dude named Brance. Not Vance. *Brance.* He was very particular about that.

It was strange at first. I went straight from learning to hunt, protect, fight, and kill to learning to breakdance, disco, waltz, and vogue. Instead of learning to torture someone into singing soprano, I was learning to actually do it with my voice on key.

That's how I spent my days, but evenings were mine. Now, I'd never actually been told this, but it was fairly obvious that I was expected to go to the gym at night to keep in shape and not get too rusty when it came to being a Shadow—you know, my real job. Tonight, a week into my new life as Bobby, I'd decided to take the night off. My first one since, well, ever.

There was a *ding* the moment before Claire's face appeared on the cracked screen by the door. With her blonde hair so tightly pulled back, she almost looked bald.

I'd been alone in *my* own apartment, so I was only wearing a pair of shorts.

"Whoa! Pervert alert," I joked as I got up to look at her.

"Put some clothes on," she said, looking away.

"Not gonna happen. You're the one creeping on me."

"It's part of my job."

"Riiiiiiight," I mocked as I stood up, raised my arms, and slowly began to spin. "Drink it in. It's okay to like it. You're only human. No shame in these feelings."

"Are you done yet?" she asked, trying to sound annoyed.

"Are you? Never woulda took you for a Peeping Tom, but . . ."

"Jane."

"What?"

"I'm a woman, so I would be a Peeping Jane," she corrected.

"So you've researched your disease. Guilty conscience."

She didn't acknowledge me and chose to go with the silent treatment. Two could play this game. I gave her another turn, granted her the luxury of a "Zeus with the lightning" pose while I "yawned," and then pretended to "knock" an apple off the table so I had to bend over to pick it up. No reaction. Nada.

"Fine, I'm done. What?" I finally asked, taking a big chomp out of the apple.

"You're to go to the gym immediately and swim two miles in under an hour. After that, a man named Luka will approach you to grapple and spar as he sees fit for as long as he sees fit. Go now."

This was my veg night. I had not planned on this. I spat out the apple.

"But I just had cereal . . . with milk," I offered as my excuse.

"The real world doesn't wait for your digestive tract."

"Can I put clothes on first?" I asked.

"I've been begging you to do that since we began. Yes, but no dillydallying."

I rushed to get into a shirt and my shoes. I'd expected her to "hang up," but she stayed on-screen watching me, making sure I hurried.

"Bobby," she called as I was rushing out.

"Yeah?"

"Next time, don't presume you can take a night off."

The screen went black.

CHOREOGRAPHY, I'D ASSUMED, WOULD be my downfall, but once it dawned on Leggo that she could use my background in martial arts to her advantage, it was easy. She computed dancing to learning new fight combinations, which I was darn good at. Right hook, left jab, straight jump kick translated well to right step, left spin, leap.

Singing, well, I knew I had some real talent, but no one was going to hear me and think an angel had fallen from heaven. The main hurdle was that apparently, real singers can "read sheet music" or something like that. I could mimic a song pretty good if I heard it, but my mind was not made to read notes. It just wasn't. I struggled. Lucky for me, I had plenty of time to work on it.

I'm also guilty of not trying as hard as I could at it because I didn't want to be there. Singing meant being with Brance, who was nice enough, but I really only wanted to spend time with Leggo. At first, I thought that if I sucked enough at singing, they'd let me focus more on the dancing, that is, spend more time with Leggo. It didn't happen. If anything, it went the other way. I got more "Brance" time. And it was probably for good reason, too, because every minute I spent with Leggo made the crush worse. The pull to see her was getting black-hole strong.

(All you C students, feel free to ask your smart classmates to explain that one to you.)

The morning my dance alarm didn't go off was one of the most depressing mornings of my life. I ran up to room 1979 anyway. It was empty. Deserted. No trace of anyone having used it in years.

While I stood in the bare room remembering our last lesson, I slapped my forehead. How'd I miss it? Yesterday we'd tossed the choreography, which I'd mastered, out the window and just danced. Had fun. It'd been hot, sweaty, and at times a bit dirty, but in a mostly harmless way. At one point, I pulled her body to mine and when our faces were inches away from each other, I looked at her. Really looked at her. Whoa. What a rush. Before I could do something stupid, like try to kiss her, she'd quickly pulled away to dance on her own. All I could do was watch.

I'd forgotten what feelings like that could do to you. How they could make you feel on cloud nine one second and then crappy the next.

Then I realized something else. As depressing as never seeing my Leggo again was, my alarm not going off could mean only one thing: it was go time.

I headed back to my room double time and tapped the cracked screen next to the door to bring up my schedule for the day. There was nothing. Not a thing on my calendar. Huh.

RING!

The sudden burst of noise and the flashing indicator from the screen made me jump. I quickly tapped it to answer it, causing another crack to spread across it, and a soldiery-looking guy's face was there.

"Yeah?" I asked, trying to hide how excited I was.

He cleared his throat and said, "Mr. Sky."

God, that terrible name.

"Your escort will arrive at 2 P.M."

The screen went blank. It was happening. It was finally, actually, truly happening. I was getting out of here. Like *out-of-here* out of here. Like real world, real people out of here. Like . . . okay, you get it. I'll stop. Even the lameness of being in a boy band couldn't weigh me down. Hutch and this place were finally breaking up. I was moving on. *Oh, hi, FATE Center, we need to talk. It is you, not me. We're totally over. Peace out in . . .* I looked at my watch.

. . . five hours? How could it only be 9 a.m.? What am I supposed to do now?

BEFORE I'D STOPPED FEELING pain, they'd literally tortured me here—tying me to a chair, using butane torch, razor blades, the works—but the next five hours were worse than any torture I'd gotten. The time dragged on and on like nothing before. I swear it even went backward at one point. Like, I honestly believed someone had snuck into my room and turned back the clocks. Ugh. TV was boring. Music was annoying. Even training didn't work.

And then, as time is known for doing, it snuck up on me. Suddenly it was time to go. Right at 2 P.M. there was a knock at my door.

It was Claire. I hadn't seen her since she appeared in the screen on my "night off," but from the neck up she looked exactly the same. Actually, she looked exactly the same as when I'd first met her at Blake's bizarro cottage by the sea: business suit, heels, and a tight blonde ponytail. I wondered if she even owned other styles.

"Hey," I said casually.

"Ready?" she asked, meeting my casualness.

"Uh, heck, yes. Please, God, get me outta here."

She laughed. "Come on."

I followed her to the elevators.

"What's your last name?" I blurted out as the doors closed. I wasn't sure why. Maybe this brief time in the apartment, this sort-of taste of sort-of freedom, had empowered me.

"Why do you want to know?" she asked. At least she was still smiling.

"So I know who to send my first autographed picture to," I joked. "I just want to know," I admitted.

"Claire Marsh," she said.

"Claire Marsh, the future Mrs. Bobby Sky."

She laughed. "This picture better sweep me off my feet."

I nodded. "Consider yourself swept."

The doors opened a second later, but I paused. We were back at the cottage. But it was stormy—there was actual rain falling. Hard. A true thunderstorm: flashes of lightning, deafening thunder, the whole deal. I couldn't move. Not because I was afraid. This wasn't right. We were kept in the dark about the process of being linked, for the most part. Still, I knew that linking had to occur in a controlled lab. This was not a lab. This was . . . wrong.

Claire shoved me out of the elevator. "He's inside," she half shouted over the wind and rain.

I turned and squinted at her. "You're not coming?"

"In that?" she laughed. "Not in these shoes." The doors began to close. "Good luck!"

I grimaced and pulled my training jacket over my head, then bolted for the cottage. I was soaked by the time I reached the cover of the porch.

Blake must have heard me land on the wooden porch because he called out, "Come on in."

I hung my soaked jacket on a hook next to the door, shook my wet hair dry like a dog, and went inside.

Man, it was warm in here. Toasty and comfortable. Blake was sitting by the fire sipping tea and there was a bottle of Dr Pepper next to a glass of ice on the table for me. He looked different. Older. Like some great stress had been slowly eating at him since we spoke last. His face looked tired and the charm that seemed to radiate from him was gone. Even his clothes felt off. The khaki pants were frayed at the bottom, and the blue sweater had seen better days.

"Sorry about the weather," he told me as I took my seat and poured a glass of soda. "It's programmed to reflect my mood."

"You mad about something?" I asked.

"A little, but mostly sad," he said with a pained smile.

"So you're 'smad.'"

He chuckled.

My fake smile didn't reach my eyes. "Not about me, right?" Was this why I'd been called here? Was the stray dog finally being put down?

"No, my dear boy, no. A decision was made that affects us and I do not agree with it. Backs me into a bit of a corner, if you will."

"Sorry?" I offered. No clue what he was talking about, but glad it wasn't about me.

He downed the rest of his tea, put the cup on the table, and sighed. "Not your fault in the least, but I appreciate your politeness. You always were a good kid. So, are you ready?"

I nodded. "I've been waiting a long time to be linked." Hope springs eternal.

"Linked?" He seemed genuinely surprised. "You're not getting linked. Not now and especially not here. No, if we linked you now, there would be no way you could go to your audition. You would only care about Ryo."

"Oh, then . . ."

"Why are you here?" He stuck out his hand. "I just wanted to wish you luck."

I shook it, baffled.

"And to stress on you that this isn't a done deal, Bobby. Our inside man can only grease the wheels so much. If you're terrible, no amount of grease will cover your squeak. You have the look, but you still need to give him something tangible to work with when he champions you to others. You have to impress." Now *he* seemed baffled. "Why do you think we went through all of this if all you had to do was show up?"

How could this *not* be a done deal? You have the power to kidnap teenagers and turn them into walking weapons, but you don't have the power to manipulate the outcome of a boy band audition? That's where your reach stops? How is that possible? How could you honestly *not* know the outcome of the audition? This *mattered*?!

"If I don't impress?" I asked, pissed.

"Then all of this would have been for naught—a waste of time and resources, and we will have no further use for you." His tone was polite. But the subtext was clear: they would put me down like an animal.

He wasn't serious, was he? I mean, no further use for me, really? Didn't need someone to change lightbulbs in the training center even? My life had suddenly boiled down to one simple this or that: boy band or die. Hilarious. Of all the "or die" scenarios Shane had ever considered for his great opening speech, I bet boy band had never been one of them.

"I'll do my best," I offered.

"For your sake and ours, I hope that's good enough," he said absently. His eyes met mine, and he straightened. "I have no doubt it will be."

Nice try with the morale booster, buddy. Lesson learned: never threaten someone with death and then try to give them the old "you'll do fine."

"You should get going. I'm shifting from 'smad' to plain mad. A hurricane is coming."

I WAS DRIVEN DEEP into the woods to a private airstrip, where a row of bare-bones no-frills military cargo planes sat. I climbed inside the one they dropped me off at.

"Claire?" I blurted out.

There she was, strapped into one of the standard jump seats that unfolded from the walls. She motioned for me to take the seat across from her. "What are you doing here?" I asked as I sat down.

"I'm your chaperone."

"My *what*?"

"You didn't think we'd let you go alone, did you?"

"Training wheels are coming off soon anyway, so yeah, I guess I did," I admitted. "So how'd you get stuck with me on this trip?"

"It was my idea," she admitted.

"Of course it was," I said, toying with her. "Like I said, there's no shame in these feelings, Claire. They're mutual."

She rolled her eyes as the plane began to move. I instinctively tried to open the window shade so I could look out. But these weren't shades. In fact, they were painted black. Dang, the mystery of where exactly the FATE Center was would not be solved today, I guessed.

"So what, if anyone asks, are you like my sister or something?"

"If anything, I'd be your mother," she corrected me.

"My mother? What?! Did you have me when you were like twelve?"

She waved off my comment, but I saw a bit of blush there.

"No one should ask, though. I'm only here to get you to the audition and back. For everything in between, you'll be on your own. Which brings us to . . ." She reached into her bag and pulled out a folder.

"Okay, you will be auditioning for the role of the bad boy. Shouldn't be much of a stretch for you."

She handed me the folder.

"This is your new cover. We kept it simple. Instead of a

kid from the streets of Austin, you're now from Tyler. In that folder you'll find information about the city, why no one will remember you, the fact that you were homeschooled, and any other information vital to pulling off the ruse. Read it. Know it. Believe it."

"You gonna quiz me on this?" I joked.

"Yes, actually," she said in all seriousness.

She really did it. Periodically she'd stop me and quiz me on what I'd just read. She was relentless throughout the entire flight and it didn't stop on the cab ride to the convention center either. By the time we got there, I really was Bobby Sky from Tyler, Texas, and my dream was to be in a boy band.

Now, I knew there'd be a crowd, but I hadn't expected this. Yeah, I'd seen pictures from when *American Idol* had come to Austin back in the day, but I'd never gone near the auditions. It really wasn't my thing. But seeing pictures of something like this and actually being in the middle of it is not the same. This was total madness. A cattle call of teen boys.

"Showtime," Claire said as she slid out of the cab.

I took a deep breath and slid out behind her. She got back in.

"Whoa, what?" I asked.

"You said it yourself: the training wheels have to come off at some point. And besides, wouldn't me being there be an issue?" she asked, raising her eyebrow. One last quiz of my cover.

I racked my brain and came up with, "I had to sneak up here because my parents don't support my singing. I'll probably catch hell for it. Oh, and a real bad boy wouldn't have his mom with him."

"Not even a hot one like me," she joked. "Good luck."

"Boy band or die," I teased and gave a mocking fist pump.

"Text me when you're done, and we'll meet back here."

I nodded.

"You're not going to run, are you?"

"Only if you're coming with me."

She rolled her eyes and shook her head playfully. "The Drake, please," she told the driver.

IN TRUTH I HADN'T even considered making a run for it. The thought lasted for a second, tops. Boy band or not, this was who I was, what I was. There was also the knowledge of what, or specifically who, would come after me if I even tried to run. Yeah, not gonna test those waters. I turned and headed to join the mass of teenage boys waiting to get inside the center.

A young skater kid stopped by and asked, "What's going on?"

"Open auditions," I told him.

"For what?"

"Singing. A nationwide search for a (gulp) boy band."

"Lame," he said, putting his earbuds in and skating off.

I hear ya, buddy.

Surrounded by competition, I started to feel a little nervous. I couldn't remember the last time I'd been to any audition, let alone something as big as this. I wonder if anyone else here was facing an "or die" ultimatum like me. I doubted it.

Some kid with an amazing voice was singing up ahead of me. Oh, great, the nerves are really coming back now. Wait, I can practically kill a man with a look at this point. How can any of this make me nervous!?! I knew the answer to that: no matter how many singing lessons I had, no matter how good Brance said I was, in my mind I was still the little kid in elementary school who always got tossed into the chorus. Tree-number-seven-type roles. Or once I was even "doorknob." My singing confidence was built on those super-solid foundations and no amount of world-class training could change that self-doubt.

The line surged forward and my heart beat harder. *Okay, enough is enough, stupid nerves. Sit back down. If you get up again, I'll beat the crap out of you.* I don't suck. I know that. Yeah, I'm not as talented as probably most of the kids around me, but that didn't matter. I don't think FATE would have wasted their time on me if they didn't think I was good enough, right? *Good enough.* That's what I'm going for. Great? Not a chance, but good enough? That I had. My whole life could be called good enough. At the Pearly Gates if St. Peter asked me how I'd say my life had gone, I could have shrugged and honestly answered, "Good enough."

As the line moved closer and closer, I got calmer and calmer, so by the time the herd reached the inside of the convention center, I was good to go again. At one point during the march we passed a pair of police officers and I instinctively ducked my head and avoided eye contact. Old habits die hard. Their radios were crackling as usual, and their eyes scanned the crowd, but neither gave me a second look.

I followed along with the mass of boys, some of whom were accompanied by a parent or two, down a hallway, around a corner, and into a massive open space the size of at least a few football fields. The space was sectioned off into walled zones, but to our immediate left the wall was lined with tables. On the wall above each table was a sign with a range of letters such as A-B and C-D, etc. Lines were already thick and heavy for each table.

"Using your last name, please check in at the appropriate table," yelled a hoarse, exhausted girl in the middle.

I immediately went for G-H and stood there for five full minutes before remembering my last name now started with an *S.* I quickly relocated to the S-T line. I couldn't see anyone singing, but I could hear it coming from all over somewhere beyond the makeshift walls. My line was long, but it moved along steadily enough to not be annoying.

When it was finally my turn, I told the guy manning the table, "Sky, Bobby."

He looked at me like "Are you serious?!" but scanned through his list and tapped on my name when he saw it. He scribbled down a six-digit number on a piece of paper that looked like the bib thing marathon runners wore and handed it to me.

"Hold this up under your chin and look here," he said, sounding tired and bored.

"Like a mug shot?" I joked. Finally, some familiar territory. I knew I could ace mug shots.

"Uh, sure," he said, not amused. After snapping the picture, he added, "Now put it on and head to audition queue . . . thirty-seven."

I peeled off the sticky tape on the back, slapped it on my stomach, and looked around for queue thirty-seven. It took some wandering, but I found it after a few minutes.

As I reached the end of my designated line, someone yelled, "Hey, you!"

I ignored the yell, even though I got the feeling it was directed at me. No way. Nobody knew me here.

"I said, hey you," the same voice said directly behind me as a hand touched my shoulder and spun me around.

Standing behind me was a small, nerdy girl with an iPad, glasses, and an earpiece connected to a walkie-talkie, looking up at me like she would rather be anywhere else. *I feel ya, sister.*

"I think I found him," she said flatly into her earpiece.

I think I found him? Huh? Then it hit me, right, the insider was probably greasing some of those wheels Blake had been going on and on about. She held up her iPad next to my face, which had my mug shot from earlier on it.

"Yeah, he does actually look like the picture . . . It's not just a perfect angle . . . Will do," she said in response to whoever was on the other line. "Follow me," she told me.

"Where?" Even in a rigged game, it's always good to know where you're going.

"To your audition."

"Isn't that what's going on here?"

"You don't want to audition here. Come on."

That caught me a bit off guard. Greasy wheels or not, the point of all this was I'd go through the motions. It had to look legit. How could not auditioning like everyone else be okay? "Or die" began dancing along sadistically in my head.

She leaned in closer and whispered, "You want to have a real shot at being in the band?"

I nodded.

"Then you don't audition here; you audition somewhere else. That call I got meant they saw something they liked. These other kids"—she motioned with her head to the others—"are just crossing something off their bucket list. If they're auditioning here, it means they don't actually stand a chance. The call I got means the way you look means you do, so come on," she practically commanded while nodding back at the door I'd entered through.

"Bobby Sky, really?" she asked me as I followed her.

"Yep."

"Seriously, is that your real name?"

"Yep." *Nope.*

"Growing up must have sucked."

"Yep."

"You know more words than 'yep'?"

"Yep." I smiled widely.

"Cute."

We exited the main room out into a side hallway. She asked me to confirm my address, cell number, and birthday—all made up, of course—as she led me up two escalators, down another long hallway, and into a smaller, more private room. It reminded me of the ones in singing reality shows on TV, except there were no cameras and no elaborate decorations. A group of ten or so people ranging in age from twentysomething to fiftysomething sat in generic foldout chairs behind a couple of collapsible buffet tables. Sodas and a few trays of snacks were on a table off to the side. Nothing fancy. Once we'd entered, all eyes shifted to us, or more precisely, to me. I wondered which one was my insider buddy.

"Oh my God, he's perfect," said a heavyset man still comically trying to look young and hip. His thinning hair was in a frosted fauxhawk, his collar was popped, and his jeans had more bedazzling than a chandelier.

"He's even better in person," a younger but even more stupidly dressed man muttered.

The reactions of the other members of the audience were equally as strange and enthusiastic. Most of it was inaudible, but I for sure heard "bad boy" and "rocker" thrown around repeatedly in a giddy discussion amongst them. Okay, so this was already going well, but it was weird, too. These people, whoever they were, seemed important and for some reason genuinely excited to see me. No one, aside from my mother, had ever been excited to see *me*, and even that had been rare. Maybe these wheels had been a bit overgreased. What had this guy told them about me?

"Thank you, Genie," said a confident, attractive, well-dressed fortysomething woman in the middle of the group. "We'll handle it from here."

The girl who'd brought me up, Genie apparently, nodded slightly and walked out.

"Bobby Sky?" the woman asked me once Genie was gone.

"Yes, ma'am."

"I love the manners, but my friends call me Linda, please."

"Yes, ma' . . . I mean, Linda," I corrected with a smile.

"Okay then, Bobby . . ."

"Hutch," I interrupted softly. "My friends call me Hutch." No sooner had the words left my mouth than I cringed. It was habit. I'd spent my whole life telling people to call me Hutch, so it was second nature.

"Hutch then," she said with a smirk as she scribbled something down.

"You know what? Bobby's fine," I blurted out.

"You sure?"

"Yeah, yeah, let's go with Bobby. Sorry."

"Not a problem. It's your name," she said. I could tell some of her excitement was gone now, thanks to my awesome name snafu. I needed to get her back on the Sky train. Oh, wow, that sounds so terrible I bet it becomes a thing. All aboard the Sky train. Ugh, I think I just threw up in my mouth a little.

"Okay then, Bobby, tell us a little about yourself," she asked me.

"Like what?" What did this have to do with singing?

"Whatever you want. Just be yourself. Tell us who you are." She held up the "application" I'd submitted online. "Something not on this."

"Okay, well," I said as I took a deep breath and tried to figure out where to begin or what to say. The application had basically been my entire cover.

This had not been part of the plan. Sing my way up the food chain until I reached the decision makers and then show them I was at least worthy of consideration for boy-band-ness—*that* had been the plan. Our man would do the rest. There was no "Tell us about yourself or who you are." I hadn't practiced this. I wasn't really prepared for this. Yeah, I had a fake cover that I knew inside and out, but that was for answering questions about *where* I was *from*, not *who* I *was*.

What could I tell them? For two years I've been trained by a super-secret organization, and their amazing plan to save the world is me joining your boy band?

Then I remembered those stupid creative writing classes we had to take and an idea hit me. I couldn't help but smile. I had this. It was easy. They wanted me to be myself, huh? Well, I was not Bobby Sky. I was Hutch and always would be. Hutch *was* the bad boy they were looking for. He *was* the reluctant rocker. So pre-FATE Hutch—all dirty, grimy, and unpolished—was the one who should answer this question.

"I've been arrested nine times but only convicted four times," I started. Then I raised my fist as I added, "Point of pride. No, I haven't learned my lesson. You need money to eat, right? Either I get away with it and my folks and I get to eat a bit better for a while, or I get busted and then not only do *I* get three squares a day in juvie, but my parents don't have to split up their paycheck to figure out how to pay bills and feed me. It's a win-win."

All eyes were on me. No one took notes. No one blinked. I had them.

"Today will also be the first time I've been allowed to sing in over two years without being afraid of being punished. My . . . dad and my family weren't too fond of it, so I had to sing in secret, where I knew they couldn't hear me. Said it was something I had to give up to become a man. I just like to sing, but when you live in the world I do, it's not really something people respect. 'Tough guys don't sing,' he liked to say. Figured this could be my chance to show my dad and the world, maybe they do. So I snuck away, hopped on a freight train headed north, and here I am. Oh, and I stole a car to get here from the station. I'll return it when I'm done, hopefully before anyone notices. I'll change the oil, check the tires—you know, Good Samaritan stuff—before I put it back. And that's me. That's who I am underneath it all."

"Any of that true?" Linda asked.

"At least half," I replied coolly.

"Ha." She chuckled. "Which half?"

"Which half do you like more?"

She smiled, enjoying the game. "A few more questions, if you don't mind?"

"Shoot," I said, playing along.

"If you weren't here right now, what would you be doing?"

"Running for my life," I replied.

They assumed I was joking, of course, and loved the response. If only they'd known the truth.

"From who?"

"The man, the fuzz . . . Take your pick. I'm a popular guy."

They got a kick out of that one, too, and one member of the audience quietly muttered to another, "God, I hope he can sing and dance."

"Who cares?" the hipster girl whispered back. "I can teach a fish to sing and dance. I can't teach that," she concluded, referring to what I assumed was my attitude and best attempt at smug swagger.

"Would you say you're a good person or a bad person?" Linda asked.

"I'm a good person who's good at being bad." Man, that felt cheesy to say.

More excitement from the crowd.

Someone said, "He's the genuine article. Wouldn't even have to coach him."

"Ever been in a fight?" Linda asked.

"Not on a Tuesday," I replied, which was true. I'd never been in a fight on a Tuesday. It was my lucky day.

"He's so saucy," a sweaty, gross, heavyset man in a suit said. I assumed that was a good thing, but I hadn't heard the term before and made a mental note to google it later on. You lost touch with new slang at FATE.

Linda looked at the others. "I'm sold," she said, dropping her notepad to the table with finality. The others nodded in agreement. "I mean, assuming, of course, you can carry a tune?" she asked me. "You can, can't you?"

"I've been told I have the voice of an angel, ma'am," I said cockily, though internally I'd gotten a bit nervous again. The singing was coming. Judgment was coming.

"I bet. Okay, so what'll it be? What tune will you grace our ears with today?" she asked me, playing along with my carefree, jokey attitude.

It had taken Brance and me a long time to figure out what I should sing. I could hit a few notes really well, but as Brance liked to put it, my voice was "limited," so it was tough to find something that worked for me. As a joke, I tossed out doing something from the '80s. Like some GNR. On top of my mother's Christmas carol obsession, she had a thing for '80s metal, so I had one, too. I never thought my comment would ever be taken seriously. To be fair, it wasn't either, not at first. But the more I thought about it, the more it made sense, so I pleaded my case.

Brance, like most others, only saw '80s metal as stadium-pumping, electric-guitar-screaming anthems, but there's more to them than that. There's heart in them. The lyrics are raw and unfiltered, but they're real and relatable. More so than most music is now by a long way. Yeah, the heart of it is drowned out by bouncing hair, tight leather, pyrotechnics, and guitar solos that last for hours, but when looked at as words on a paper and nothing else, there's real beauty to some of them. Once I showed Brance this, he was in.

Now, I wasn't about to go into the audition and unleash an electric guitar ballad on the panel, so Brance and I compromised. The song we chose was still decidedly "metal" because of the band, but for all other purposes it wasn't. It's a simple song about heartbreak, written in a laundry room, after a guy found out his girl was cheating on him. The guy? Bret Michaels of Poison. The song?

"'Every Rose Has Its Thorn,'" I said with a grin. By the reaction of the audience, Brance and I had made a wise choice. All smiles and head bobs in my direction.

MEH.

That was how I felt about the singing. I hadn't butchered it. The dance number, though? Nailed it. Leggo woulda been proud. I even added a bit of Moonwalk at the end. *You know it!*

After the song and dance show, I hung around for another thirty minutes, chatting with them about my life and upbringing, pre-FATE, of course. I held nothing back about my run-ins with Johnny Law, making absolutely sure to lay it on thick that I was the most legit bad boy they'd find with a heart of gold underneath. They'd bought it hook, line, and sinker.

So while my singing hadn't really blown them away, all were still convinced I had the genuine look and attitude they were going for. And I think this was before any extra greasing. They actually seemed to like me. It still felt weird, very weird. Linda herself walked me out and told me she'd "be in touch."

It's strange how a few hours ago, heck, an hour ago I

hadn't given two craps about the boy band part of any of this; it was only what had to be done. Now that they actually liked me, though, I was sorta into it and, dare I say, excited?

As I left the convention center, I passed by another group of excited youths heading into the auditions. I almost felt bad for them. Almost. They were all probably more talented than I was, and had probably been taking singing and dancing classes since birth in preparation for this moment. They honestly thought that if they were the best, they'd have a shot. If only they knew the powers that be were looking for a certain type rather than talent.

"Suckers," I called out to none of them and all of them as I headed toward the street.

Claire was sitting on a bench waiting for me. I'd texted her I was done after Linda had walked me out.

"So?" she asked.

I bobbed my head. "Okay, I guess?"

"When will they let you know?"

I shrugged. "No clue. Now what?"

She checked her watch and looked around. "Want to go to the aquarium? I've never been and hear it's great."

Go to the aquarium? It was such a normal-person thing to do. So spur of the moment. It felt weird. I was so used to structure, a schedule that cannot be deviated from.

"Shouldn't we be going back?"

"Do you want to?"

"Not really."

She checked her watch again. "We have a few hours. Come on. We can grab a hot dog while we walk."

It took us a good thirty minutes to reach the Shedd Aquarium, but I didn't care. The air was fresh and brisk as we grabbed some sodas and dogs from a vendor and took the route through the park to the famous Soldier Field. I'd been cooped up inside for so long I'd forgotten how big the world really was, or what normal everyday people looked and acted like.

Two hours later, while watching the penguins play in the polar zone, we got the call. The gig was mine. All aboard the Sky train.

chapter 13

THE MISSING LINK . . . GET IT?

Immediately after landing back at FATE, Claire escorted me to the elevators. From there, we were whisked to the hallway and into a round room—where there was nothing but a single circle of light on the floor with my name in it.

Oh, memories.

Claire pointed at the circle. She was about to speak when I cut her off.

"Yeah, I'm not an idiot."

I moved into the light. A woman in a white nurse's uniform scurried over from out of nowhere, holding a small syringe in her latex-gloved fingers.

"What's that?" I asked her.

"Assists with the link."

"Link juice," I joked.

She didn't laugh.

"Ow!" I cried out when she stuck the needle into me.

Her head jerked up. Her eyes were wide.

I grinned. "Just kidding. Didn't feel anything. Come on, lighten up."

Claire laughed at least, and someone was chuckling from somewhere behind me. A slow clap started, too. I spun around to look.

Blake was walking toward me with a big smile, smacking

his hands together. He was just so dang likable it was annoying!

"That was funny, Bobby," he said. "Well played."

I shrugged and repeated, "Couldn't help it."

He stood over by Claire and asked, "Any questions, concerns, what-have-yous?"

Of course, but none I'd bring up here.

"All good," I said. "Let's kick this pig."

Blake walked over toward me and shook my hand. He looked like he'd recovered from whatever funk he'd been in at the cottage.

"Best of luck, Bobby."

"Yeah, thanks. You too," I added automatically like we all do. *You too?* What was wrong with me?

"I eagerly await your first album," he said before walking away and calling out over his shoulder, "I expect a signed copy."

"Do I get to keep the money I make?" It had only recently occurred to me I could be a millionaire soon.

"Not a dime," he called out before disappearing around a corner.

Once he was gone, the creepy, appears-out-of-nowhere nurse was suddenly right next to me again, holding a black metal box that had a pair of those clear, plastic-looking science-class glasses. I didn't wait for any go-ahead or indication of what to do. I grabbed the things and put them on.

His name is Ryo Enomoto and he is from Shinjuku, Japan.

I'LL ADMIT IT, I really didn't know what to expect. Yeah, we'd all heard stories, but until you experience being linked, no amount of describing can do it justice. Basically, imagine that every single priority in your life vanishes and is replaced by one thing and one thing only. That's the best way to explain it, I think. In my case, that one thing was to protect Ryo. There was nothing else. All I cared about now was keeping him safe. All of life's other problems? Poof! Gone. I had one singular focus. It not only felt good; it felt *right.*

Ryo was now the beginning, middle, and end of all my thoughts. His face was always front and center in my mind. He was good-looking with elf-like features and kept his hair shaved on the sides, but longer and slicked back on top. He was tall and thin, like borderline unhealthy thin. Like he'd had a growth spurt and his physique hadn't caught back up yet. A gust of wind could knock him over. I only had images of him in my head but was well versed in reading people now. His eyes—and the way he held himself—confirmed that he was shy and nonconfrontational. Was it something in his head, or was it the fact that underneath those lips were some of the biggest, Chiclet teeth I'd ever seen? Wow, those were some honkin' chompers. No wonder he never did more than smirk.

I don't really remember leaving the spherical room or even getting on the elevator. My mind was buzzing and too busy working through how quickly I could find him to worry about crap like walking. Now I understood why I had to audition first. No way I'd have even gone to the audition, let alone been any good. Finding Ryo and making sure he was okay was all that mattered to me now. I couldn't rest until I did. All I knew was that he was in LA, so I had to get there like yesterday.

Claire was waiting for me in my apartment with a stack of empty boxes. "Pack up whatever you want."

"Huh?" I had barely heard her. I felt like I was on drugs or something.

"Anything you want is yours."

"Oh, right, yeah." I didn't move, though.

"Are you okay?" She seemed genuinely concerned.

"Yeah, a little out of it. Sorry." I tried to shake it out. Not much help there, either.

"How does it feel? I've always been curious."

"Like a crush, but without the love part. It's like how I felt when I met Leggo. I wanted to see her so badly it hurt. Same for Ryo, but minus the 'wanting to make out' part."

Had I just said that out loud? I did, didn't I?

"Better get packing," I blurted out, embarrassed.

Clothes, gear, and a "care package" (wink, wink, my arsenal) would be sent for me so I didn't have to worry about them. I didn't want anything in the room, but I also didn't want to not pack anything, either. Felt rude. I took all the Dr Peppers, in case they didn't have any in LA, and all the Doritos. What? I like Doritos. Lie to me and say you don't. Exactly, everyone likes Doritos.

"Done?" Claire asked.

"Guess so."

"Then let's go," she said.

I picked up my box of munchies and headed out with her.

"You do this for everyone?" I asked as we got on the elevators. It had been eating at me for a while. She was the boss's assistant. Surely she didn't see out every Shadow, right?

"No, you're special."

"Aww, thanks."

"When I told Blake that you hit on me when we first met, he insisted that I be around to motivate you."

"Sneaky."

"It worked, though, didn't it?"

I didn't have the heart to tell her that my crush on her disappeared the moment I met Leggo, so I lied and told her, "It did."

We got on the elevator.

"So why are you with me now?"

"Seemed like the right thing to do. Why ditch you on the last ride?"

"Thanks."

She shrugged. In a case of total déjà vu Claire led me down and outside the building, where the same two security guards and the golf cart were waiting for me. I eyed the one in the passenger seat until he reluctantly got out and slid around to the back. I hopped into the front seat like before.

"Next time you see me, I'll be famous," I teased.

"It will be strange," she admitted.

"How old are you?" I asked as the cart pulled away.

"Thirty-four," she called out.

"What?!" I blurted out before quickly adding, "You look fantastic for an old chick!"

She laughed as she called out, "Goodbye, Bobby."

THE GUARDS DROVE ME deep into the woods again to the same private airstrip where the same row of bare-bones no-frills military cargo planes sat waiting. I climbed inside the one they dropped me off in front of, and strapped myself into one of the standard jump seats that unfolded from the walls. I wondered if it was the same one that had taken me to Chicago and shamed myself for not scratching my initials into the wall or something to mark it. Oh well. Unlike my last plane ride, though, I'd come prepared. I cracked open a Dr Pepper and ripped into a bag of Doritos. Plane snacks! And you thought I'd simply grabbed this stuff by accident. A little faith, please.

I leaned back, as comfortably as one can, in the hard-as-stone seat and took a moment to reflect. This flight would mark my last and final hours as Robert Hutchinson. Once we touched down, I'd officially be Bobby Sky from Tyler, Texas.

I'd pitched them Austin, since I knew the town pretty well and could answer any questions about it, but they'd shot it down. Yeah, I looked different now, but my mom, assuming the band took off and she eventually saw me, was going to freak out. Anyone I'd known back home would probably. Being from Austin would have been too coincidental for them to ever let it go, so I was from Tyler. Bonus time—if my mom ever did get a bug up her butt that Bobby Sky was actually her son, which he was, then they had plenty of lies and stories to convince her or anyone else that it wasn't me. I knew, though, that if my mom really thought it was me, there was no chance in the seven hells she'd listen to them, and the only way to get her to drop it would be me telling her I wasn't her son. Wasn't looking forward to that and already hated myself in advance for doing it, even though I hadn't even done it. No way I'd get through that conversation without crying. Yeah, I admit I'd probably cry, so deal with it. Hopefully it'd never get to that point.

Nope. Hutch was almost gone now—nothing but a blip in the old memory banks. A typed-out line on the computer, highlighted and cut into nothingness. Nothing but screaming fans, private planes, and first-class livin' for your pal Bobby Sky from here on out. No, seriously, this clunker was dropping me off at the Tyler airport, where I was flying first class to LAX. That's right, the rich seats where the tray tables come out of the arms and you get served hot nuts. LA and, more importantly, Ryo, here I come.

Having polished off two cans of Dr Pepper and a whole bag of Doritos, I snoozed as the white noise from the airplane engines and total darkness inside the plane got the better of me.

Chapter 14

Eighteen-ish Months Later . . . Same Recipe, Just New Packaging

"You sure you want to mess up that pretty face?" Marko asked me. He had a heavy Russian accent, so it sounded more like: *"Yoo-shore vant meez-up dat-prit-fiss?"*

Marko was leaning casually against the metal door that led to the fighting pit, nonchalantly picking dirt out from under his fingernails. Muffled cheers reverberated from the "arena" on the other side. There were a lot of places now that I couldn't go without being recognized; thankfully an illegal, underground street fighting pit in London was not one of them. I knew what I was doing was risky, but I couldn't help it. My FATE training had made violence a part of me. I had an itch to scratch and this was the only way to scratch it, so every month or so, I'd sneak out and find a fight. It helped me stay sane.

"You think this guy's pretty?" I joked, nodding at the fighter next to me.

My opponent had a shaved head. He was obscenely thick with muscles and was inked all over. He basically looked like he had been cloned in the cliché B-movie bad-guy-enforcer lab. He spoke no English and only grinned at me through a grill of solid gold teeth.

"You have no idea what I'm saying, do you?" I said to the man, making sure to smile and nod as I asked. The man nodded back and smiled wider in return, not understanding a word. "You are a giant, giant man by the way," I continued. "I mean, good God, did you see a Punisher comic and be like, *that* . . . *that* right there. I'm going to become *that.*"

"Pyun-eeesh-er," the man repeated, grinning sadistically as he latched on to the one word he understood.

It always amazed me how far-reaching American pop culture was. I guess I was part of the problem, too, though, huh?

"You're funny, American. I like you," Marko responded with a chuckle. He eyed me. "You look familiar. What's your name again?"

Okay, maybe even here I had to worry about being recognized. One less fortress of solitude. The world sure shrinks when you're famous.

"Hutch." I used my old name whenever I did stuff like this. It felt right. "I've got one of those faces. Happens all the time."

There was an especially loud cheer, followed by a *thump-thump* on the door. Marko banged back twice in response.

"Well, Hutch, you ready?" Marko asked me, and then repeated the question to the other man in what sounded like broken Slavic.

It was time to focus. In a well-practiced motion I pulled my shaggy hair into a ponytail. I had the advantage of youth and stamina, but the human hulk had experience and size. I was no slouch, but compared to the monster next to me, I looked like a skinny child, and there were no rules in these types of fights. Blood, guts, and glory were all one could hope for in the world of underground fighting. I took my shirt off and tossed it to the side. I liked that shirt and didn't want it ruined.

Marko took his weight off the door. It slowly began to open. Warmth, dust, and the smell of sweat and dry booze wafted into the room. I caught a glimpse of my not-too-distant future: a packed house, warehouse lighting, and a small circular fighting pit. I cracked the bones in my neck and started to loosen up my arms.

A crowd rushed past us—first, two bouncers dragging an unconscious, beaten, and bloody fighter; then a doctor (or what could pass as one in this place) babbling on about spine stabilization. The last one into the waiting room was the victor. He was still hamming it up for the crowd. He paused at the door and gave the people one last fist pump, which was greeted with a wild response. As he passed me, he gave me a smile and wink through one of his disgustingly swollen black eyes. He could walk, though. His opponent, not so much.

"Okay, let's go!" Marko slammed his fists into our shoulders in an attempt to rile us up. All it did was annoy me.

Before going out I glanced over my shoulder. The doctor was tending to the unconscious man and the pack of fighters going on after me were doing their best not to watch him, not to let even an ounce of fear or doubt enter their heads. I liked a bit of fear; it kept you honest.

When I took my first steps out into the warehouse, the cheering hit a deafening level. It was not on my account. The size of my opponent had them in a near frenzy. Heat, sweat, and violence—yes, you can smell violence—filled my nose and lungs. It triggered something primal inside me, as it would for anyone. No doubt my opponent felt the same.

This felt right. Like home.

THE BELL RANG AND the monster sprang off the wall and came charging right at me. He threw a heavy, looping punch at my head. Casual as you like, I ducked under the swing and countered with a left punch to his liver—followed by a vicious overhand right that connected flush with his jaw. The combo sent him crashing to the floor in a heap. Facedown and totally still, he was out good and cold.

The room fell silent, everyone in shock at what had happened. Half the eyes in the place were on me, the other half on the unconscious mountain in the middle of the ring. I scanned the crowd and then gave them a smirk as I shrugged. The cheers erupted like a bursting volcano.

From the corner of my eye I saw his friends shaking their heads in disbelief. The crowd by the betting board quickly became mobbish, as some felt a fix had been in, and demanded their money back. Before it got out of hand, or they switched their focus on me, I hopped over the wooden barrier of the pit and headed for the locker room. Some fans slapped me on the shoulders and back as I left, while others shoved, spat, and threw beer at me, obviously pissed off about the outcome. A few scuffles broke out around me as those who'd felt cheated fought with those who'd either won money or were simply in awe at what I'd done to my much larger and heavily favored opponent.

Things were really beginning to get out of hand when I reached the metal door that led to the safety of the back room. I quickly went through it, walked to the far bench where I'd left my stuff, and checked my phone. A few missed calls from our manager and some texts, too. I checked the time. 7:09 P.M.

"Crap," I muttered to myself. I was cutting it close.

A hand slapped down on my shoulder and I nearly reacted in a very violent way. Lucky for Marko, I didn't.

"That was impressive, friend!" Marko raved. He shoved a wad of bills into my hand. "Your winnings. When will you be back?"

"Uh, I don't know. Next time I need money, I guess," I lied.

"Well, I hope good fortune *does not* shine on you, then," he joked.

"I bet. See ya."

I threw on my hoodie, pulled on my baggy sweatpants, and went outside. The nighttime cold hit me like a sledgehammer and I regretted my outfit once again. A simple sweat suit was not appropriate attire for a proper London winter. It was quiet out here though, the sounds from within the warehouse practically nonexistent. You could almost call it peaceful.

To my right I heard a train whistle and was about to start jogging toward it when movement up against the wall on my left caught my eye. A homeless man sat up and coughed. It was a painful cough. An old, hopeless cough. Our eyes met.

"Little cold out here," I said to him.

"Just a bit o' winter is all," he said. "Seen worse in my life."

I took the wad of cash Marko had given me, a couple thousand pounds if I had to guess, and handed them to the man. He looked shell-shocked.

"Promise me you'll get that cough looked at, okay?" I said as I started to jog away from him.

"God bless you, lad. God bless you!" he cried out after me.

The road spat me out into a main industrial loading area. Another train horn blared not too far away. I could make it if I sprinted. I crossed the open space and shot down an alley toward the sound of the horn. The alley dead-ended at a ten-foot-high chain-link fence, but on the other side was a mass of train tracks, with a metro line slowly pulling away from Neasden Station. I hit the fence at a full sprint and scaled up the side and over the top with ease. My feet kept moving the moment I landed on the ground on the other side.

It would be close. The train was creeping away from the station, but it was picking up steam fast. Had giving my money to that guy cost me my ride? Only time would tell.

I held nothing back now as I tore down the tracks toward the back of the train. A service ladder sat bolted to the side of the last car and was my only option for getting on. I reached out for the ladder, but my hand closed on nothing but air as the train surged ahead. My lungs were aching, and my legs were burning. I could dance for hours now, but my overall physical fitness had gotten a little slack. I gritted my teeth and with everything I had left hurled myself at the ladder. My fingers caught and curled around the cool metal rung of the ladder. Once I reached the top of the car, I checked my phone again. Another text from our manager.

Where are you?!?!?!?!?!?!?

Around. Relax.

After sound check we had a few hours until showtime to do what we wanted. Some lay around and relaxed, while I snuck away to find a fight. To each their own. I texted: I've got something special planned. That was a lie, of course. I didn't. Unless showing up late was the "something special." Either way, it would buy me time and keep him from looking for me.

Do I need to worry? he asked.

Nope. Start the show as planned. I got this. You'll love it.

The wind up here was almost unbearable. The cold air cut right through my sweats. Luckily, the trip was only one stop, and a short one at that. Now, famous or not, hitching a ride on the top of a London metro is both illegal and hard to explain when you're me, so when the train reached the station platform, I waited for everyone to get off and the platform to empty out before jumping off.

I GOT MY FAIR share of sideways glances from the crowd outside the stadium. I now realized I hadn't really thought this part out too well. I ducked my head deep inside my hoodie and pulled my hair over my face.

Loud music blared from the arena, distant and echoing. The preshow. A gaggle of young, frantic girls in near hysterics were shoving their way past the others so as not to miss anything. I saw my own face on one of their shirts. I tried not to do a double take. Even now, it was still a very odd sensation.

I allowed myself to be carried toward the main front gate with the others, but I didn't follow them inside. About fifty yards away from the main entrance, I started heading perpendicular to the flowing crowd until I reached the edge of them. Once there, I snuck away and headed toward the back entrance at a full gallop again.

I hurdled the metal barricade surrounding the bevy of fancy tour buses and equipment rigs, sped past a throng of men in all-black roadie attire, and moved so fast the guard barely had time to yell, "Hey!" as I flew past him and into the belly of the stadium. I kept going down a long hallway until it opened up into the arena. A huge black curtain cut the stadium in half, keeping the crowd and stage on one side and the workers, crew, and me on the other. Not stopping, I snaked my way through the mass of people scurrying around with clipboards, costumes, instruments—you name it. Everyone was too busy with their own work, too preoccupied with their own responsibilities to give me a second look.

"Gooooooooood evening, London!" boomed the announcer's voice through the deafening sound system.

"Crap," I said to myself and scanned the area for . . . "Bingo."

I jogged over to a rack of clothes. I stripped down and threw on some weathered jeans and a torn, sleeveless pearl-snap shirt, before slipping on a pair of comfy, gray New

Balances. I balled up my other clothes and tucked them into a space behind the shoe rack.

"Are you ready?!?" the announcer yelled. It was met with a roar from the sold-out crowd.

On the table next to the clothes were microphones. I hurriedly grabbed one.

"I said, are you ready?!?!"

The response from the crowd this time was so loud and shrill it hurt. I began to run again, making my way toward the curtain and the stage.

"London, England. We give you . . . Interrrrrrrrrrrnational!"

The lights went out, swallowing the arena in darkness. A deep, rhythmic bass began to boom. The timing, the schedule was so well rehearsed that I knew I'd never reach my spot in time without a bit of improvisation. I had an idea and it would definitely be "something special," as I'd promised. I'd piss some people off, but I had to do it. Behind the black curtain, I clawed and scrambled up the intricate sets all lined up and in order for their use in the show. When I reached the top of an elaborate, steampunk-style tower, I leapt off of it.

I burst through the black curtain at the same time the stadium lights came on and the show started. The intro of our hit, "The Start," blared to life as I soared through a waterfall of sparks and past the explosive pyrotechnics that opened the show. I landed on one knee in the middle of the stage right on my spot. The four other members of the boy band were already in their places and shot me some quizzical looks. All I could think of doing in response was grin mischievously and wink at them.

I slid right into the choreography along with them without missing a step.

"I wanna go back-back-back, back, back to the start,

The night you stole-stole-stole, stole, stole my heart.
My stomach turned-turned-turned, turned, turned to knots,
You can't controooooooooooooooOOOOOOOl what the heaaaAArt wants . . ."

chapter 15
INTERNATIONAL!

"Bobby, you are doing it again," Ryo said from his bunk.

We were on the tour bus. My bunk was right across from his. His dark eyes were boring into mine, so I knew exactly what he meant.

"Sorry," I blurted out. I quickly looked back at my tablet.

Dang it. I'd gotten a lot better about staring at him since I'd first met him, but I still got caught from time to time. What? I can't help it. I'm chemically programmed to want to stare. You know when you're out with friends and someone says, "Don't look?" What do you do? You look. We all do. That's sorta like what it was like—but all the time. I knew he was there and my mind was telling me not to look, but for some reason I had to do it anyway. But like I said, I've gotten a lot better. At first it was borderline creepy how long I would look at him. It was really awkward a couple of times. Really . . . awkward. Moving on. I pretended to be totally focused on my tablet. I was practicing disarming bombs. The FATE techs designed me an app in case anyone ever planted a bomb on our bus or plane.

There was an eruption of laughter from the front. My other bandmates were playing a yet-to-be-released video game.

"We are housed with animals," Ryo said with a yawn.

I snuck a quick glance. He had groggy written all over his face.

"You should have your Yakuza friends put a hit on them," I joked.

Before you get up in arms at my total non-PC, take a breath. This dude is like my brother now, beyond, but when we first met, he asked in total seriousness if I'd ridden a horse to school every day. Because, you know, that's what all Texans do. I met his fire with fire and immediately made a Yakuza joke. He dropped the horse bit, but I kept going. He hates it.

"Humorous as always." He smirked. English was one of four languages he knew, and he spoke it like a robot: perfect wording, perfect enunciation, zero emotion.

I nodded and then hovered my finger over two wires on the bomb app. The fate of Paris hung in the balance. I chose to cut the green wire. *Boom.*

"Dang it," I muttered to myself, this time out loud. I was barely at a 10 percent disarmament rate. If a city ever actually hung in the balance and I was tasked with disarming the bomb, the city would be toast. Pulling a random person from the street and letting them try to disarm it using dumb luck gave them better odds than sending me in.

"Is everything all right with you?" Ryo asked me genuinely as he swung his legs over the side of his bunk.

I'd tried my best to keep my distance from him at first, you know, to respect the rules of the game, but I couldn't do it. It was impossible without looking like a jerk. I tried to play it like these boys were my new family, and Ryo was my favorite little brother. Hey, don't judge. Blake said it was cool, remember?

"Yeah, just tired." It was true. I'd been tired since Leslie busted me out of the clink.

"We have a three-day break soon. Do you have plans?"

I shook my head. "Probably just tool around the city like always."

I never made plans during any of our breaks. How could I? I went where Ryo went. The staring was bad enough; I had no clue how I'd explain dead-on stalking. So my go-to excuse was that as a poor kid from Texas, every city we were in was new and exciting to me. I'd yet to be called out on it.

"You are always welcome at my home," Ryo offered for the umpteenth time.

He was from a perfect family. His father was a professor and his mother ran some kind of online business. Every break we got, whether it was two days or two weeks, he always went home and came back fully refreshed and ready to go. I never took him up on the offer, though. I didn't know why, but for some reason vacationing with the guy felt one step too far. Like somehow that would be over the line.

"Yeah, maybe," I said as always but meant no.

Ryo slid off the bunk and asked, "Would you care for a drink or snack?"

"Nah, I'll be up in a minute," I replied. "Thanks, though."

OKAY, OKAY, OKAY, CALM down. Yes, we've skipped ahead a bit. No, you really didn't miss that much. Trust me, I was there. Yeah, there were a few hiccups at the beginning, like my inability to stop staring at Ryo, which we covered, but that was about it. We began recording our album within hours of me landing at LAX, and our first single, "Love Weekend," was on the air the next Tuesday.

"It's a love weekend,

So our love won't get weakened . . ."

Oh, it was cheesy, but it was number one for eight weeks, so there you go. On week two we began rehearsal for our summer tour. Heck, I'm pretty sure they had T-shirts and posters for sale before we even knew the name of the band, which was . . . drumroll, please . . . International. Yeah, ugh is right.

But, and I hate to admit it, I'll give credit where credit is due. These people knew what they were doing and they were frighteningly good at it. Like, as good as I am with a submachine gun. International was, like the name suggests, an international boy band built solely to steal money from young girls' wallets, or, more accurately, their parents' wallets. Every part had been researched and audience tested to ensure success. I'm the bad boy American; Seamus is the Irish practical joker or class clown; Karim is the super good-looking Moroccan heartthrob; Amit is the cute, innocent Indian baby face; and Ryo, who rounded out the group, is Japanese. The fact that he's Japanese helps to bring in the massive Asian market, but mainly the guy's the real talent. Like Freddie Mercury and Mariah Carey had a kid and then that kid had a kid with Whitney Houston and Andrea Bocelli's kid. Dude can sing, for real.

Every moment of the next twenty years was planned for us. They were not idiots. There would be a "fight" and a "breakup" in three years. We'd each launch solo careers, then combine for a few duets, and then two years after that regroup and dominate again. And that was just us. We quickly found out we weren't the only play they were making. The label, realizing how well a Biggie-Tupac-esque rivalry would help sell records, went all in and created a rival boy band called Universal. We were the "just like you" boys who'd won the lottery in the worldwide casting call, while Universal were the "silver spoon" boys plucked from only the best Disney and Nickelodeon shows.

Hate was to be fabricated. Words would be exchanged between International and Universal, and these words would get heated and eventually get "physical." Fences would be made, and a double tour would take place. But "issues" would arise and the tour would be canceled one year in after a backstage "brawl" (fully caught on camera and choreographed by only the best movie-fight folks in the biz).

And to hedge their bets even more, they also created three all-female acts. There was the girl band Forever, the rock band Steam Runners, and the singer-songwriter country-pop girl Ecko Kelley. They made up the Solar One Tour, which quickly became the hottest show on Earth. Still is, but we're catching up.

The members of the Solar One Tour and both boy bands were encouraged to date and live off the constant rumors of love triangles and in-fighting.

I'm telling you, it was all laid out to the day. There was nothing left up to chance. They simply paid chance off.

So here we are, a little over a year and a half down the road, with seven number one hits, two double-diamond albums, a Christmas collection under our belts, and we've been on tour nonstop. Oh, and we did a movie, too. And I thought my FATE training had been exhausting.

See, I told you it wasn't much, and now to catch you right up to the present, after our London show, we stayed the night in King's Cross, and then loaded into our buses to head to Brussels, where we've got the European Kids' Choice Awards. We're expected to win a bunch of stuff for our second album, *It's Always You for Me.*

And those are all the holes I feel like filling in right now. You want to know more? Our all-inclusive, behind-the-scenes memoirs will be out next year. US $29.99.

I ROLLED OUT OF my bunk and made my way to the front of the moving mansion that was our tour bus. Technically we had two, but for short rides like this we all crammed into one and hung out together. The label liked to call it "band unity." It didn't hurt that we still liked hanging out with each other.

"'Mericaaaaaa," they all called out when I entered the room. Seamus had come up with the greeting way back when and it had stuck.

"Fellas," I greeted them tiredly with a weak wave. "How much longer?" I asked the group.

"Hour or so," Karim answered, his eyes still glued on the game like the others.

Oh, how convenient. Everyone speaks English? I hear ya, but yeah, they do. We're the only country that's so lazy we look at learning a second language as some ridiculous chore to get through high school. And shockingly, everyone assumed I was the dumb one. I know, right? Wherever could they get that idea from? But when people think you're dumb, they'll underestimate you, so I never denied it. I played it up actually. So out of pity English was chosen as our default language. They "took a vote" to make it seem like they weren't doing it out of charity, but come on. There were two native English speakers in the group, so the vote was rigged from the beginning.

I helped myself to a Dr Pepper from the fridge and took a seat in one of the marshmallowy soft chairs. I was almost nineteen now, so I was legally allowed to drink in Europe, but being who we were, there were strict rules about booze. And by rules, there was only one: can't have any. Even tucked away in our hotel rooms, drinking was forbidden. "Would ruin the image," they told us, which was believable. Of course, the label had it all planned out for the first time one of us was seen with a beer. It would be the beginning of a fake rift among us boys. The guilty party would go to rehab and be welcomed back with open arms. Total PR fluff that the entertainment world would eat up. Seamus, playing to all the terrible Irish clichés you could imagine, would be the "drunk." But that was still a year out from now on the schedule.

The bus slid to a stop outside our hotel, the Warwick Brussels, in Brussels, Belgium. As usual, a legion of adoring fans had been tipped off to where we were staying and the masses were out in force. Posters, hats, shirts, what have you were waving about, ready to be ruined by some markers and the chicken scratch that counted as our signatures. *So much glitter*, was and still is my instant reaction to our merch. For our name they'd used a type of diamond-like ink that acted like glitter and it was plastered across everything in all caps. This stuff could catch light and sparkle in total darkness. I was half impressed by the science and half disgusted by the flashy stuff. They'd even given us Sharpies that had the same glittery effect when used. What was wrong with classic black? Or, if you're feeling frisky, blue?

Okay, so confession time. You know all that crap I talked earlier about boy bands and how embarrassing it all is? Well, it's still totally true and I don't take any of it back, but, okay, it's sorta fun sometimes. A lot of fun. Tons of it. Still totally lame, of course, but lame in a good way? There's the parties, the hotel suites, the money (which I don't see much of), seeing the world, getting to hang out with my best friends all the time . . . I could go on, but you get it. And believe me, having tons of money and being famous *is* all it's cracked up to be, trust me. It's awesome and anyone who tells you otherwise has forgotten what it's like to be poor and normal. And you're probably sitting there thinking, *Man, that sounds like a pretty cool life.*

I WILL NEVER ADMIT THAT IT IS. *Ever.* I can't. I won't. Please don't make me admit I like it. Please . . .

chapter 16
THE INTRUDER

Getting through the crowd hadn't been that bad really. As usual, the European fans had been polite and waited calmly for their turn without bull-rushing us. They use "please" and "thank you," and mean it when they talk to you, and they never try for a selfie without asking. They respect boundaries. They don't feel entitled to anything from you. Americans, take note. We were able to work our way through them in under thirty minutes. I kept close to Ryo, ready to snap bones if anyone tried anything, but no one did. They never did. With the autograph and selfie-happy crowd behind us, we could finally retreat to our rooms. As usual, each of us had our own suite on the top floor, so we crammed into the elevator together.

Now, when you spend as much time riding up and down elevators as we do, you learn to have a little fun with it. We had a rule: if we were all in an elevator together, and the doors happened to open up, we had to sing something to whoever came in. "Elevator music," we called it. (I know, it's so clever!) It always scared, surprised, and confused the unlucky. It was fun at first, but like most great traditions it got old pretty quick. Karim was still way into it though, so for his sake we played along. He really bought into this whole "brotherhood" thing and it didn't take too much effort on our part to play along.

We made it up without stopping, thank God. I didn't think I had an a cappella version of "Hold Tight" (our current elevator music song) in me that night.

"Maybe we should go up and down again? For fun?" Karim asked hopefully.

Ryo gave me a pained look. Seamus and Amit did the same.

"I'm pretty beat," I offered.

"Oh, all right," Karim said, accepting it, but his eyes brightened. "We should have dinner as a family tonight. To celebrate our awards."

"That would be bad form," Seamus argued. "You never celebrate the victory before you have it in hand."

"Excellent point," Amit agreed.

Okay, so aside from Karim, we were all in agreement that dinner as a group was not something we wanted to do. We were a good, close group, but we were around each other enough already for everything else. Not to mention being in a bus for hours wears you out. Little tics get bigger, and then there's the overall smell of BO, burps, and farts that come from five teenage boys on a bus together that makes you need some time away to reset, charge the old batteries, and generally unfunkify yourself.

"Tomorrow night, for sure," I offered.

"I will make the reservation!" Karim said excitedly. "And arrange for the cars, of course."

Once I got to my room, my eyes found the overly huge and ridiculous welcome basket from the local tour promoter sitting on a table. Another iPad, countless gift cards, and local snacks. Never in my wildest dreams did I think I'd roll my eyes at an iPad, yet here I was. I'd kept the first few, but then started anonymously donating them to sick kids in local hospitals. Still your beating heart, ladies, *I* wanted to hock them on the street for some extra folding cash, but Ryo insisted we all do the sick-kid thing.

Eyes on the basket, I caught the golden corner of what could only be a pack of Haribo gummy bears peeking out and made a beeline for it. It was well known that they were my favorite candy, so they were always included in my baskets. The band dentist was not a big fan. This bag would be toast before bed, but first . . .

I flipped open my laptop and powered on my gear. Over the years I'd hidden near-invisible cameras and microphones in all of Ryo's luggage: his backpack, Dopp kit, wallet, and half of his shoes. I'd also hacked his phone, laptop, and tablet and could hijack them for their mics and cameras at will. This way, I could always know what he was up to and if he was okay since rooming together would have been weird. It wasn't a perfect system, but it was the best I could do since we were never in the same place for more than a couple nights. Ideally I'd have his room fitted with a gazillion cameras and mics, leaving no corner hidden or silent, but you have to play the hand you're dealt. Besides, the band had pretty good security guards. One of them was former SAS, like a British Navy SEAL, so I knew if the s ever really did hit the fan, I could count on him. The others? I mean, they were big, and I would hope they'd do right, but once bullets start flying, butts start running.

Ryo was talking with his parents. Yes, I speak Japanese, okay, sorta. I'd listened to enough of his conversations with his folks and watched enough anime and old samurai movies "as research" to be able to get the gist of what he was saying most of the time. If he was talking to his *Oya* (told you I spoke some *Nihongo*), it meant we'd been in our rooms for five minutes. The boy was consistent as a clock. The moment we got to a new hotel, he checked the room for intruders (adorable), put his bags neatly in his closet, washed his hands, and then called them at the five-minute mark. His life was so regimented that I felt bad for him sometimes. The others joked behind his back about whether he has to call home before going to the bathroom. The sad thing is we're not a hundred percent sure he doesn't.

Next, as always, Ryo hopped in the shower. So the good thing about my Ryo Creepster Gear is I can always hear what he's up to, but unless one of my random hidden cameras is set up just right, I'm usually blind to most of the room. That's where Ryo's regimented life was a godsend. Once he was in the shower, I grabbed a camera from my gear and shoved it into my pocket.

OUT ON MY BALCONY the bitter Brussels winter almost knocked the wind out of me. Man, Europe was cold in the winter. I tip my hat to you, World War I and World War II soldiers. Being in a foxhole in this must have sucked. After making sure no one was watching, I climbed up on the banister and rock-wall-climbed my way over to Ryo's balcony. Picking the lock was easy enough and within seconds, I had my camera placed in the top corner of the room. I'd have a perfect view of the room from there.

Ryo sang in the shower, by the way. And not our songs or Top 40 stuff but bluegrass like Doc Watson, Hackensaw Boys, Foghorn Stringband, and Old Crow Medicine Show. Not even he knows why or how he ever found it, but that's his jam. That alone would have made us friends. He was belting out "Fall on My Knees" right now. A classic.

Back in my room, I patted my own back at the placement of the hidden camera. You know, if this whole Shadow thing doesn't work out, I'm going to Hollywood to be a camera guy. I kicked off my shoes, put my feet up on the desk, grabbed the edge of the treat basket, and slid it over.

As I was sifting through the swag, my hidden mics picked up the click from Ryo's front door lock.

Someone had entered Ryo's room.

I lunged for my roller bag, ripped open the hidden compartment in the bottom, and took out my Glock .45—preloaded with a clip of armor-piercing bullets. Holding my breath, I eyed the screen on Ryo's room, cursing that I didn't have a clear view of the door.

The door closed, and a girl crept silently into view. No hello. No noise. Nothing. She knew what she was doing. I immediately went to my door and began to mirror her every step with one eye on the monitor. I kept the pistol raised. Yes, it would be a shot through a wall, but I aimed dead-on at her head. One move I didn't like and I'd drop her.

She sat down on the couch and pulled out her phone. She looked relaxed. She didn't have any weapons I could see, but that meant nothing. I didn't need a weapon to kill, either. She wasn't much older than Ryo or me—Asian, thin, and not very tall. Her hair hung in two loose pigtails, the tips frosted pink. She had on a pair of black jeans, a black V-neck shirt, and what looked like black, full-leather Chuck Taylors . . . All right, I'm gonna come right out and say it. She was hot. It would be a shame if I had to kill her. Maybe she was just a Ryo fangirl. There were millions.

Her head snapped up, seemingly without warning. She looked right at the hidden camera. We were suddenly staring at each other. How the . . . ? No way she could know that; no way. Her eyes seemed to hold mine for a few seconds before she smiled and went back to her phone. Must have just been coincidence. Maybe she randomly spaced out while she was thinking of something . . .

The water in the shower turned off. Moments later the bathroom door opened.

I took aim again as Ryo came out in a robe.

The girl didn't move.

The moment Ryo rounded the corner, she said in Japanese, "You should get better security here."

Ryo screamed. A lifetime-of-embarrassment kind if your buddies heard you. He stumbled and tripped, then scrambled backward into a closet, terrified. I was a nanosecond away from pulling the trigger, but the girl still hadn't moved. It was the only reason she was still alive.

"And you wonder why we never dated," she added, pocketing the phone and standing up.

This got my attention. Ryo's, too. He crept out from his hiding spot and peeked into the room.

"Akiko?" he gasped.

"Surprise!" she shouted, bursting out with a wide smile, her arms extended for a hug.

"What are you . . ." He struggled to stand.

"I was in Rotterdam for a gig and thought I'd surprise you. Surprise!" she repeated.

I kept my gun trained on her as she ran over to hug him, only relaxing when he hugged back.

"You frightened me," Ryo said in a shaky voice.

"No, really?" Akiko mocked.

"I am a bit ashamed of my reaction."

She stepped away from him. "I won't tell anyone."

I lowered my gun and sighed.

They sat down on the couch and began catching up. Nothing that interesting. She asked about the tour. He asked about her work. It was pretty boring stuff, so I took the moment to eat some snacks and take a shower of my own. I took my gun and Creepster Gear with me, of course.

A LITTLE WHILE LATER, as I was getting out of the shower, there was a knock on my door.

"Bobby, it is Ryo," he called out in English. He had no idea how well I understood Japanese. As far as he knew, I was still a novice and spoke a few phrases in broken Japanese.

"Yeah, gimme a sec," I called out, sweeping the room to make sure I'd stowed my gun and Creepster Gear.

There was another knock.

"Bobby?"

"Yeah!" I yelled out as I walked to the door and opened. Yeah, I was still in just my towel.

"What's up? Oh, hi," I said, pretending to be surprised by his friend. I even pretended to be a little embarrassed by my seminakedness.

"Allow me to introduce you to my good friend, Akiko," he said.

"Hey, nice to meet you," I said, offering her my hand to shake. "I'm Bobby."

"Bad timing?" she asked, looking at me and my towel-only attire.

"Pretty girl surprising you in a hotel room is never bad timing."

Not even a blush. In fact, what was that, pity? Harsh. They followed me into my room.

"Do all of you shower at the same time?" she joked. "Cute."

I ducked into the bedroom and threw on my jammies before joining them back in the living room.

"So, uh, how do you know Ryo here?" I asked her.

"We were neighbors as children," Ryo answered for her. He sat down on the couch. Akiko was still snooping around the room, as if looking for something.

"So why are you in Brussels?"

"Her work," Ryo answered again.

I was beginning to wonder if she'd ever answer herself.

"What do you do?" I asked, making a point to look right at her and not Ryo.

"Information security," Ryo said, like it would mean something to me.

"I'm a hacker," she said, finally turning toward me. She looked satisfied—like whatever she'd been looking for she'd found . . . or hadn't found. "Ryo wants what I do to be something more professional-sounding, but I'm a hacker. That's what I do. People pay me to hack their systems so they can make them stronger."

"Seriously?"

She nodded.

"Cool. So basically you're, like, paid to break stuff."

"Yes," she said, sitting down on the couch with Ryo.

"So are you two, uh, you know . . . ?" I asked.

"No," Ryo said quickly. Too quickly, and with an embarrassed laugh that was too forced to hide how he really felt. *I've been there, buddy. It sucks. Oh, Leggo, where are you . . .*

"Oh, okay."

There was a nice, long pause of super-fun, awkward silence after that. Akiko stood up. "Sorry to interrupt your evening. Ryo's told me so much about you that I wanted to meet you."

"Oh, really?" I looked at Ryo. He nodded. He'd never mentioned her to me. How he could never tell me that one of his closest friends was a hot hacker was something we'd discuss on the bus later. "Yeah, Ryo goes on and on about his Yakuza friends, too, so it's nice to finally meet one," I joked. I thought it was funny, but no one laughed. Ryo looked embarrassed. Akiko looked pissed.

"Sorry," I muttered.

"It is an insult to our culture and history that the world stereotypes us into a nation of criminals," Akiko said.

"I'm really sorry. I just—"

"Good night, Bobby," she said, and immediately left the room. Ryo followed her out but hesitated at the door.

"Sorry, Ryo," I said.

"It is okay. I know you are only joking."

"Can you make sure she knows that?"

He nodded. "Go drink the horses before you sleep, cowboy," he said with a smile.

"It's water the horses," I corrected him, but gave him a polite snort.

"Water the horses? They are not plants. That does not make sense."

"Neither does drinking horses."

"No, it doesn't, does it?" He laughed. "Now I must go speak with Akiko before she calls her Yakuza friends and gets you killed."

I gave him another polite snort, but it was only to acknowledge the effort. I felt like a world-class a-hole and I deserved to feel bad. I didn't want to know what she was saying about me, so I turned the volume on my Creepster Gear down and did my best to ignore them. I couldn't mute it, though, and had to keep some volume. It's hard to ignore words like "ignorant," "witless," and "stupid American."

chapter 17
TOUCH ONE HAIR ON HIS HEAD

I don't sleep much since I don't really need it, but the little bit I got that night was garbage. It was some of the worst sleep I'd had in a long time. My mind ran wild with visions of Akiko as a cowboy giving me her disappointed face as she shot me.

Even though we didn't have a show, it didn't mean we had the day off. Every city meant the same daily routine, our regular round of local PR. "Surprise" hosts at a radio station, guest stars on a local TV channel, some type of local honor. It was all pretty repetitive. The day flew by and before I knew it, I was with the boys in a limo, heading to the awards show. Akiko was with us and was going as Ryo's guest. She still hated me and didn't make any effort to hide it, so the ride was wonderfully awkward. She looked really nice, though. I mean, she was pretty darn hot in her scruffy hacker clothes, but all fancied up like this? Wow. Just wow.

It took forever to get down the red carpet. I know what you're thinking: *Poor guy has to suffer through people wanting to take his picture. Life must be so hard.* But you have to remember I have to make sure no crazy hops the fence and tries to stab Ryo, so it's doubly exhausting for me. Once we got inside, it was more fun and much less stressful. There was a lot of legit security and no press, so everyone could relax.

No one needs an excuse to come to Europe, so even

though it was a kids' awards show, everywhere I looked there were A-list movie stars and musicians hanging out and joking. Ryo was my regular wingman, but tonight he had Akiko, so I was on my own. I had nothing in common with these people and hate schmoozing, so I figured I'd head backstage and snoop around. Like anyone would stop me. Plan in place, I turned to leave. As I turned, a shoulder bumped into me. It was hard and done on purpose.

Tug Mansfield.

TUG WAS "ME" IN our archnemesis, Universal. The feud between our bands was totally fake, of course . . . or it should have been. But it wasn't to Universal and especially not to Tug. He seemed to be especially into it. I think the label had forced them to say that they hated us so much that now they *believed* that they hated us. Weird how that happens. They never shied away from trying to pour fuel on the imaginary fire. Apparently this now included shoulder bumps at awards ceremonies. Have you no class, sir?

"'Sup," Tug said to me, trying to sound tough. He had on a dark blue suit that was strategically dirty and ripped, a pink V-neck, and a black checkered scarf. A scarf?! I can't even . . .

"Yeah, okay," I replied, sounding as uninterested in this as I could and trying to walk around him.

Tug blocked my path and I kid you not, chest bumped me.

"Dance-off, son," he said seriously.

I almost laughed. "Here?"

"Dance-off," he repeated.

"There's no music," I added. Now, I'd heard he was a bit dense, but this was amazing.

He chest-bumped me again as he said, "You scared, boy?"

He looked over his shoulder toward a girl, his date, I guess, who seemed to be really eating this macho crap up.

She looked like the trashy, bitter maid of honor who'd had too much to drink at a bachelorette party. Well, at least they have each other? Do two stupid parents make a smart baby? That whole two negatives equal a positive thing? Man, I hope so. If not, Earth is screwed.

"Let's go, Sky."

He began to bounce.

Oh my God, you're serious. I didn't know what to do. Instinct told me to hit him and put an end to it, but my instincts were something I'd learned to ignore because they'd always given me horrible advice. So then . . . good lord, was I really considering having a dance-off in the middle of this room to shut this situation down? How could that somehow even be an option? Tug raised his palms to taunt me.

"Maybe . . . later." I slowly backed away.

"That's right, son. Back on up."

He clucked. Like a chicken.

I turned away. God, I wanted to punch him.

"'Sup, son," he said to someone else.

It was the grunt that followed that got my attention. I knew that sound: pain. I knew who made it: Ryo. Every nerve in my body spiked as I whipped around. Ryo was massaging his shoulder. The pain courtesy of a Tug shoulder bump. Akiko was at his side, glaring at Tug. She'd looked like she was about to throw down herself. I was sorta starting to like this girl. A waiter passed with a tray of beef satay hors d'oeuvres and I had to fight the urge to grab one of the skewers and stab Tug to death with it. I took a deep breath and strode over, planting myself between Tug and Ryo.

"Go make sure I'm sitting with you, huh?" I said casually to Ryo.

Ryo nodded, grabbed Akiko's hand, and pulled her away.

"'Sup, son," Tug said to me, raising his palms up in the air. "Back for more?"

If you didn't know, there's a major pressure point in your forearm. If you know where to grab, you can press down on the radial nerve and cause intense, knee-buckling pain with little effort. My mind shot back to the past for a moment. Like learning a new curse word and using it to death—that was all we did to each other at FATE the few weeks after we learned where to press. Walking down the hallway? Nerve pinch! Eating lunch? Nerve pinch! About to rappel out of a helicopter? Nerve pinch! Pretty stressful few weeks while we got it out of our systems. You had to assume that around every corner someone was waiting to cripple you.

I snatched Tug's arm and dug my thumb right into the sweet spot. He whimpered and his knees buckled almost instantly.

"On your feet," I whispered into his ear. I slapped a fake smile across my face as I grabbed his other arm and kept him from crumbling to the floor. "Don't look around for help, and don't make a sound, or I'll press"—I added a bit more pressure with my thumb—"harder."

Tug's eyes began to water. He whimpered the saddest and loudest high-pitched squeal I'd ever heard come from a grown man.

People began to stare.

"We're just two old friends catching up," I said calmly while smiling and pressing. "Smile, Tug," I ordered.

He tried to smile, but it looked more like he was showing the world his teeth. Satisfied that he would never forget this moment, this pain, I relaxed my grip. He immediately grabbed his forearm with his free hand.

I leaned over and whispered into his ear, "If you ever touch him again, I'll break your legs."

He stared back at me as if I were a stranger. Good. I'd scared the crap out of him.

I smiled, straightened up, and slapped him on the shoulder like an old buddy as I said loudly, "Great seeing you, Tug. Good luck tonight. Say hey to the boys for me."

BACKSTAGE, A HUGE TROUPE of dancers caught my eyes. They were doing some really crazy dancing that looked oddly familiar to me. I couldn't take my eyes off it.

When it ended, the choreographer in charge yelled out, "Okay, great, last chance for makeup and costumes, everyone!"

My stomach jumped. I knew that voice. The group scattered, and when I saw who was still in the middle talking to a couple of dancers, butterflies exploded in my stomach.

"Leggo!" I blurted out, and stepped out from the shadows.

She turned around and it took her half a second to recognize me. For that half second I felt like garbage. How could she not remember me? But then a huge smile burst across her face. "Bobby?!"

Like a zombie, my long-buried crush burst up through the hard ground and back to life.

She ran over to me.

"Hello, person I don't know and have never met," she joked.

I'd hoped for a hug. She delivered. A good hug too. A hug that meant something. Or one my crush convinced me meant something.

"I was hoping I'd see you," she admitted when she let go.

"What are you doing here?"

"I'm the choreographer for the dancers in the Solar One Tour," she said like it was nothing.

My jaw dropped. "That's awesome!"

"Thanks."

The small group she'd been talking to before running over to me was still waiting and one called out, "Leggo?"

"Yeah, I know," she said to them before looking back at me. "I gotta go get changed and stuff. We open the show. Good seeing you," she said as she turned and started to skip off.

I had to say something. This couldn't be it. Get her number, address, email, something, you fool. Do something.

"You wanna hang out after?" I blurted out.

"Yeah, totally. I'll find you," she said as she ran off with her group. "Good luck tonight!"

I looked around to make sure no one was looking before allowing myself a congratulatory "You know it!" out loud.

THE SHOW WAS ABOUT to start, but I needed to head back out to the front anyway. I hadn't seen Ryo or heard his voice in over ten minutes. Whenever that happens, my insides start to squirm and the feeling won't go away until I know he's safe. I knew he was, of course. This place was crawling with security and then there was something about Akiko that gave me the feeling that girl could tear a man in half if she had to. But I had to know for real with my own two eyes (or ears would do).

I found Ryo safe and sound, like I knew I would, over in a corner with Akiko, laughing about something. And don't think I didn't notice that the moment I appeared, Tug quickly left the room. I met up with Akiko and Ryo as everyone started heading for their seats and the three of us went inside the auditorium.

We won Song of the Year, Album of the Year, and somehow the Lifetime Achievement Award, too. How that makes any sense for a band that's only been together for a year and a half I have no idea. Someone, someday will have to explain it to me. I didn't care about any of it—on many different levels—but mainly because all I could think about was Leggo. Had there even been other dancers up there during the show?

The end of this thing couldn't come soon enough and when it mercifully did, I hurried out into the main lobby, where the after-party would be, and waited.

"Bobby!" I heard her call out behind me.

I spun around, stupid grin and everything.

"You were awesome," I told her.

"Thanks," she said shyly.

"I mean, it was no Moonwalk, but it was pretty good," I joked.

She laughed. Her laugh was adorable. A good-looking dude suddenly appeared and handed Leggo a drink.

"Here you go," he said with an Italian accent.

"Thanks, babe," she responded.

Babe? Did I hear that right? Uh, what the . . .

"Oh, Bobby, this is Evander, my boyfriend."

Boyfriend?!? What . . . Who . . .

"Hey, nice to meet you, Bobby. I'm a big fan," Evander said, offering me his hand to shake.

I shook it, because that's what you do.

"So how do you two know each other?" he asked me.

Deer in the headlights, anyone? It took every bit of control I had to not pull him in close and snatch the life out of him.

"Oh, uh, I consulted for a few days for their tour," Leggo quickly answered for both of us. "Helped Bobby learn to Moonwalk."

"Cute," he said.

Cute?!? CUTE?!? I hadn't had anything to do with "cute" since I was three. I would show him "cute" when I ripped his spinal cord out and wore it like a necktie. I would call it my "cute jewelry."

"Oooh, crab cakes," he said, and walked away.

"You okay?" Leggo asked. I can only assume my face had given me away.

"Oh, yeah, fine," I lied. "I just, you know, uh, you look happy."

"Love, you must try these," Evander called out, waving her over to the server with the tray of crab cakes.

"Gotta go," she said with a big smile. "Great seeing you, Bobby!"

"Yeah," I muttered.

I watched her hurry over to Evander Crab Cakes. It was hard being mad, seeing how excited she was. And besides, who was I kidding? Like I could ever have a normal relationship. I'd been linked. I'd given up everything when I became what I am. Why would dreams of a happy life with a family be any different? Love wasn't in the cards for me. Not now. Not *ever*.

I mean, what did I expect? I get married and then tell my new wife that Ryo has to come on our honeymoon because he can't be out of my sight for more than ten minutes? Come on. Pretty awkward if they don't know why and even more so if they're into it. No, Leggo was much better off without me in her life and I knew it. Every girl was. For the second and decidedly final time in my life, I had to leggo my Leggo.

You can't control what the heart wants.

Oh . . . my . . . God, did I just use the lyrics to "The Start" to describe my feelings? Excuse me, I need to go beat the crap out of myself in the bathroom.

chapter 18

THAT BLENDER YOU SOLD ME IS CRAP

Tour dates in Lisbon, Madrid, Barcelona, Nantes, Paris, Amsterdam, Liverpool, Glasgow, and Dublin came and went without issue as I slowly got out of my funk. No matter how hard I tried to play it off, I was still really bummed about Leggo and Evander. What a stupid name. It wasn't until after the Dublin show, our last show in Europe, during the flight back to the States that I finally, honestly got over it.

It was like a switch flipped somewhere over the Atlantic and I was back. Like Leggo had been a European problem that couldn't cross the ocean. An Old World issue that had no business being in the New. Like monarchies.

We made a pit stop in New York to do a couple days of PR work to promote the upcoming US tour—a few appearances on some morning and late-night TV shows, the big radio stations, the usual. None of us really understood why we had to do this since the whole tour had sold out in minutes, but when the label says "do," you do.

With the PR machine nice and greased we needed to get over to Seattle, where the US tour would begin. A helicopter took us from midtown Manhattan directly to LaGuardia, where the plane was waiting. But this wasn't some ordinary, private charter like we usually got—no, this was one of the official jets of the record label. This was reserved for the real heavy hitters of the company. The Stones got one of these jets. Coldplay got one of these jets. The girls of Solar One got these jets. We all shared a knowing look. The "just like you" boys had finally caught up to the rest.

We'd been on our fair share of private charters, but nothing like this. Talk about awesome. Daaaaaang, this thing was nice! Flat screens, couches, and a buffet! Love it. The itchy fingers of old Hutch would have stolen so much stuff in here.

"Universal's going to be so mad," Amit said with a chuckle.

Seamus agreed. "Will definitely ruffle their feathers. Wish I could see it."

"We should take a picture, as a family, for our memory book," Karim said.

"Memory book?" I asked.

"I'm making one for each of you," Karim said, as if we were the weird ones.

"That is quite kind of you," Ryo acknowledged, staring me down, knowing I wanted to make fun of the kid. "I will agree to your picture."

He looked at me, knowing that if I agreed, Seamus and Amit would, too.

"Yeah, why not."

As predicted, Seamus and Amit agreed. Karim took a few selfies, with each of us strategically placed behind him, and then asked the copilot to take some more. Thirty minutes later—pretty short for a Karim-inspired photo session—we finished.

"Maybe we'll take some more once we're in the air?" Karim said, sounding hopeful.

No one answered.

"Gonna be a bit," the captain told us. "Got a lot of planes stacked up, thanks to the storm in Florida."

It didn't matter. Once you're on a plane like this, delays don't bother you. Oh, you mean I should just have another lobster roll while I watch a movie that's not even out yet? Man, okay, I guess . . .

Most of us were still on Europe time anyway, so when you combined that with waking up early for the talk show, naps were high on everyone's to-do list. And the super-comfy chairs and couches on this plane were made for napping. While everyone got comfy I got a call on my phone. The number was blocked, but that didn't mean anything since half the numbers of people we dealt with came across as blocked.

"Hey, what's up?" I answered, assuming it was one of our producers or something.

"The blender you sold me is crap," a person I didn't recognize said on the other end of the line.

"Not my problem, bro," I responded automatically, and immediately looked out the window. I couldn't believe this was happening. This was FATE calling. But why? They'd only contact me if something was wrong. What was wrong?

I looked around. None of the boys were paying attention to me, which was good. Seamus (not surprisingly) was already asleep. I got up and moved toward the front of the plane to be farther away from them.

"I want my money back," the guy on the other end replied.

"Fine. Where can I send it?"

"Hangar 16C."

I looked back at the guys. All of them were busy texting or watching movies, so I turned and asked the pilot, "Okay if I go for a walk?"

"Absolutely, but don't go too far," he said. "When we get the go-ahead, we'll need to move quick."

I HAD NO IDEA where hangar 16C might be. Given who I was dealing with, I shouldn't have been surprised to see it was the next hangar over. I took one last look at the plane to make sure none of my bandmates were watching and then quickly walked away.

The metal side door opened quietly enough as I pushed it. In my imagination the hangar would be pitch black except for a single light from the ceiling shining down on a black Lincoln. Oh, and there'd be a man in a black suit and trench coat, with black gloves and black sunglasses, standing next to it holding a manila envelope. Reality, as I'd learned, is quite different in comparison.

The hangar was well-lit and fairly dirty, and had seven planes jammed inside it. It was quiet in here, though. At least my imagination had gotten that part right. A guy in a hoodie and jeans stepped out from behind a plane and waved at me to follow.

I tailed him into the middle of the hangar, where the pieces of a small Cessna plane were scattered around, along with a bunch of tools.

"Everything okay?" I asked him. I needed to know what was going on.

He held up his finger silently, asking for a moment. He looked midthirties, had a mess of curly black hair with a touch of gray, and wore black-rimmed glasses. He didn't look a threat with his pudgy frame, but I knew better. Anyone and everyone can be dangerous. I mean, yeah, I could take him—whether I could or couldn't was a thought that went through my head every time I met someone new—but we were on the same team, so I knew I wouldn't have to. Not to sound too egoistic, but I'd never met anyone I didn't think I could handle. Comes with the gig, I guess.

"All clear," a man behind me said.

"No one followed," said another in the same area.

Where in the heck had they come from?! Talk about silent. Were they part-cat? I looked over my shoulder to see two men wearing black combat fatigues walking toward us. Both had short-cropped hair, black combat boots, and don't-mess-with-me attitudes. Unlike Floppy here with the glasses, these guys were legit—trained soldiers of some kind. They stopped a few feet behind me, one on the left and the other on the right. I wasn't scared, but it did make me feel uncomfortable.

Floppy reached into the front pocket of his hoodie and pulled out a pair of the clear linking glasses. "Here," he said.

I reached out and took them, but I didn't put them on.

"What's going on?" I asked him.

"You're done. Your assignment's over. Now, put those on and unlink. You're still a valuable resource and we have a new assignment for you," he said, as if reading it all from a cue card.

"I sorta like the one I have now."

I couldn't believe those words had come out of my mouth, and that I'd actually meant them, too.

"Well, that's too bad. It's over, and you're needed elsewhere."

"But, how?"

Had I missed Ryo doing the miraculous, world-changing thing I was here for?

"The *how* is not your concern," Floppy said calmly, but I could tell he was getting annoyed. He jerked his head toward the exit. "Your assignment is completed. He is on his way. The rest will take care of itself."

"On his way?" I repeated. I felt a prickle at the back of my neck.

"On the plane."

"What happens on the plane?!" I demanded. When he

didn't answer, I repeated, angrily and slowly, "What . . . happens . . . on . . . the . . . plane?"

"How should I know?" he admitted, a bit annoyed.

"Look, buddy, I know you're just doing your job. I get it. But I joined a boy band for this. *A boy band.* Whatever makes this kid so special I'm gonna be there for it. I'm gonna see it," I said seriously. "Give me the glasses, and I'll put them on after he does it, and I'll meet you wherever you want."

He didn't respond. For a moment I thought he'd agree. But then it happened: a flick of the eye to the men behind me. Nothing more. Barely noticeable, but I saw it. I'd been trained to see it.

I reacted in the only way I knew how—also the way I'd been trained—without mercy. In a flash, I slammed my left foot into Floppy's chest, sending him flying backward into a mess of parts. At the same time a hand grabbed my right shoulder. I reached up with my right hand, grabbed it, and twisted until I heard things break. The attacker fell to the ground clutching his arm. There was another on my left. So my left foot, which had never touched the ground after hitting Floppy, swung over and caught him in the throat. The whole thing lasted precisely one second.

I looked at the men. Floppy was on the ground, clutching his chest and trying to catch his breath through . . . three—no, four broken ribs. The man on my right was still growling in pain, holding his mangled arm. The man on my left was silent and turning blue, gurgling through a crushed windpipe. He'd be gone soon and was no longer a concern. *Kill or die. The only enemy you don't have to worry about is a dead one.*

My focus went back to Floppy. He was the one with the answers.

WE AREN'T TRAINED TO simply maim or injure and move on. *Kill or die. The only enemy you don't have to worry about is a dead one.* I'd only done what I'd been trained to do. I reminded myself of this as I shoved the last of the bodies into the luggage compartment of a random plane in the hangar. As I was about to close the luggage hatch, Floppy's glasses fell out. I picked them up and gently put them back on his face.

What? I'm not a total monster.

He'd told me nothing, of course. Not anything useful. He didn't know what was going on any more than I did. He was a Collector for FATE. I'd never heard the term before, but it wasn't hard to figure out why they were called that. Guys like him were sent to collect Shadows who were no longer needed on their assignments—and presumably those Shadows would be killed or recycled or stuck permanently at the FATE Center.

All he knew was that after the flight to Seattle, Ryo's protection was no longer needed and I was being reassigned to some place called the Nest.

Apparently they had assured him I'd go willingly. Uh, nope. I'd made it quick out of respect for his honesty. His friend with the jacked-up arm had known even less and quickly joined Floppy for whatever afterlife he believed in. Luckily, no one had come in during any of this. Try explaining that one to the press.

With the bodies safely tucked away, I headed back to my plane. Whatever was going on, I was sure as hell gonna be a part of it until the very end. I would see this through. They'd linked me. What did they expect would happen? I only did what they'd trained me to do. Or so I kept telling myself. Then again, I'd disobeyed orders, and I'd killed some of their people—my people. The killing they probably wouldn't mind, but the disobeying of orders? That was a big no-no. Maybe when we landed, I'd fall off the grid instead.

Oh yeah, that would totally work. It wasn't like I was in a world-famous boy band or anything . . . I'm not hugely recognizable with my face on posters in girls' rooms across the world . . .

I'd figure it out. All I knew was that whatever lightning-to-the-brain moment Ryo was about to get, I wanted to be there for it. I'd joined a boy band for this, so for God's sake, at least let me see the pot of gold at the end of the rainbow.

The closer I got to the plane, the more nervous and excited I got. What was about to happen? How long would it take? Would I even know when it happened, or would it just be a thought Ryo has and a small smile? I knew as I reached the stairs I was going to really have to focus on not staring at him.

I climbed on board and within minutes we were taxiing. No one had questioned where'd I'd gone or why either. The hangar had never happened. I took a seat where I could watch Ryo without him knowing it. He was playing a game on his tablet. Was this what inspired him?

"I have that game if you want to play it," Amit offered.

Wow, I must have been staring hard that time. Oops.

"Oh yeah?" I asked, pretending to be excited.

"Here," he said, handing me his tablet.

"Awesome. Thanks," I lied and started to play it.

It actually ended up being a good cover. I held up the tablet at eye level so it looked like I was staring at it instead of Ryo. Three cheers for Amit.

An hour after takeoff, Ryo reclined his seat and dozed off. Ah, right, the old dream inspiration. Classic. He'd wake up, shout, "Eureka!" and then explain his world-changing idea to us. All I had to do now was wait.

And wait.

And wait—

My pocket vibrated.

Dut . . . dut . . . dut . . .

I bolted up in my seat and my hand wrapped itself around the phone. That pulse was unmistakable. An alert.

Dut . . . dut . . . dut . . .

My phone—normal-looking, but developed and made by FATE specifically for Shadows—had a warning. I made sure no one was watching me before looking at the screen.

Incoming Missile – Heat-Seeking flashed on the top of the screen.

Below that was a lovely map showing our plane cruising happily along with another blip screaming toward us. Impact was imminent. There were seconds to spare.

I tapped my phone to bring up the only option available to us. It wasn't ideal, but given that the other option was the guarantee of dying in a fiery explosion five miles up in the sky, I had no other choice. My phone, packed with a lot of really other cool features, can release an electromagnetic pulse, or EMP, which fries all electrical stuff within its blast range. My finger hovered above the spot to detonate.

With the engines killed, there would be no heat signature and the missile would miss us. Yeah, by shutting down the plane I'd most likely be killing us anyway, but a missile strike guaranteed death. Crappy odds beat crappier ones every time. Still I hesitated. We'd have to glide down from thirty thousand feet with no hope of getting the engines back online. It was possible, just not likely. It all depended on the pilot. Maybe ours was *that* good. Maybe he was on par with the "Miracle on the Hudson" guy, you know, the one who landed a plane on the Hudson River after hitting a bunch of birds. Okay, more likely we'd die on impact. But at least that wouldn't be death now. The gift of time is the greatest of all.

I tapped the button.

Everything shut off. A collective gasp of panic erupted

among my bandmates when everything, even the lights, shut off. Well, not Ryo. He was still asleep. For the most wonderful of half seconds the plane held steady. Not bad, I thought. Then it got bad. The plane lurched, the nose dipped, and we all got that super-fun feeling in our stomachs as the plane gave in to gravity and fell. After that, the cabin was all shrieking terror. I glanced out the window and I caught sight of the tail smoke from the missile as it zipped past us like we weren't there. Obstacle one down. Obstacle two, here I come. I needed to get to the cockpit. The pilot would need help.

My body wanted to go up toward the tail, not down, so I practically had to pull myself down the aisle. Halfway there we began to spin. That didn't help, either. Not only did it become near impossible to keep my bearings, but crap kept smacking me in the face. Eventually I got to the cockpit door and climbed inside. The pilot was clutching his chest and crying. Okay, so he wasn't as good as that "Miracle on the Hudson" guy. *Bang up job, buddy. Way to keep it to together.*

I grabbed him and unhooked his belt.

"I'm sorry . . . I'm sorry . . . I'm sorry . . . I'm sorry . . ." he was repeating over and over. What the hell? Don't they train pilots for catastrophic power failures? *I* did when FATE gave me flying lessons.

"Ugh," I growled. I shoved him hard out of the cockpit and into the main cabin to get tossed around like a rag doll for a bit; maybe that would snap him out of it. I slammed the cockpit door shut, strapped myself into the seat, and took a breath. I'd done this before, sorta. I'd had to recover planes in free fall plenty of times on the simulator. It all came back to me and instinct took over.

Within five seconds—which seems like not a lot of time but

is an eternity when you're free-falling—I was able to stop the spinning. Ten seconds later, I had us in a controlled glide. Okay, maybe not controlled, but these planes weren't meant to "glide," so a better way to say it would be a controlled dive. Yeah, that's more like it. Whatever you want to call it, the big takeaway was it gave me some time to think and a chance at us not dying. A chance.

"Where do I land?" I called out to no one.

We were somewhere over the Grand Tetons. These are particularly sharp and snowy mountains that are also rocky and steep. Not ideal. But it looked like there was a break where the ground could be flat up ahead.

I gritted my teeth as I kept one eye on the altimeter and the other on the terrain, trying my best to steer us to the crash zone. Yeah, it would be a crash zone, not a landing zone. Gotta have wheels to land, but the controls for those were fried along with everything else. We were crashing. There was no way around it.

I reached behind me and unlatched the cockpit door.

"Ryo, strap in and hold on!" I yelled, realizing I probably could have said "everybody" instead of "Ryo," but at this moment I couldn't care less about them.

Ten seconds to impact. I gave the plane a little turn while I kept pulling up on the yoke with everything I had.

Five seconds to impact.

I pulled harder, trying my best to flatten us out. The trees and ground were flying by below so fast it seemed fake. The simulator was more real than this. Then again, you got to walk away from a crash in a simulator. Up ahead, the tree line gave way to a wide open grassy plain. I could make it. I *had to* make it.

Three . . .

Two . . .

One . . .

The last of the trees clipped the underside of the plane with a sickening jolt.

Plane, say hello to ground.

Ground, you play nice, please.

chapter 19

SIMPLE LIVIN'

Dirt, grass, and hunks of airplane exploded up from the ground and blinded me as the nose of the plane dug into the earth. Noise, the rumbling of the ground on the metal, the creaking of the hull—it was deafening. We began to slide to the left. Something caught the wing and jerked us back around to the right. I didn't care which way we slid as long as we weren't . . . rolling.

Why did I think that?!

At that moment the wings finally gave in and allowed the ground to rip them off. After that there was nothing standing between us and some super-fun rolling.

We began to roll. Of course we did. I'll admit it, we got lucky. If we'd started rolling earlier while we'd been going a lot faster, we'd have all died. Planes aren't built to handle that and we'd have been torn apart along with it. Luckily, we were going slow enough that the hull held, and after only three sluggish rolls the plane groaned and finally came to a stop on its side.

Hey, coulda been upside down. Yeah, it's not much of a bright side, but it's a start.

The dust was thick, but I knew it would clear soon. I was worried about fire.

"Everyone okay?" I called out while I unbuckled my seat

belt and dropped to the floor. Well, technically the side of the plane.

"Yeah," a chorus of voices called out all at once. I only really heard Ryo's. It was the only one I cared about. I blindly made my way to the back of the plane. Hearing is not seeing, so I had to see he was really all right. I had to know he was really okay. Until then I couldn't focus on anything or anyone else. The dust was starting to clear, but I could still only see a few feet in front of me as I moved.

"I'm stuck!" Karim called out.

"I gotcha," Seamus told him and then added, "Ryo, help me out, would ya?"

I could see figures ahead of me working to help someone down. The moment I saw Ryo with my own eyes, I felt better. The knot in my stomach untied itself, the block in my brain crumbled, and I was me again.

Knowing a fire could burst to life at any second, turning us all into brisket, I looked for an easy way out. All the windows were busted out and there were some holes in the skin of the plane, but none of them were big enough to escape from. I tried the main exit, but it was dented and jammed tight and wouldn't budge. It left only one way out.

"Everyone, through the cockpit windows," I instructed. They were busted out and were the only openings big enough for us to fit through.

I made sure I was the last one left inside before climbing out myself. There was a crazy contrast between the dusty, cramped interior of the plane and the bright blue skies, open fields, and clean air that I now found myself in.

Once we were a safe distance from the plane we all took deep, clean breaths and did our best to shake, pat, and brush the dust off.

Somehow, everyone was okay. I was beginning to wonder if

there was a limit to how many times you can call it luck and have to start calling it something different. Super luck? Or maybe it wasn't luck at all and it was because we all had our seat belts on, and science is awesome, and I remembered my training. Anyway, aside from some bruises, twisted knees and ankles, and a ton of small cuts, everyone was good to go. Ryo had a nice gash over his left eye, but he didn't seem to care.

"What the hell happened up there?" Seamus asked the pilot.

The pilot raised his palms and shook his head in disbelief. "I have no idea. We were fine and then"—he snapped—"everything died. Some . . . electrical glitch, I guess. I . . . I didn't know what to do."

No one seemed to argue, but why would they? Glitches happen.

"How did you manage to land?" the pilot asked me.

I knew this question was coming and was still trying to figure out how I'd explain this away. I went with a classic and something I was really, really good at: when in doubt, play dumb.

"You mean crash? Pretty easily, actually," I joked.

He shook his head. "I couldn't have done that."

No kidding.

"Um . . . I don't know. Flight simulators? Too many action movies? All I did was pull up on the stick thing as hard as I could," I lied with a shrug to top it all off. "Just luck, I guess."

"Well, whatever it was, you saved all of our lives," he said. His voice shook with emotion. "Thank you."

"Seriously, all I did was yank up on a stick. But thanks."

The other guys all thanked me, too, but Ryo walked over and hugged me. When the others saw him do that, they all came over and hugged me along with him. I hated every second of it, but when I saw the pilot looking on like he wanted to join in, I couldn't help but motion with my head for him to join in, too.

He practically sprinted over to join the all-dude band hug. Well, satellites, I hope you're catching this. A boy band group hug in the middle of . . . where the heck were we again?

"Anybody know where we are?" I asked.

And no sooner had I asked it than all of us took out our phones to look because that's what you do now. Don't know the answer to the question? Look at your phone! Even I did it out of habit, even though I knew it wouldn't work, thanks to the EMP.

"Mine's dead," Ryo said first.

"Me too," Karim added.

"Same for me," Seamus chimed in.

"Me too," admitted Amit.

This many teens in one place without a working cell phone might be a world record. And since no one was pointing out how strange it was that none of our phones worked, I wasn't about to be the one to bring it up.

"Yeah, dead," the pilot said, tossing the dead brick of a phone to the ground before adding, "The crash must have jumbled their insides. I think we're in Wyoming."

Ah, Wyoming. No offense, she's a gorgeous state but also one of those states most people know absolutely nothing about. It looks sorta like Thor's hammer and it gets really cold in the winter. That's about all most people can say. Oh yeah? Wyoming's capital, go. Exactly. You don't know. No one does. It's Cheyenne, by the way.

"Now what?" Seamus asked. It was the million-dollar question: Now what? Of course he meant where to go or what to do, but the question was a lot more complex for me. Now what?

Where had that missile come from? Had FATE fired it

because of what I'd done to Floppy? Or was it someone else? Had to be someone else, right? FATE doesn't kill FIPs. So it had to be someone else. Was the missile supposed to hit us, but Ryo somehow survived and because of that he changed the world? That did make some sort of weird sense. He lives and champions something awesome because of it.

But then . . . How badly had I screwed things up by what I'd done? Oh no, had Floppy just been trying to save my life? But really, who fired the missile and who gains anything from shooting down a boy band? There were too many questions and no chance of answers. I didn't know who or why, so there was no point wasting the energy on it. I'd find out when I found out. I needed to focus on the here and now, and the here was somewhere in Wyoming and the now was avoiding the massive storm front heading right at us.

Everyone looked at the pilot, because that's what kids do: we look to adults for help when we're in trouble. We want nothing to do with you every other moment of our life, but when the you-know-what hits the fan, they're our go-to. The pilot understood and looked around, but I could tell he had no clue what to do either. He'd spent about as much time hiking as Amit had. Off to our left I could just make out a small line of smoke going up into the air. It was too small to be a forest fire of some kind or natural fire. No, it was man-made and coming from a cabin, house, or campsite. Either way, it meant people.

I pointed at it and said, "Fire."

Everyone looked and the pilot, taking charge, said, "We'll go that way. Should be people there."

No kidding, I thought again.

BOOM!

We all ducked and screwed up our faces at the sudden explosion. The leaky gas had finally hooked up with a spark and, well, the plane was toast. We were far enough away from it, so we were all okay except for some ringing ears. Normally, I'd have been worried about starting a forest fire, but with the wall of threatening clouds heading this way, I knew Mother Nature would be doing us a solid on this one and putting out the blaze. I also knew that a fire was the least of our concerns. There were about a thousand rounds of bullets hidden in my bags and some explosives, so when the fire got to them, they'd start going off. We needed to get moving before that happened.

THE TENDRIL OF SMOKE was farther away than it looked. For the next few hours we walked in pretty much silence. At one point, I tried to get them to whistle "Heigh Ho" with me, but only Seamus knew it. Meanwhile the storm got closer. The guys were all worried about how their parents were doing, probably knowing by now that the plane carrying their children had disappeared but not knowing that their children had survived. I didn't have that worry. Six months after joining the band, my "family" tragically "died" from carbon monoxide poisoning, leaving me all alone. It was an "awwww" story that not only helped sell records but allowed me to promote carbon monoxide awareness. It also helped explain why I never went home or had anyone visiting me.

The grassy plain gave way to the woods, and the woods eventually gave way, revealing a postcard-quality ranch in the middle of a valley.

Everyone sighed in relief.

Cows grazed and a group of horses ran wild in a green field. A small farmhouse sat next to a large stock pond. A huge red barn and riding arena finished off the property. I bet every one of us at that moment saw this ranch and dreamed of retiring on it. It was beautiful. It was simple. It was perfect.

The storm was right upon us now and would be releasing

the hounds, so to speak, any minute now. The trees had protected us from the wind, but now that we were clear of them, the gusts were strong. Sporadic raindrops were beginning to hit us, and there was constant thunder now, too. This thing was a whopper. Holy hell, that last clap was close. The animals instinctively were heading for cover under trees or going back to the barn.

We reached the fence surrounding the field at the very moment a farm truck came tearing through the grass toward us. The driver swung the truck around and slid sideways to a stop in front of us.

A kindly looking old man in a flannel shirt waved at us and yelled, “Get in! This thing’s about to blow!”

We didn’t need to be invited twice and scrambled over each other to get into the bed of the truck. Sitting on the wheel in the back of an old beater? Felt like home to me. Halfway to the house the skies opened up. Lightning flashed, thunder boomed, and the wind, somehow, got even stronger.

The old man screeched to a halt inside the red barn. It was raining so hard that water was leaking through the roof.

“Out of the truck!” he cried, then ran over to a trapdoor and opened it. “Down here fast!”

One by one, on shaky legs, we followed him down a set of rough wooden stairs that led to a tight, concrete tunnel. Hmm. Could this dude be a cannibal or something and here we were willingly following him into his slaughterhouse? What? It could be true! Maybe cannibals were common in Wyoming, I don’t know. Eventually the old man pushed through a closed door that opened up into a proper-looking basement. Jars of eyeballs, fingers, and brains lined the walls. Just kidding. But the jars of assorted vegetables and fruits sort of did look like body parts.

Another set of stairs led back up again. No sooner had the old man clomped up the first step than the door at the top swung open. A gray-haired woman, also in a flannel shirt, appeared. She was holding a double barrel shotgun. The old man stopped dead in his tracks and we all backed in behind him. I instinctively reached for the knife I kept in my pocket but stopped when the man snickered.

"Jesus, Charlotte, it's just me."

"Just you, Frank?" she said in that tone that only a wife uses with her husband. She peered over him at the rest of us.

"Well," he said shyly, "you know."

"Got tired of picking up stray dogs and moved on to people, I see."

"What was I supposed to do? Leave them outside in this?"

Charlotte's hard face softened and she sighed. "No, of course not. Come on in, boys. You look frozen and half-starved."

Frank led us up and into the house. When he kicked his boots off next to the cellar door, we all followed suit. I couldn't help but smile at the sight of our name brand, wildly expensive shoes all piled up next to Frank's beaten-to-hell brown boots and the double barrel shotgun that Charlotte had left leaning up against the wall behind the door.

The cellar door opened up into a kitchen that had a small dining nook. A pot was boiling on the stove. On cue, Charlotte opened up the deep freezer and pulled out two giant frozen bags of brown glop.

"Hope you like stew," she said.

The others responded with sures and yeahs, while Karim whispered to Ryo, "What's 'stew'?"

"Anything is appreciated, ma'am," I said as my southern manners came back with gusto.

She smiled at me and nodded in appreciation before

turning to Frank, who was pouring himself a cup of coffee from a pot, and clearing her throat.

"Oh, right," Frank remembered, and put the steaming cup down. "So," he started and his eyes found our pilot, "what, uh, brings y'all out here?"

A fair question and I'd wondered what had taken so long. Then again, these people were so polite and accommodating it didn't really surprise me they'd waited until now to press us for information.

"Plane crash," I told them.

Frank gasped and Charlotte said, "You don't say."

They both looked at the pilot, who nodded and said, "Yeah, thing just died on us. No clue what happened."

"And then it blew up after we got out," Karim added a bit too excitedly. "Barely made it."

"Is everyone okay?" Charlotte asked.

"Yeah, we were the only ones on it," Seamus answered.

"Well, thank goodness for that." She sighed.

"Southwest of here?" Frank asked.

I nodded since I knew the others had no clue. Charlotte slapped him on the arm.

"Told you I heard something."

Frank shrugged and muttered, "Sorry."

"So this wasn't one of those big commercial jets, was it?" Charlotte asked.

We shook our heads.

"Small private charter," the pilot answered.

"You boys on a school trip or something?" she asked.

We shook our heads.

"Church mission trip?" Frank asked, trying a guess of his own.

The half of us who knew what he was talking about shook our heads.

"Family reunion?" Really, Charlotte? *Really?*

We looked at each other. Did she see a family resemblance in this group of misfits? Even Seamus snorted, he found it so ridiculous.

"We're International," I offered. Hoping that hearing the name would trigger something. It didn't. They shared a look but were still lost. "We're sort of famous."

"Really?" Charlotte said in disbelief. Now it made sense why they were treating us like they had no clue who we were. They honestly didn't.

"We're a band," Seamus told them.

"Like a rock 'n' roll band?" This had gotten Frank excited.

"Sorta. We're a boy band. We sing and dance."

"So like New Kids on the Block?" Frank wondered.

Tip of the hat to the Godfathers of boy bands. But no, sir. The members of that band are old enough to be our dads. Maybe even our grandpas. I'd like to say we're a bit more evolved. If this were the military, they would be the Continental Army and we would be Navy SEALs. Not that I said any of this. I was laughing too hard. We all were.

"We're *like* them," Ryo finally said. He's so dang polite.

"Our daughter was a huge New Kids fan," Charlotte mused. "Big crush on that Joey boy."

"Well, if you're famous, there's gotta be something on the news about y'all," Frank said, flipping the TV on.

"You have cable?" Karim asked excitedly. He was the TV nut of the group. Eyes usually glued to a screen of some kind.

"Nah, not out here. Over-the-air stuff."

"Oh, like satellite? Cool." Karim was not following.

"No, free TV. We use an antenna," Frank said, equally as confused.

Karim mouthed *antenna* to me. I laughed.

Frank flipped through a couple of static-filled channels

until he found the local news. A somber-looking weatherman was talking about the storm.

On and on he rambled about the wind and the rain and hail. Then I saw it. We all did. A news ticker was sliding its way across the bottom of the screen. *Plane carrying band "International" missing over Wyoming. All passengers presumed dead.*

We all got a decent laugh about that, but it quickly turned serious.

"My parents," Seamus blurted out. "I have to talk to them."

The others echoed their own worries about reaching out to their folks.

"And I have to talk to the NTSB," the pilot said grimly. He looked at Frank. "Do you have a phone we can use?"

"Not a landline. But here," Frank said, taking one out of his jeans and tossing it. "I guarantee it won't be working though. Never does in storms like this."

The pilot confirmed it was dead. "No signal. Is there a town or a working phone nearby? We need to get the word out that these kids are okay."

Frank shrugged. "Down the road a ways, but no way we'll be able to get there in this. It's a rough ride in the best of weather. We'll have to wait until morning."

"Five minutes until stew's ready," Charlotte announced. "Frank, go grab some of Caleb's old clothes. These boys must be freezing."

When Frank disappeared, Charlotte offered us warm coffee.

"Glass of water would be a godsend," Seamus said for us all. Parched didn't really begin to explain how thirsty we all were.

Charlotte pointed to the cabinet and said, "Cups up there. Help yourself. It's well water, so might taste a bit off to you, but I promise it's safe. Fire's going in the living room, right through there," she said, pointing at the only other way out of the kitchen except for the basement and what looked like a back door.

We chugged a few glasses of water each—it actually tasted delicious—before going into the living room. Like everything else about this house, the living room was small but perfect. Two rocking chairs sat in front of a roaring fire and there was a large brown leather couch behind them. I think the fire reminded us all we were soaking wet and freezing, so we all rushed to crowd around it. The warmth felt awesome.

A few minutes later, Frank appeared with some boxes of clothes.

"Some of our son's old stuff. You're welcome to it," he offered. He tossed me a sweat suit and added, "Probably the only thing we have that'll come close to fitting you, hoss."

While the others dug through the old clothes I stripped down and put on the sweats. The pants fit more like capris and the top barely reached my forearms. Still, the warm clothes felt amazing. The others found clothes that fit them well enough. Seamus was a bit snug in his T-shirt and jeans, but Karim, Ryo, and Amit, all pretty skinny, were swimming in their flannel shirts and jeans.

"I feel like a cowboy," Ryo said, looking down. "This is what you wore every day, right, Bobby?" he asked me jokingly.

Amit quickly added, "So this is what being Bobby Sky feels like." Then doing his best impression of me, " Hi, I'm Bobby. I'm a tough cowboy. Don't mess with Texan."

Everyone laughed.

"I don't sound like that!" I laughed. "And it's 'Don't mess with Texas.'"

"Frank, you left the barn doors open!" Charlotte called from the kitchen.

"I left them open for the animals," he called back.

"Don't lie. You just forgot."

Frank had barely sat down in his rocking chair and grumbled at being called out.

"I'll do it," I offered.

"Appreciate the offer, son, but have you met my wife?" he joked. "Back in a few," he added as he got up and walked out.

The others went back to warming up by the fire. I went to the kitchen.

"Thanks for having us, ma'am," I told Charlotte. "Can I help you with anything?"

"No, I'm fine. Thank you, though." Then she paused. "Actually, can you get all your wet clothes for me?"

"Sure, why?"

"So I can toss them in the wash."

"Oh, I can do that. Where's the wash?" I asked, even though I fully remembered it being down in the basement.

"Cellar. Thanks."

"And really, thank you."

It felt strangely nice to do an honest-to-goodness chore again, even if it was only a load of laundry. I was still down in the basement tossing in the detergent when Frank came down the tunnel. He was soaked to the bone.

"Wanna toss in your clothes?" I asked him.

"Nah," he said, waving me off. "Appreciate it, though."

"Get everything closed up?"

"Yep, all good."

He took a deep pull of air and smiled. "Mmmm. Stew's ready."

We couldn't all fit in their small dining nook, so we took our stew into the living room. We were all starving and still a bit cold, so you could chalk it up to that, but I'm not going to lie. This was one of the best meals I'd ever had.

chapter 20

SOLICITORS NOT WELCOME

Car tires splashing through puddles in wet, muddy gravel.

I was dreaming, right? Or was I in that gray area in between? The wind had died down and the rain was only a patter now, but the lightning was still flashing, and the thunder was still booming. It was so relaxing . . . so nice . . . (yawn) . . . Sleep, here I am. Let's get back to this.

Car doors quietly clicking open.

Okay, *that* I heard. For real. What time was it? I checked my phone, because that's what you do, and the stupid thing was still broken. Why was I still even carrying it around? It was unfixable after the EMP and I knew this. The tick-tock of the clock on the wall to my right called to me. 1:15 A.M. Yikes, that was really early. Or really late, depending on your night, I guess.

I'd volunteered to take the couch in the living room. They thought I'd done it out of politeness since there were only four guest beds, but really it was so I had quick access to both entry points of the house. I tiptoed to the window by the front door and looked out. It was pitch black out there. I waited. A crack of lightning hit. For half a second the burst of light showed me a parked SUV a hundred feet away and four figures in black creeping toward the house. Armed. Silhouettes with machine guns. Another burst of light from above.

The men were silently spreading out in a line across the front of the house.

Questions? Oh, you bet I had them, but this was not the time. There would be time for questions later.

Ryo.

I sprinted to the room he was sharing with Amit and had barely shoved open the door when the first explosion of gunfire came ripping through the walls. One snagged me in the shoulder and knocked me down. I knew right away it wasn't too bad—just some tissue damage, a lot of blood, but no broken bones. Not that it hurt, of course. The fire shots I'd endured at FATE had numbed my pain receptors for life long ago, but I was annoyed that the shot had knocked me down. Probably saved my life, though. Another round of fire sliced through the air above my head. Ryo was lucky. The heavy wooden headboard was a shield. Bullets were tearing through the wall like it was made of paper, but the bed was like an armored vehicle and took the fire like a champ. Nothing was getting through it.

Amit popped up in his bed—mouth open, eyes wide. The next second, bullets tore his chest open. He fell to the floor next to me—dead. I'm not gonna lie. My first thought was *better him than Ryo,* who was staring in horror at me, frozen, and still under the covers. There was yelling and screaming from the room across the hall where Seamus and Karim had bunked. And I could also hear Frank and Charlotte yelling and moving around in their room upstairs.

More gunfire.

"Stay down!" I yelled.

I could tell that the attackers were moving counterclockwise around the house. The movement was methodical and timed. I knew this pattern. Heck, I'd practiced the same tactic myself. You do a clean, sweeping circle around the house, killing, injuring, or flat out scaring anything inside. Once you've finished the loop, you go in and mop up. The bad news was this meant the guys were well trained. The glimmer of good news was their decision to go counterclockwise meant they were moving away from us.

Time would run out fast, though. Ryo was safe here, at least for the moment, so my only option was to stop the shooters before their sweep brought them back around to this room again.

"I'm gonna go check on the others and get help, okay?" I yelled at him. "Stay here and stay down! Don't move! Swear it."

He nodded. I'd have preferred an actual "I swear," out loud. But it was time to move.

Staying low, I ran to the cellar door and grabbed Charlotte's double barrel shotgun. It was loaded but with only one shell. I didn't have time to look for more. The gunmen were in the backyard now, halfway done. As I passed back through the kitchen, I grabbed a knife from the cutting boards.

Forcing myself not to dash straight back to Ryo, I sprinted out the bullet-riddled front door instead, which was barely hanging on by a lone hinge. Rain pelted me. My bare feet sloshed in the mud, but gunfire drowned out any sound, and I knew that the storm and the darkness gave me natural cover. I reached Ryo's side of the house at the same time the first of the attackers was rounding the corner from the back. I hurled the knife at him and it struck him right in the throat. He fell to his knees. I yanked the knife free as he collapsed to the ground and plunged it into the heart of the next shooter in line. Bad move. The knife got stuck in bone. The dead man fell backward, taking my knife with him. I had no choice but to unload the shotgun on shooter number three. The blast caught him square in the chest, picked him up, and hurled him backward into the final attacker. They crashed to the ground in a heap. Perfect. Before he could scramble free, I flipped the gun in my hand and swung it like a bat at his head. The butt connected with his skull with a sharp crack. His body slumped back into the mud. He was out cold, but he'd live. When he woke up, I'd finally get some answers. Tossing the shotgun aside, I grabbed his assault rifle and stood over the bodies.

Adrenaline like I'd never felt before coursed through me. That . . . was . . . awesome! I'd performed in front of two hundred thousand fans in Shanghai. We'd given a private concert to the Pope. I got to drive an actual F1 supercar 240 miles per hour for our "Rush of Love" video. None of it—nothing compared to this. I wanted more.

My ears perked up at a faint rumble. Engines. I turned toward the road. The headlights of two cars were bouncing down unevenly toward me, their beams dancing in the rain. Oh, world, sometimes you're just the best. I raised my new and improved weapon. It was an SR-3 Vikhr. I almost felt giddy. I loved these things. Compact, extremely deadly, and very fast. I pulled the trigger and sent a stream of my bullets into the beams. The cars went swerving off the road. When the clip clicked empty, I dropped the gun and picked up another dead guy's. Rinse and repeat.

The headlights winked off.

I stopped firing and squinted. A bullet whizzed so close to my head that I felt the heat of it. It was followed by a hailstorm of others. I dove to the ground and started to bear crawl–sprint back to the house. I took the risk and grabbed a SIG SAUER pistol off the body of the first attacker. It wasn't much, but it would give me a better chance than not having anything. Judging from the gunfire I knew there were at least five unique shooters out there. The SIG clip held ten rounds, so I had two for each of them. Come meet me inside, fellas.

I ran straight to Ryo's room and pushed the door open. He'd broken his promise and was on the floor. I instantly understood. He was sitting next to Amit and I could tell from the blood on his hands and clothes he'd tried to do CPR on the kid. Ryo looked up at me, and when our eyes met, his eyes filled with tears. I wanted to hug him. That, and punch him in the face for breaking his promise. Trying to save Amit was a very Ryo thing to do, but a better use of Amit's body would have been as a shield. I kept that to myself.

"Come on!" I grabbed him and forced him to his feet.

"We can't leave him!" Ryo cried.

"He's dead, Ryo."

The shooting outside had stopped and it was eerily quiet.

My voice fell to a whisper. "We gotta go."

I dragged him all the way out into the hallway before he got his footing.

The shooters outside would be careful, but they'd come inside soon and Ryo needed to be anywhere but out in the open when they did. My bandmates didn't matter, I knew this, but I also knew Ryo couldn't leave them behind, so I had to play the *yeah, I'm worried, too* part. I peered into the next bedroom. It looked like Swiss cheese. Seamus's arm was hanging over the edge of the bed, blood streaming down his fingers into a pool on the floor, but Karim was still alive somehow. He'd been hit in the chest.

"Can you move?" I asked him.

"Yes," he wheezed.

He tried to get up but started to fall. I didn't have time for this but knew there was no way Ryo could leave him, so I caught him, threw his arm over my shoulders, and wrapped my arm around his back.

"I got you. Come on," I grunted.

The tunnel to the barn was our best and only chance. Halfway to the kitchen, I heard a creak on the wooden floorboards outside the back door. Whoever was out there had a straight view of the cellar door through the kitchen window. The stairs to Frank and Charlotte's room were to our right and were our only option now. I didn't like it, but it would have to work.

I looked at Ryo and held my finger up to my mouth. He nodded. I then motioned silently with my head for him to go upstairs. One creak, one slip and we'd have been toast, but the stairs miraculously didn't betray us. In the master bedroom, Frank and Charlotte lay dead. Charlotte was still in bed; Frank was slumped over by a window. Ryo nearly let out a scream, but I slapped my free hand across his mouth before any sound got out.

The layout of the upstairs was simple: the master bedroom and a bathroom. Nothing fancy.

"Closet," I whispered to Ryo and silently reminded him to step quietly.

Karim was struggling to hold his weight, so there was no chance he'd be able to walk softly. I adjusted my grip, heaved him off the ground, and carried him over.

The clomping of boots on the hardwood stairs started.

There wasn't room for all of us in the tiny closet. I shoved Karim on one side and pushed Ryo toward the other. I then halfway closed the accordion-style doors, leaving the middle of the closet totally exposed. It was a simple trick but one that had to work. I quickly slid onto my belly and ducked under the bed right as someone entered the room. All I could see were their tactical, Special Ops–style boots. I'd had a pair just like them once.

The boots came toward the bed and paused. I got my

pistol ready. Whoever it was spun around, checked out the bathroom, and then paused in front of the closet. My heart was pounding so hard I was shocked they couldn't hear it.

"All clear," a man with a French accent called out. "Just an old man and woman. No sign of Hutch or the others."

My stomach dropped. Whoa, whoa, whoa. *Hutch?* Had I heard that right? Hutch didn't exist anymore. The only ones who know Hutch is Bobby are . . . FATE? What in the hell was going on here?

"Well, there are three missing, so come on down," an oddly familiar female voice crackled over a radio. "We need to find them."

How do I know that voice? Who is she?

"Roger that." The boots began to walk away. "Have you already started?"

"Told you to hurry," the female voice said.

"Dammit, S."

Karim let out a deep, gurgling wheeze. I cringed. Luckily, the man was too busy thundering down the stairs to hear it. *Started what?* It didn't take long to figure it out. Smoke. It was pitch black in here, but that didn't mean my nose didn't work. They'd set the house on fire. Destroy all the evidence and smoke out anyone hiding—all in one go. Exactly what I would have done. Tip of the hat, gents. We were screwed nice and good now. No attackers would be inside anymore, though, so at least we had that going for us.

I slid out from under the bed and opened the closet doors as I whispered, "It's me."

Ryo untucked himself and got up. Karim was fading fast.

The smoke was starting to get thick. We had a few minutes, tops. I had Ryo sit down with Karim on the bed while I snuck glances out each of the windows. Yeah, we were screwed. There was an attacker stationed on each side of the house, ready to take out anyone who tried to escape. Correction: tip of the hat *and* a nod to you, fellas. They were giving us no chance.

Someone would have to be the distraction, pay the ultimate sacrifice, and die, leading the men away from the others, so the others, more specifically, Ryo, would at least have a shot. This was it. This was my purpose. Time to pay the fiddler. It's been a helluva ride, folks.

I was about to tell them the plan when Karim spoke up in a choked voice: "I'll distract them while you two escape."

I shook my head. So did Ryo.

"I mean it. My final breath will come soon enough. Please allow me the honor of using that last breath to save the lives of my brothers."

Ryo swept him into a hug. I did the same.

I pulled the gun out from my sweats and offered it to him as I lied, "Here, take it. I found it under the bed a second ago." Neither of them had any clue what I'd done outside to the first wave of attackers, and it was better they didn't.

"I don't know how to use those," Karim said, waving it away. "The Texas cowboy should know how to use that, right? All you Americans have guns, no?" he joked, cracking a pained smile. "I don't have long, so . . ." He nodded and stood straight.

After another deep, labored breath, Karim climbed out the window, shambled across the roof, and dropped to the ground. He was spotted instantly by the attacker watching that side of the house.

"Runner!" he shouted. He raised his gun, but before he could fire, I took aim with my pistol and dropped him. Karim took off running into the field. I waited until I saw that he was being chased before saying to Ryo, "Let's go." We headed out the window on the opposite side of the room.

The heat of the roof was hot enough to burn our bare

feet. We jumped off quickly, thankful for the cool, soft, and muddy ground.

We reached the barn and practically crashed through the side door to get in. The lights inside were a welcome contrast to the night outside. I smiled at the sight of Frank's truck. The smile disappeared quickly, though. From the corner of my eye, up in the rafters, a black figure popped out from behind a line of hay bales and opened fire. I bear-hugged Ryo and launched the two of us behind the side of a horse stall for cover. A line of bullets pinged across the metal barrier. After a quick glance to make sure Ryo was okay, I took out my pistol and popped up, ready to fire. The figure was gone.

"Go for the door. You can make it," the strangely familiar female voice called out from somewhere on the level above us.

"You think?" I joked as I played along, ducking back behind the safety of the metal stall. I knew this voice for sure.

The voice had a point. The door wasn't too far away. If I used myself as a shield, I could get Ryo through it, but then what? I'd be dead and Ryo had already proven he was a bit of a freezes-in-the-moment type. How far would he get? And then there was the chance of a bullet going through me and into him. No, Frank's truck was it. But how to reach it? No doubt whoever was up there had called her friends in from wherever they'd killed Karim. We had thirty seconds, tops, before they reached us.

"What about the window? Think I can make that?" I asked, looking around for anything that could help us. Ryo raised his eyebrows, confused by what was going on. I raised my hand for him to relax.

"Oh, for sure. Bet ya a loonie you can," she said. My heart jumped. I knew someone who used to bet me a loonie all the time . . .

"Sam?" I gasped.

"Good to see you again, Hutch," she said.

I wish I could see *her.* She'd set us up perfectly. So much for whatever history we'd had or I'd imagined we'd had. She had a job to do now and would do it. Still didn't stop me from wanting to see her.

Again, Ryo tried to question what was going on, and again I had to shush him. I knew I'd have to explain all of this to him at some point, but now was not the time.

"You miss me?" I asked.

"You miss *me*?" she shot right back at me.

"Up until about ten seconds ago, yeah."

She laughed. I missed that laugh. I wanted to see the smile that went with it.

"So, uh, hear from any of the others?" I joked. I needed to buy time.

"Nope. I've missed the alumni cocktail parties," she answered dryly. "But I did hear there's some girl in Texas who is best friends with her FIP. Just like you."

"Idiot. At least my bromance was preapproved."

"Yeah, I don't think it was meant to be a trend. They may send me to Texas next."

Of course, I thought. "So you're a Hunter now, huh?"

"Sort of. In training, I guess. Right now I just go where they tell me," she admitted lightly. "Better try *something* soon, Hutch. My friends will be back any second now."

"Oh, you know me. I do my best work at the last possible second."

I was beginning to panic. I had nothing except my go-to: bull in a china shop, which wouldn't end well against someone who was better armed and in a better position. But when you're a bull, it's sorta expected that you destroy the china shop when you're trapped in it.

"I'll cover you. Get outside and run, okay?" I whispered to Ryo.

Before he could nod, though, Sam called out playfully, "Good thing these lights are on, or I wouldn't be able to see a thing in here." Then for good measure a bullet clanged into the metal wall across the barn from us, right next to the main electrical breaker box.

"I knew you still loved me!" I sang out playfully. Why hadn't I thought of the lights?! Obviously, hearing Sam had thrown me off my game. Maybe that was the point of them sending her here. They liked to do stuff like that.

"I don't know what you're talking about," she responded coyly before adding, "I'll still be trying to shoot you, though." I knew she was serious, but from her tone I could tell she was smiling.

"As you should. Thanks."

"See you around, *Bobby Sky*." She laughed.

I took aim and plugged a shot into the breaker box. Sparks flew out and it zapped wildly as the lights flickered out. I grabbed Ryo by the collar and dragged him at a full sprint to Frank's truck. Fast as I could, I opened the driver's side door, shoved him inside the cab, and slid in next to him. Bullets clanged against the roof, but only one got through. Luckily, it puffed into the seat between us.

Like most people who live on a farm and own old, beater farm trucks, Frank had left the keys in the ignition. Thank you for taking us in, Farmer Frank. I am so sorry it cost you your life. I mean it. Somehow I'll find a way to watch over your kids for you and help them out. I promise.

The moment the engine turned, I slammed it into gear and stomped on the gas. The old truck's tires spun out in the dirt and hay before catching and sending us flying toward the closed barn doors. We blasted through them—and what made it even better wasn't what, but who, was on the other side. Sam's team couldn't have chosen a worse place to be.

Two became roadkill instantly and the third barely managed to dive out of the way. I still clipped his leg as he dove.

We weren't out of danger, not yet. We flew down the muddy farm road, cleared the pasture, and were about to reach the tree line when I started to believe we'd made it. Maybe a few more seconds and . . . a pair of lights appeared far behind us.

Of course, this was just the end of the second set. I'd performed enough shows to know that there's always an encore.

chapter 21

NO ESCAPING STEREOTYPES

This old girl had power, but speed? Not so much, especially with how muddy it was. Even with four-wheel drive the truck was struggling, which was why I couldn't understand how whatever was cruising up the farm road after us was moving like the mud didn't bother it at all. Then I remembered seeing a four-wheeler in the barn. This had to be it, but the other vehicle that was keeping pace with it? No clue. Had there been a second one? Luckily, or unluckily I guess, they'd be on us soon enough, so I'd know then.

Once the road hit the forest, it began to climb upward with brutal switchbacks and was so sloshy with mud I understood why Frank had told us we'd have to wait for morning. Driving in this slop was impossible and dangerous.

With every near 180-degree turn in the road I'd lose sight of our chasers, but each time the road straightened out for a bit they were a little closer than before. The turns were slowing them, too, but they were still gaining on us. A few minutes and they'd be on us.

We weren't going to outrun them and going off-roading in an unknown forest at night wasn't something you did. We really only had one option: plant our flag and dig in. They probably wouldn't be expecting it, and maybe that way we could catch a break.

"I'm gonna stop the car and we're getting out, okay?" I told Ryo.

"What? Why?"

"They're gaining on us. We have to get out. Ready?" I asked as we approached a tight switchback. He nodded.

The second we cleared the next turn I jammed the parking brake on and spun the wheel. The truck slid to a stop sideways in the middle of the road. There were maybe a few feet of clearance on either side. It was the perfect roadblock.

"Now!" I yelled as I jumped out on the muddy road and reached back for Ryo to slide toward me, but he was already hopping out his door. "That way works, too," I yelled, frustrated at the miscommunication.

I ran to the rear, but he ran to the front.

"This way!" I yelled out angrily.

He circled around the car toward me and we ducked down on the side of the road behind an old log. Within seconds, the whining sound of (yep, I knew it!) a four-wheeler engine, and whatever other vehicle was with it, came screaming up the road toward us. The headlights lit up the woods on the turn as they got closer and closer, but thanks to the thick woods and switchback, the truck wouldn't be seen by whoever was coming until the last second. It's like I planned it or something . . .

A man on a four-wheeler slid around the turn, saw the truck, and tried to brake and swerve. The moment he appeared, I opened fire and caught him in the chest and neck. He lost control and smashed into the side of the truck. A Polaris, a super-awesome off-road golf cart, was right behind him and couldn't react much better. I popped off a shot that caught the middle of the windshield. The driver swerved hard. They came right at us, clipped the log we were hiding behind, and flipped off the side of the road into the woods down below us. As it flew over us, I was pretty sure I saw a long ponytail, a girl's ponytail.

I ran over to the side of the truck where the four-wheeler had crashed, grabbed the nearly dead man, and finished the job. Clear of danger up here, I called out to Ryo, "Get in the truck."

He did so as quickly as he could. Once Ryo was safely in the truck, I grabbed the machine gun from the dead guy and headed toward the Polaris. I did a controlled slide down the slick pines of the forest floor toward the flipped Polaris. It was upside down and the wheels were still spinning. I carefully circled around to the driver's side.

Halfway out from under the wreckage, but hurt, stuck, and struggling, was Sam. She sensed more than heard me and looked up. Emotions that I'd buried and convinced myself I'd forgotten about washed over me. Leggo had only been a crush—a fun one—but just a crush. It wasn't real—not like this, not like my Sam. These emotions had history; they were living scars. I wanted to drop down to her side and hug her, but I knew better and pointed the gun at her instead. She gave me a weak smile and stopped struggling.

"Make it quick and clean, please," she said as she closed her eyes and rested her head in the pine needles.

"Not sure what you mean," I said as I dropped the gun. "Lucky you fell so far down the hill, or I would have been able to find you."

"I knew you still loved me, Hutch," she said playfully like I did before.

For a couple seconds I forgot who and where I was and dreamed of dropping everything and running away with her. But FATE would never let it happen. So I echoed her earlier words with the best smile I could muster: "I don't know what you're talking about."

I grabbed the side of the Polaris and lifted it up just far enough for Sam to pull herself free. Her leg was mangled and it looked broken.

"You gonna be all right?" I asked.

"'Tis but a scratch," she said, quoting something I thought sounded familiar but couldn't place.

"Want me to make you a splint?" I offered.

"How very Prince Charming of you. No, you need to get out of here. You need to disappear."

I understood and nodded.

"I missed you, Sam."

She smiled. "I missed you, too."

I didn't want to go. I wanted to stay with her, help her, just be with her, but I knew I couldn't. I could care about her and she about me, but we were on different sides of the coin now. The Capulets and Montagues. Hey, that's actually a pretty good comparison. (Take that, eighth-grade English teacher who said I never paid attention.)

There was so much more I wanted to say to Sam, but I didn't. What was the point? So without so much as a goodbye, I slid down the rest of the hill to the road below and started my hike back to Ryo. When I finally reached the truck, I climbed in muddy, exhausted, and depressed.

"Is she dead?" Ryo asked me.

"She won't be an issue anymore," I said as I turned the wheel of Frank's truck and headed toward town. I beeped the horn twice as we left. I could argue that it was a standard gesture, some professional courtesy to Sam so she would know we were leaving. I *could* argue that, but it would only be a half-truth. I'd also done it to serve as one last goodbye. The horn had said what I couldn't.

My adrenaline was pumping like crazy and I was driving a bit more recklessly than I probably should have, but I didn't care. That had been intense. That had been crazy. That had been one helluva emotional roller coaster. A shootout, a lost love, and a last-second escape—my mind didn't know what to focus on, so bits and pieces raced around in my head. And I probably would have kept going that way if Ryo hadn't been there. He was staring at me as we drove. It was awkward. Oh, the irony wasn't lost on me. I'd done so much weirdo staring at him that this was quite the reversal of roles.

After five minutes of hard, silent staring Ryo calmly said, "I believe you owe me an explanation."

It was so formal, so perfectly Ryo, and so not how a normal person would have reacted that I couldn't help but smile. He was such a robot sometimes and I loved that about him. Cracked me up.

"This is not funny. What was that and who are you?"

"You're right. I'm sorry," I coughed out as I stopped laughing.

Never reveal who you really are is one of our basic rules. Remember that creative writing class I had to take that we all laughed about because it made no sense? Who's laughing now? Here goes the big lie I came up with when I first joined the band.

"I'm CIA."

"Since when?" he asked. The flat, stone-faced look he gave me told me all I needed to know. I'd hooked him, and I only needed to give him a reason to believe me. Oh, buddy, I had it . . . I think.

"I was recruited after I got into the band. They came to me and asked if I'd be interested in being an agent as well on the side. Like any teenager I said yes. 'Hell yeah!' I think was my actual answer. So while the label was grooming me to be a celebrity, the CIA was grooming me to be a spy. Bobby Sky, pop star, super-spy, they called me. I rehearsed and hit the studio during the days with y'all, and at night I trained with them. Didn't you ever wonder why I went straight to my room each night after we were done, instead of hanging out? I was sneaking out for training."

There was a tree lying across the road in front of us. I had to swerve hard to miss it.

"Why would they recruit you?" he asked. I could tell by his shaky voice that he was starting to believe it. I was reeling him in.

"'Cause celebrities like us are allowed to do whatever we want and go wherever we want. Even the most reclusive of people and world leaders want to meet us and stupidly let us into their most secret, secure places. How many times have we been allowed to go in somewhere that no normal person could ever get into?"

"Many times."

"Exactly, and the best part is, it's all done with open arms. People want us there. They bend over backward to have us there and show us their cool stuff. We touched a nuclear bomb in Moscow, for God's sake, remember? A long time ago the CIA figured, why not take advantage of stuff like this? Get people who could use their celebrity status to gain entrance to the most secure places, and actually come away with useful intel? Every time we went somewhere awesome, I planted a bug or something."

He nodded. This was it. I almost had him.

"And I'm not the first. Jagger? MI6. Steven Tyler? CIA, and a heck of a shot with a sniper rifle. The Hoff? CIA and BND joint agent."

"BND?"

"German CIA. Great folks, but that's not the point. Point is, you asked, and that's why I can do all the stuff you saw."

"You're an agent with the CIA," he said, trying the words out in his mouth.

I nodded as I said, "Yeah, crazy as it sounds, but yeah."

"So all that has happened is your fault?" he suddenly asked, as if accusing me, and to be honest I hadn't been ready for this. "Our brothers have died and we are running because of some . . . some line you crossed or some mission you failed?!" he added angrily.

"No, no way," I said defensively. "You heard the same stuff I did. They were after *all* of us. I mean, yeah, I knew one of them, but it's a small world for people like me and that was just coincidence. I have no idea why they were after us."

Had he bought it? That last part had been true. They had been after all of us, not just me. God, I hoped he believed me. I needed him to believe me.

"Yes, you are correct. They were after all of us," he admitted after thinking about it. "I do recall hearing that. But it still could be your fault. You don't know for certain."

I could use this. No, I didn't want him to blame me, but I could twist the idea into something useful.

"Yeah, I guess it could be. You're right, I don't really know. I can find out, but there's no way you should have to be in danger for something *I* may have done. We need to get you somewhere safe so I can go figure out what's going on."

"So when we reach town, we must find a phone and alert the authorities. I will be safe in their custody," he offered.

Oh, dear sweet Ryo. Like everyone in the world when the s hits the fan, they think calling the magic authorities will help it go away, and for the most part they're right. But "normal" and who we were dealing with aren't even the same sport. It'd be like if you were swimming in the ocean and you yelled at a sea horse to go get help when a great white started circling you. What are they gonna do about it? Make their weird sucky face and float away in a current, that's what.

"No, these kinds of people *own* the authorities, Ryo. We call the police and we may as well save everyone some time and call the bad guys directly."

"So what, then?"

"I don't know," I admitted. The last resort for any Shadow was "call FATE," so I had no idea what to do now that I couldn't. "The problem is we're sorta recognizable," I went on, "so we can't just go anywhere and expect to stay hidden for very long."

All I could think of was grabbing some gear and disappearing into the Canadian frontier, but looking at Ryo I knew he'd never even seen a tent, let alone slept in one. The guy tried to shower at the same time every day of his life; woods wouldn't agree with him.

"We need a safe house," he said. "Ideally a secret location, unknown to the law. Maybe with some level of protection, too? Like guards?" He sounded like a waiter reading me my options of sides.

"Can I opt for armed guards with a side of attack dogs?" I couldn't help the joke but quickly added, "Yeah, we need a place to lie low. You got one of those in your back pocket?"

"I may have an idea, but it is painful to admit it to you because of our history."

Okay, that got my attention. What the heck did that mean? *Our* history?

"Your offensive jokes aside, I may . . ." He took a long pause before quickly and quietly adding, "I may have a connection to the Yakuza." Even in the dark cab I could see a sneaky smile spread across his face.

"What?!" I practically laughed out.

"Akiko may have had some past dealings with them," he added, avoiding my eyes.

"You mean after all the crap she gave me about it, I was right?"

"It is still an offensive stereotype."

"But I was right! When it's true, it's not offensive."

He turned to me. "Yes, it is. You are quite stupid sometimes. That does not mean I should assume that all Caucasian boys from the United States are stupid."

"You should, though. You watch the news. We are all very stupid."

He simply looked at me.

"Okay, fine, good point. So how do we reach her?"

"A phone?" Ryo said sarcastically.

If I hadn't been linked to him, I might have smacked him. "I meant, do you remember her number? 'Cause I don't know any number in my phone." That part was a lie. I had every single one memorized forward and backward. Problem was, they were all for FATE, so it was sorta like I didn't know any. I had been right to ask Ryo, though, because he looked deer-in-the-headlights lost. Nobody actually knows numbers anymore. They are just a name in your phone you tap when you want to talk to them. Or not even a name, just a picture. Picture!

"She on Instagram?" I asked him.

Ryo nodded, but he still hadn't put the dots together.

"So we can find her on that, right?"

He nodded, but this time he was smiling. "Yes, yes, we can. She checks it all the time."

"Then we have a plan."

ABOUT TWENTY MINUTES LATER, we reached the small town and it couldn't have come soon enough. No, we weren't being chased again—that would have been better. The shock of it all had worn off about fifteen minutes prior and since then Ryo had been crying about our bandmates. And no, not like quiet *I-still-want-to-look-brave-but-I-can't-help-the-tears-from-silently-streaming-down-my-emotionless-face* crying, but blubbering, snotty, choking-yourself crying. It was really, really awkward sitting next to that, so reaching town was a godsend. Don't get me wrong, I felt bad for what happened to the boys. I'd miss them, and I'd mourn them in my own way at some point, but in my mind the best way to honor them was through vengeance. That's what I did best, so that's what I was focused on.

"We're here," I said loudly, hoping it would snap Ryo out of his groaning sobs.

It was barely three-thirty in the morning, so the roads were dead and empty. Good. Yeah, we were in a small town, but if anyone saw us, recognized us, and snapped a picture to post online, we'd be toast. I cruised down the main drag toward the local gas station and parked a few hundred feet away. The lights for the pumps were on, but the convenience store was dark and closed.

"Wait here," I told Ryo as I got out of the truck. He nodded as he sniffled.

Like most good ranchers, Frank kept spare hats, gloves, bandannas, and rags in the back seat of the truck. I put on an old, beat-up straw hat, wrapped a blue bandanna over my nose and mouth like an Old West bandit, and slid on a pair of gloves. In my soaking wet, muddy sweat suit I looked ridiculous. Good. The less chance anyone had of recognizing me, the better. The last things I grabbed were a hammer and flashlight from Frank's toolbox.

I ran toward the convenience store and when I was close enough, I flung the hammer at the glass front door. It hit the door but bounced off like it was nothing. Well, that's embarrassing.

"Oh, come on . . ."

I picked up the hammer and tapped it on the door. The stupid thing was made of bulletproof Plexiglas. Great. So instead of walking through the door like a respectable criminal, I had to break the small glass window in the bathroom and shimmy my way in all gracious like. The smell was enough to make me gag, so I was really happy it was dark in here and I couldn't see whatever wetness my gloved hands were touching.

I crept out of the bathroom and into the main part of the store. When I flipped on the flashlight, I smiled. Even in a small town like this they had burner phones behind the counter. I grabbed two, undid the lock on the front door, and was about to run back to the truck when I paused. Clothes. My sweats were soaked, muddy, and had blood on them. Ryo's pajamas were about the same. I ripped open a box of trash bags and filled one with some shirts, jeans, socks, and boots. Loot in hand, I quickly ran back to the truck.

"Here," I said, tossing the phones to Ryo.

I tossed the bag of clothes in the back seat, along with my disguise, and started driving. We'd stop to change later. Having a chore helped stop Ryo's tears, and by the time he had ripped one of the phones out of the package and turned it on, he had stopped crying.

"Looking for a signal," he finally told me, right as I was about to ask what the holdup was. "Got it," he finally said.

His fingers flew across the keyboard as he logged in.

"Done," he said. "Now we just have to wa . . ."

Ding.

"Told you she always checked," he said smugly.

"Get her number."

Ding.

The response was almost instant.

"I have it," Ryo said.

"Good. Show it to me."

He showed me the number and I memorized it.

"Now call it."

He dialed.

"Akiko, yes, I am alive. It has been a very . . ."

"Here," I said, practically taking the phone from him. We didn't have time for chitchat. "Akiko, it's Bobby. Can you use your little hacker skills on this phone and make it unreadable, untraceable, un-everything?"

"My little hacker skills? Do you aim to insult me at every opportunity, or is it chance?"

"Can you do it? Yes or no?"

"I already have."

"Holy crap, that was fast. Color me impressed."

"That means so much to me." The sarcasm oozed through the phone.

"Look, I'm sure you've seen the news. We'll explain it all later, but right now we need your help. Ryo says you can help us hide. Can you?"

"I'll find something."

"Good, we'll be waiting. Hurry."

I tossed the phone to Ryo as I said, "She's going to find us something."

Recognizable or not, our best bet to stay out of FATE's gaze was to be in a massive city where we could cover our faces and get lost in the crowd. The closest was Denver, so that's where we were headed. We stopped at a rest station and changed into the clothes I'd stolen. In matching flannel shirts, dark blue jeans, and boots we felt a bit silly, but neither of us cared. Being dry and warm trumped everything.

The phone rang.

"I have a plane for you," Akiko said. "Park in Lot F at the Denver airport. Someone will find you."

"How do you know we're heading to Denver?" I asked. Not even Ryo knew that.

"Even though others cannot trace your phone, it does not mean I cannot. Get to the airport."

"Got it."

"And, Bobby," she began, "if he is injured when we meet, I'll . . ."

"Yeah, yeah, you'll kill me. I got it," I said, interrupting her.

"I was going to say I'll be quite angry."

"Oh. You can be that, too."

"I'll see you both tomorrow in Tokyo," she said before the line went dead. Tokyo?

Running low on gas and without a penny to our name, I stole a car in the next small town we passed. I left Frank's truck as collateral. Ryo insisted on writing down the address so that he could pay them back. He would too. He's that kind of guy. Off the grid and warm—with a new car and a tank full of gas—I was starting to hope. Ryo dozed off next to me as the mile markers ticked by.

150 miles to Denver.

149 miles to getting closer to some answers.

148 miles to vengeance.

chapter 22

NIHON, NIPPON, YAMATO!

I have to say that I love, *love* Tokyo. It's the most wacked-out, fast-paced, hyper-real, bizarro city ever. It's like the neon lights and sounds of the Vegas Strip took over all of Manhattan and then someone packed the streets full of really, really nice, polite people. Like so nice it's disturbing. Like, I bumped into *you*; why are you apologizing to *me*?! It's bursting with people and energy and excitement, and then there are the random temples, which are so cool but so out of place in the middle of the city that they feel fake. Tokyo is a place with what feels like endless possibilities, where you seriously never know what is around the corner.

I was going to see none of it.

The private plane Akiko had arranged to steal us away from Denver landed in the Tokyo airport at dusk. Ryo had slept most of the fifteen hours (including three pit stops), thank God. I probably should have slept more, too, but I didn't. I wasn't any closer to answering the questions *I* had—as in, why we were on the run in the first place—but I knew Ryo would start pestering me about the CIA the moment he woke up, so I spent the flight adding layers to my fake CIA cover.

After we taxied over to one of the private hangars off the main terminal, the door opened, and the little stairwell folded onto the tarmac. We waited for someone to come get us, or tell us to get off, but no one did. After a few minutes, we shared a look, got up, and got off. I never even saw the pilot; the cockpit was shut the entire time. No customs official stood at the ready, and no passport was required. Instead a black Mercedes with gold trim awaited us. It was a signature of Yakuza rides. Once you were at a certain level within the organization, you had one of these. I had my "learning Japanese" by watching old movies to thank for this bit of useless knowledge. The back door of the car was open and waiting for us. Still looking like twin hipster lumberjacks, we hurried off the plane and climbed inside.

Ryo greeted the driver in Japanese: *"Ohio."*

The man ignored us and began to drive. He ignored all our questions like we weren't there. Or he was deaf, and in that case I apologize for cursing at him for fun to get a reaction from him.

TRAFFIC WAS TERRIBLE. RYO told me it was normal for Tokyo. I decided not to argue. It took us two hours of snail-like inching until the driver finally turned down an alley.

We were in the middle of the city, so I had my doubts about how "super secret" this hideout could be. I held my tongue. Maybe this alley led to a shady, rusting hovel hidden between skyscrapers and protected by snarling dogs and unfriendly types?

But then the driver turned the car and plunged us into the garage of a huge modern skyscraper.

Okay, Yakuza, I don't mean to criticize, but no self-respecting criminal organization would have a hideout in a skyscraper. You're adorable.

The driver threaded his way through the garage, which was crowded with men and women in business clothes headed home for the day. *Too* busy. Too many eyes would recognize Ryo, a national heartthrob and uber-celebrity. in half a second. I knew the windows were tinted, but I now really doubted how "safe" this safe house really was. I'd need to come up with a plan B and quick. The driver eventually parked the car in front of a service elevator. The back door of the Mercedes clicked open automatically and no sooner had Ryo's boot touched the ground than the elevator doors slid open.

Akiko was alone in the elevator, waiting for us.

She wore a pantsuit and had her hair perfectly parted, the final touch being black-rimmed glasses. She looked super professional and totally miserable. Wait, that sounds bad. She looked great, but you could tell she was miserable having to dress like that. Better.

We ducked our heads and ran to her. The doors slid shut behind us. Ryo hugged Akiko and seeing his old friend brought back a lot of the emotion of the last twenty-four hours and he teared up. I stared at the floor. Thanks to the link, seeing him cry affected me in a way I could barely handle. It gutted me.

"Put these on," she said, handing each of us a bag.

Inside each bag was a set of coveralls with a hood. Along with the coveralls was a set of dark safety glasses, one of those respirator masks that goes over your mouth and has two filters on either side, and a small backpack with a metal tank. With the coveralls, hoodies, sunglasses, and masks we looked like two plain old exterminators on a job. I felt a little better. No one was about to recognize us. Even I didn't recognize us.

"You're exterminators here to work and I'm an intern, understand?" she instructed.

We both nodded.

Most iconic evil lairs are in the penthouse, so I assumed we were going there. Makes sense when you think about it. It gives you a bunch of easy escape options: helicopters, BASE jumping, zip-lining, etc. So when we stopped at floor twenty-seven out of seventy-five, I checked another box in the *I-don't-think-they-know-what-they're-doing* column. This wasn't even close to the top. They probably didn't even have a balcony.

On the plus side, neither Akiko nor Ryo was asking me any questions. Gotta recognize the small victories, right?

The elevator opened up to an empty hallway. We followed Akiko to a nondescript office. As in literally, there was no signage. A receptionist was chatting on the phone. When she saw us, she waved us in. Akiko took us past the desk, through a door, and into a sea of cubicles. Half were empty, their owners having left for the night, but the other half still had black-haired heads popping out of the top, their faces staring at glowing computer screens. So this was what real life was like. How depressing. As we followed Akiko past the cubes toward the far end of the office, we got a few glances but nothing to worry about. I could guess what they were thinking from the glances: *Oh, bug guys are here. Gross. Well, better get back to it.* Lots of quick glances, but everyone went back to work.

This was all very strange. Where were the gangsters? Where were the scary-looking, dark-suit-wearing, tattooed-up thugs with samurai swords and Uzis like you see in the movies? This was an office, and from what I could tell, a real one. These were normal people who, unless they're amazing actors and have ninja stars hidden under their desks, would be worthless in a fight. Thanks, Akiko, but the first chance I get to sneak Ryo out of here, I'm gonna take him. I need something remote, dirty, and totally off the grid. This was none of those.

Another receptionist sat guarding a large office ahead of us, and as we got closer she picked up her phone, waited a second for the other end of the line to pick up, and said, "They're here."

A sweaty, middle-aged man in a nice gray suit burst out of his office door, grinning from ear to ear.

"Hello, hello," he called out. "Yes, yes, please come inside. The infestation is right this way," he added a bit louder than would have been normal to make sure others could hear it. "So pleased you could make it on such short notice."

Once we were inside the office, the guy closed the door and his whole cheery demeanor disappeared. The sparkle in his eyes and the smile on his face were replaced by a hard glare and flat, pursed lips. He'd gone from the guy you'd laugh with at the bar to the one you stayed far, far away from. He strode over to a door off to the side of his office and opened it. It was a bathroom.

"Inside," he ordered.

We crowded inside the bathroom. It was big for a bathroom. There was a toilet, a shower, and a changing area. So it wasn't small, but with four people inside, it was a little cramped.

The man pushed through us to the far wall. On an end table sat a tiny little bonsai tree in a bed of small white rocks in a black bowl. The man gripped the trunk of the tree, twisted it, and then pulled it toward him like a lever. Something clicked. The table and wall swung toward us, revealing a vast shadowy space beyond.

Now we were talking.

"In," the man grunted in English.

We followed him into what looked like a dorm room. There was a set of bunk beds, TV, small fridge, and (I could only guess) a bathroom behind the door on the far side. It wasn't luxurious. It didn't meet my own personal standards for what makes a good hideout, but I had to hand it to him, this was pretty legit. Assuming no one knew about this place, no one was going to find it. Okay, it wasn't ideal for long-term comfort, but for a short, get-off-the-grid break? This would do.

The man didn't stay. Instead he turned back and closed the secret bathroom door behind him, leaving us alone. I was instantly struck by the silence. The room was soundproof. Okay, maybe I'd jumped the gun judging these people's hideout skills. After all the driving, flying, and then driving again, it felt pretty damn nice to finally be still and quiet.

"Is this sufficient?" Akiko asked me.

I nodded. "It'll do, but I have no idea how long we'll need to hide, so long-term?" I shook my head.

"This is only temporary. You will be moved to more comfortable housing once I have completed a job for them."

"Job?" Ryo asked.

"Yes," she said, still staring at me. "This"—she motioned around—"did not come easy and it did not come free. I had to offer them my services, without my usual stipulations, in exchange for bringing you all here. I must now perform a job I would normally never accept, so now I'd like to know why I agreed to it."

Together Ryo and I explained what had happened. We started with the plane crash and went all the way through calling her for help. Every time I tried to gloss over something unbelievable that I'd done, like fly the plane, in an attempt to keep her from getting too suspicious about me, Ryo was quick to stop me and go back. I wasn't about to mention I was pretend "CIA" and Ryo never brought it up either, so when we somehow made it through the whole tale without Ryo spilling the beans, I couldn't believe it. I'd hoped for this, but what you hope for and what actually happens is pretty much never the same thing. Was this going to be one of those magical moments where it somehow does, though?

"Oh, and he's CIA," Ryo blurted out matter-of-factly.

Thanks, buddy. Akiko's eyes shot at me.

"CIA?"

That was it. No questions about the death squad who'd come after us, or the chase in the woods, or congrats on getting her best friend out alive. Me in the CIA was what she was focusing on? I filed that away in my brain, not sure at all what it meant. So I just nodded. "Yep."

She frowned. "*Yep*, as in I just helped an agent of the CIA get inside a Yakuza safe house?"

"Oh," I said. I started seeing where she was going with this. I raised my hands. "I am not that kind of agent. I don't care about any of this, so unless one of *you* tells our hosts, they'll never know."

We both looked at Ryo.

"What?" he asked. "I can keep a secret."

"You couldn't keep me being in the CIA from her!" I reminded him.

"I did not know it was a secret to keep and I do not keep secrets from Akiko. But I am sorry."

How could I stay mad at that? I sighed and focused back on Akiko. "We, I, owe you. Do you need help with this 'job'?"

She looked at me. Studied me. But when she didn't say anything, I gave her some more to think about.

"I'm not that great with computers, but I'm a good blunt club if you need it."

"You are an analog tool in a digital world," she said flatly. She pulled out her laptop. "I can do more damage with this in ten minutes than you could in a hundred lifetimes."

"Can you stop a man who's about to shoot a child?" I blurted out defensively. I'd tried, but I'd never been one to handle an insult very well, and she'd pushed my buttons. "Sometimes you need an analog tool."

"Well, when I need a *tool* I'll know who to call." She smiled viciously.

"I'm hungry," Ryo said, louder than necessary to break the tension. "May we order in?"

I think Akiko and I could have gone at it all night, so cheers to him for stopping us. I stared at her and she at me. We silently agreed to an uneasy truce.

"I've already done that," she said, breaking the stare and pointing toward the fridge. "Your favorite."

Ryo walked over to the fridge and inside was a huge platter of sushi with boxes full of all the fixings. Never liked raw fish, so this wasn't for me. Deep fry it, broil it, heck, smoke it and I'm all over it, but raw? My caveman ancestors didn't invent the GrillMaster 3000XL for me to eat anything raw. Looked like ol' Hutch here's gonna be eating some white rice tonight. Mmmmm. Ryo was beyond excited about the food and actually clapped, so thanks to our weird connection, I was oddly excited, too. The link does weird things to you.

"Would you two mind if I showered before we eat?" he asked.

Yes, even in life-or-death scenarios he was still compulsive about cleanliness. The question reminded me how dirtbag filthy we were. I would need to shower, too, at some point.

"Go for it," I said.

He glanced between Akiko and me. "Will you two promise to get along?" he asked.

"She started it," I said with a smile. "I promise we'll behave."

He shook his head and closed the bathroom door behind him.

Once we were all alone, Akiko looked up at me and patted the cushion beside her.

"Join me?"

I could've used a good moment of down time. I wasn't

going to get it, though. No sooner had my head hit the back of the couch than Akiko stood. Alarm bells went off; I was now in a weaker position if she were a threat. Which she could be. How much did I really know about this girl?

"What is your real name? Where are you from? And who do you *really* work for?" she demanded.

"Uh . . ." The questions caught me off guard so my "Uh . . ." was legit.

"What is your real name? Start there."

"Bobby, uh, Robert technically," which was totally true, "and I'm from Texas," which was also totally true.

"But 'Sky' certainly isn't your real name."

"It is, though," I lied. I had no tells to give it away. I could tell you I was the president of Mars and no lie detector on Planet Earth would tell you I was lying.

She shook her head. "I'm very good at what I do. Very good. And I'm also very protective of my Ryo. He has become curiously attached to you. More so than with other friends. Yes, your records do pass the eye test but not the smell test. Your digital history smells . . . fishy. There is the hint of manipulation, the ghost of someone tampering with your past before you joined the band. Not to mention that there is very little of you out there to begin with. Very rare for someone of our generation, especially for one who is a pop sensation."

I met her steely gaze. Stick to the script; that was best. "My parents were weirdos. They didn't let me use the web much. Didn't trust it and thought it—"

"It's as if your online presence has been fabricated," Akiko interrupted.

"Because the CIA scrubbed my past to make it harder to blackmail me," I explained. Even I was impressed with how quickly I'd come up with that one. And it even sorta made sense.

"That is a lie for Ryo to believe, not for me. We both know you are not a CIA agent. They do not hunt down their own and murder US citizens in their homes." She paused. "Now. Would you like to tell me who you really work for?" she asked.

Fine. Time to fall back on what had always worked for me my whole life—my *real* life—before I became a Shadow. Time to call on the old Hutch charm. "You got me," I said as I raised my hands. "I don't work for the CIA, as in the Central Intelligence Agency. Never have. That *was* a lie for Ryo. But I do work for *a* CIA. I work for Cinnabon International Advocacy. My job is to subconsciously get people to buy our delicious cinnamon buns. Sometimes I'll whisper, 'Cinnabon' during our shows and on our albums. I know it's unethical, but it's what I do." I sighed deeply. "Wow, it feels really good to finally tell someone. Load off my shoulders."

That's when I saw it. The faint hint of a smile. Point: Hutch.

I lowered my voice. "Ever wonder where we got our name 'International'? Cinnabon *International* Advocacy. They've been pulling the strings since day one. We're their bun boys."

She snorted. Two points: Hutch.

"Look, just know that whatever I am—super-agent or cinnamon bun preacher-salesman—Ryo is safe with me and I'd die before I let anything happen to him, okay? I promise."

She shrugged and pulled out her phone, flopping back down beside me. The conversation appeared to be over. Or so I thought until I saw that she was typing my name into her phone. Ugh, well, she's persistent, I'll give her that. Whatever. She'd never find anything and if she did, I'd just have to kill her.

"SO I HAD AN idea," Ryo said, stepping out of the bathroom freshly dressed. His showers usually last close to twenty minutes, so by his standards it had been a pretty short scrub. He must have been really hungry.

"Let's post a video online, let everyone know we're alive, and tell them the CIA's trying to kill us. No way they can still come after us if we out them like that."

I knew this was coming. I'd been waiting for it.

I raised my hand and said, "It's not a bad idea. The problem is, if we do that, we're still running. Yeah, the outrage of it all could shield us for a bit, but then some other issue would zap everyone's attention away and we'd be left right back where we were—only, now we've really, really pissed whoever's trying to kill us off even more. We'll always be running unless we can figure out why they're coming after us and how we can fix it. Right now we're names on a list, but if we poke the bear, well, bears can be really mean when they want to be. Give me a chance to fix this, okay? If I can't, we'll go with your plan. Deal?"

He had been munching during my whole spiel, so he had to swallow before he could say, "Deal. Can I at least call my parents?"

I shook my head. "You love them, right?"

"Of course."

"Then it's better to keep them out of this. I know these people and if they see you're in contact with your parents, they'll use them against you without blinking. Give me a few days, okay?"

He nodded, but then his eyes widened as he thought out loud, "So they could have my parents right now? We must go find them!"

"They don't have them. They are watching them, keeping tabs on them, yeah, but they don't have them."

"How can you know this?" Akiko asked for Ryo before he could.

"Because there's no play in that move right now. Look,

my people are vicious sometimes, but they're not cruel for cruelty's sake. They won't go after your parents until we give them a reason to. My advice: Don't be the reason your parents are dragged into all of this. Let them mourn. Let them believe you're dead. They're safer that way."

chapter 23

THE BLUNT CLUB SWINGS INTO ACTION

We caught up on the news while we ate. All the channels were reporting that a terrorist group had claimed responsibility for firing the surface-to-air missile that had taken us out. All members of the band were confirmed dead. There were candlelight vigils and plenty of videos of crying, once-adoring fans. I'm a cold-hearted monster now, whatever, but Ryo wasn't and it depressed him a lot and that depression seeped into me a bit, too. It made him think of his parents and how badly he needed to talk to them. I talked him off the ledge, but he was in a funk and had gone to lie down. Beaten down and tired from travel, stress, you name it, he was asleep within minutes.

"Very clever to blame terrorists," Akiko muttered. She'd been on her computer, directing only half of her attention to the TV throughout dinner.

"They're not stupid people."

"They employ you," she joked. "Well, I believe it's time I get to work."

She put on some headphones, and began hammering away at the keyboard faster than anyone I'd ever seen. It was depressing. I started to feel like the analog tool in her digital world. While she hacked away—or did whatever she was doing—I scanned the channels. No HBO. No ESPN. Great. I ended up on some really bizarre game show and couldn't stop watching. In the first challenge all the contestants stripped down to their underwear and got into a small pond. While they were in the water these small sucker fish latched on to them. After sixty seconds they all stood up and, from what I could tell, the person with the most sucker fish dangling off them won. It was disgusting, disturbing, and amazing and it kept going. Each challenge was weirder than the one before it. I was addicted and before I knew it, I'd been watching for over an hour. I hoped it would keep going all night. Japanese TV—gotta love it.

"*Kusoooo,*" Akiko hissed angrily.

I ignored her.

It wasn't until she started muttering, "No, no, no . . ." that I had to ask.

"Everything okay?"

"No," she said, knocking her headphones off with her shoulder to keep her fingers dancing across the keys. "They have live security," she said, as if I would understand.

"Ink and paper kinda guy, remember," I said, pointing at myself.

"They have an actual human monitoring their servers. They detected me and now he's trying to hack me."

"So, unplug or something."

She groaned. "I can't. The job isn't done and this is the only chance to do it. I fail and the weakness I'm exploiting will be fixed and lost."

"Oh. Sooooo . . ."

"It's an endurance battle now. I will attack him. He will defend. He will attack me, and I will defend. The first person to make a mistake or gets tired loses."

"Sounds really stressing," I admitted. Looks like someone may be in line for good ol' fashioned Hutch neck massage . . .

"It is, but it's also fun," she said and actually smiled.

Fun? Wow, we are very different people.

"Good luck, I guess. You need me to turn the TV off?"

"Actually," she said, "and it pains me to even ask."

"Anything."

"This could last all night and I'd prefer it not to. I may . . . be in need of a blunt club."

"Wait, wait, wait," I joked. "You mean to tell me that there's something this old analog tool can do that you can't? That's impossible. No way. Inconceivable," and in my best-worst English accent, "Not bloody likely."

"You're enjoying this moment, aren't you?"

"More than you could know. What can I do?" I asked seriously.

"Stop the other hacker. Be the blunt club you say you are," she added.

"Where am I going?"

Typing with one hand she pulled out a spare phone from her backpack with her other hand, opened Google Maps, and typed in a location. "Here."

"Got it. So what? I just look for a dude typing like crazy."

"The servers are on the same floor as the labs. When you get there, let me know. I'll point him out for you."

"Then what? Smash his computer?"

"You're the blunt club, so you would not dare tell me how to do my job, and I would not think to tell you how to do yours."

"Can we make out when I get back?" I joked.

"If Ryo is still asleep, yes," she said, her eyes never leaving her computer screen.

I gulped. Was she serious? I had not been expecting that. I was honestly a bit terrified of this girl. It took me a few seconds to shake it off and get moving.

I WAS STILL COVERED in dried blood and mud, so I patched up my shoulder and changed quickly into jeans, a T-shirt, and a hoodie that she'd brought for me. I also snagged her sunglasses and train pass. There were no weapons. There was, strangely, a baseball bat, signed by some Japanese slugger, hanging on a plaque on the wall. I took that, too.

"How do I get out of here?"

There was only one way in or out of the hideout as far as I could tell, and there were still people in the office who would question where'd I'd come from or, worse, recognize me.

"Open the oven," she instructed. That made no sense, but before I returned fire, I figured I'd at least play along.

Holy crap, she wasn't kidding. The oven wasn't actually an oven. When I opened it, the door swung open on hinges like a regular door, and there was a black hole in the bottom of it that went straight down. Dangling from the ceiling of the oven was about a foot of climbing rope with a nylon loop at the end.

"Do I do what I think I do?" I asked Akiko.

She nodded. "Enjoy the ride."

Wow. Okay. I sat down on the floor, dangled my legs over the edge, slid my hand up through the nylon loop so that it hugged my wrist, and gripped the rope with everything I had. And away we go. I slid off the edge. For a moment I was freefalling and got that feeling you get in your stomach when that happens, but then the rope around my wrist tensed up and I realized that, yeah, I was going fast, but it was controlled-ish. Luckily, it was pitch black in here, so I couldn't see if the ground and death were screaming toward me or not. After about ten seconds of near free fall, the rope really started to pull at my wrist and a few seconds later, my feet tapped lightly on the ground.

"Cool," I couldn't help but say. When I let go of the rope, it shot back up into the darkness. "Cool," I had to say again.

I used the flashlight from Akiko's phone to look around.

I was in a small square room and on the wall to my right was a metal trap door barely three feet tall. I twisted the lever to open it, but when I tried to push it open, it barely moved a couple inches before clanging into something metal and stopping. A dumpster was blocking me. I put my shoulder into it and shoved as hard as I could. Slowly, and with some loud screeching, the dumpster moved and the door swung open enough for me to squeeze out. I was in an alley a hundred feet or so away from the main road. Even at this time of night there was plenty of foot traffic out there. Either no one had heard the screech from the dumpster, or, and probably most likely, no one cared. Everyone walked past the alley like it wasn't there.

I put on the sunglasses, pulled the hoodie up over my head and face, tucked the baseball bat up into the hoodie as best I could, and headed out into the masses. I kept my head down and made sure not to bump into anyone as I wove in and out of the crowd on my way to the nearest train station. I used Akiko's pass to get on, and three stops later I hopped off. Even though I was only three stops away, it was a stark contrast from where I had been. This place felt almost subdivisional, residential. There were a few ten-story or so buildings around the train station, but after that it was all houses. I kept following the map on Akiko's phone until it led me to the gates of a college campus. I had to double-check the map to make sure this was right, but it was. Eventually I ended up at the Advanced Science and Technology building.

The main atrium of the building was dark and deserted, and when I looked up, the offices of the professors and PhD students that lined the upper floors were dark and empty, too. A group of young students, talking loudly, burst up from a set of stairs off to my left and passed me as they exited. I walked toward the stairs where a sign with an arrow pointing down read, among other things: LABS.

The stairs led down to a set of heavy, metal French doors that opened up into what I will call the Nerdery. It was a huge open space of tables with everything from projects with robots to smoky, boiling chemicals. The place was packed. It was past one in the morning at this point, but I guess science knows no hours. Off to the right were smaller, more private labs, but off to my left the entire wall was nothing but blinking servers behind a wall of glass windows.

I texted Akiko that I was there. How was she going to point the person out to me? Oh. It was faint, but it was there somewhere up ahead.

"Over here! Over here! Over here! Over here! Over here! Over here!"

I began to work my way through the room toward the sound. Those who didn't have headphones were craning their necks to see who was breaking the unwritten rule about noise.

"Over here! Over here! Over here! Over here! Over here! Over here!"

I think I could see him now, but it wasn't a him. It was a her. Across the room, sitting in front of some kind of main computer system away from everyone else, was a fortysomething woman with her hair pulled into a loose bun frantically slamming away at her keyboard.

"Over here! Over here! Over here! Over here! Over here! Over here!"

I slowly started walking toward her, making sure to not draw attention to myself. I slowly let the baseball bat slide out of my hoodie and held it next to my leg as I softly sang:

"Take me out to the ball game,
Take me out with the crowd.
Buy me some peanuts and Cracker Jacks.
I don't care if I never get back.
Let me root, root, root for the home team.

If they don't win, it's a shame."

I reached her at the absolute perfect timing.

"For it's one! . . ."

I tomahawk-chopped the bat down on the mainframe box, crushing it.

"Two! . . ."

I swung for the fences and swept the monitors off the desk.

"Three . . ."

I slammed the bat down on the keyboard, sending tiny little keys flying up into the air.

"Strikes you're out! At the old . . ."

I went back after the mainframe box for another good hit.

"Ball . . ."

Another good whack.

"Gaaaaame . . ."

One last crack to fully destroy it.

In total shock the woman simply looked up at me. She was terrified.

"Got a little carried away, sorry about that," I muttered. "Have a great night."

I was about to leave when an arm wrapped itself around my neck like a python and started dragging me away from the shocked lady. I dropped the bat, but before I could do anything else, I was flipped over and sent flying through the air toward the glass wall of servers. I slammed into the glass, which didn't break, thank goodness, and barely had time to stop a soccer kick headed straight for my face. I grabbed the foot and twisted it. The attacker spun out of it, but it gave me a chance to get to my feet.

From here the fight got weird. He was older. Thirty, maybe forty, but every time I would throw a punch or kick, he would dodge it like he knew it was coming. But it was the same for me, too. I also sorta knew what he was going to do almost before he did and easily dodged or slipped out of it. It was like fighting an older version of myself. It was going nowhere fast. It wasn't until he did a spinning-kicking-flipping move called the Charybdis that my mind was blown. That was a move named and invented by one of the FATE hand-to-hand combat teachers. Only Shadows learned it. This dude was a Shadow?!?! I'd never thought I'd see another in the wild, let alone an older version like himself. I mean, I knew your assignment could last years, decades even, but in my mind all Shadows were young like me. Which meant . . . I looked over at the woman whose computer I'd just destroyed and couldn't help but mutter, "FIP?"

The attacker stopped and gave me a really confused look. *Holy hell, I was right!* No wonder it had felt like I was fighting myself. I *had* been. While he was looking at me trying to figure out who I was and what I was here for, I went for it. I sold out on a fake head punch and when he reacted to block it, I dove down, slammed my shoulder into his gut, wrapped up, and drove him toward the far wall, the old linebacker bum rush from my football days. He elbowed and punched me as we went, but I was cool with it. I slammed him into a door, which broke off its hinges as we fell into one of the private labs.

He was stunned, which gave me time to place myself on top of him and slam my forearm over his throat.

“Calm down,” I hissed. I looked through the broken door to see if anyone was coming. No one was. They were all keeping their distance. “I’m not here to hurt her. I came to destroy the computer. That’s it.”

“How can I trust that?” he growled out, and tried to escape with a quick burst of energy.

I jammed my arm down harder into his throat as I added, “I woulda killed her when I was next to her if I’d wanted to hurt her.”

The truth of it made sense to him and calmed him down. In return, I lessened the pressure on his neck and sat up to take some of my weight off his chest.

“What now?” he asked.

“I’m leaving, okay?” I said and then had to add, “And how cool was this? I mean, really weird and mind-blowing, but cool, yeah?”

He smiled and echoed, “It was cool.”

“Right?”

“Was nice to get a good fight in, too,” the guy added, reading my mind.

“Totally was,” I said, rolling off him and standing up.

My disguise sunglasses had come off somewhere in the lab, so I pulled my hoodie down extra low across my face before heading to the door. I paused and looked back at him through the busted doorjamb.

“Good luck, man.”

“You too,” he said, sitting up.

I detoured to pick up the bat and conveniently found my

sunglasses near them. Having picked up all the evidence, I bolted before the Japanese fuzz got there.

By the time I got back to the safe house, Akiko was waiting for me in the alley with my exterminator costume.

"All done?" I asked.

She nodded.

"What were you trying to do to their system?" I asked as I started to change back into my costume.

"They wanted me to install a looking glass," she said, like that would mean anything to me. "They wanted an undetectable way to look at all the ideas and experiments of the students so they can steal anything worth money."

"That's not cool."

"They're not the good people," she said like she had to remind me. "They have a sense of honor and duty that can be admired, but they are still criminals."

"I know. It's just stealing from kids seems doubly mean," I said as I heaved the last of my costume on.

"Which is why I normally never would have done it."

"Well, thanks," I had to say, knowing she'd only agreed for us.

I was shocked to see that there were still a few people in the office working. Did they ever go home? Who had this type of work ethic? Once safely back in our hiding spot, I was glad to see that Ryo was still asleep.

I took a long-overdue shower.

WHEN I EMERGED, AKIKO was sitting on the couch, scrolling through something on her phone. She'd taken off the jacket of her pantsuit, rolled up her sleeves, and freed a few buttons from her collar so that a peek of her upper chest skin could be seen. Her hair was up in a classic Japanese, locked-in-place-by-chopsticks ponytail.

“Feeling better?” she asked, tossing her phone onto the coffee table.

“Much. Nice to be good and clean,” I admitted.

“You were quite filthy before. So?” she asked, taking off her glasses but giving me no clear clue what the “so” was about.

“So . . . what?” I asked, confused.

She smirked and then seductively bit the arm of the glasses. Then it hit me and I flushed red as I figured out what the “so” meant. “Oh.”

So . . . we totally made out.

chapter 24
NO GOOD DEED . . .

With the mission completed, true to their word, the Yakuza picked us up the next morning and took us to a proper safe house.

It was everything I could have ever wanted: a grimy campus of old buildings on the outskirts of town that looked like it had once been the business headquarters for some shady company. The best part, though, was that it was crawling with heavily armed and loyal foot soldiers. Now, this was more like it. We were driven to the east side of the complex and told to never leave it. There was everything we could want over here: plenty of space, our own rooms, food, heck, we even had our own *onsen*—Japanese hot baths that put hot tubs to shame—but when someone tells you that you can't go somewhere and doesn't give a good reason, well, we all know how that works out. You gotta check it out.

The compound seemed safe enough, and I knew Akiko would do anything for Ryo, but I had to check every square inch of the complex before I could convince myself that Ryo would be okay here without me while I took off to figure out why FATE was trying to kill us. Like all good recon operations I was going to have to wait until night, since "blending in" wasn't about to happen for a long list of reasons.

Until it got dark I spent as much time as possible going

over everything on "our" side of the compound. The area was surrounded by a tall, solid metal wall topped with coils of razor wire, and at any given time there were ten armed men randomly patrolling the area in twos and threes. Not too shabby, if I had to say. I'd have felt a lot more comfortable with, say, a thousand, but who am I to be that picky? Ten would do. And that was on this side, which I sensed was the "legit" side. Who knew what or how many men were on the other side. Night couldn't come quick enough, but when it finally did, we got some unexpected visitors.

A group of management-level gangsters swung by to celebrate the success of Akiko's mission. I tried to keep my distance as I had a job to do, but they were so personable the feel-good vibe was infectious. We drank sake, joked around, and enjoyed some fresh Wagyu beef, which if you've never had any, try it immediately. They stayed late into the night until red-faced and tipsy, and then they finally left. I admit, I was a little sad to see them go. These guys weren't so bad. Heck, they were a lot of fun actually. I hoped they'd come back the next night, too. But right now I had to worry about putting Ryo to bed and making sure he fell asleep.

"WHERE ARE YOU GOING?" Akiko asked.

I flashed her a dumb grin. She'd waited for me in the common area, watching muted TV and tooling around on her laptop. I'd thought she'd gone to bed, too. Oops.

I shrugged. "Fresh air?"

"Don't get caught," she said with a smirk. She went back to her laptop, adding, "I have no more favors to call in."

I crept along the shadows, dodging a few guards here and there until I reached the forbidden side. It was actually pretty easygoing and I probably made it harder than it needed to be. Was it necessary to do a backflip off a balcony to get over a chain-link fence? No, but it was fun, so I did it anyway.

Once I was on the other side, I didn't know what I expected to find. I mean, I knew it wouldn't be a My Little Pony factory, but I hadn't expected to find everything. Drugs. Check. Guns. You bet. Counterfeit bills? Stacks of them. Other normal illegal stuff you can think of? Yeah, I saw it all. But when I heard a child's cry for help and took a look through a small window in a door, I was glad I did and wished I hadn't at the same time.

Cages.

Looking through the window I could see around thirty or so metal boxes, and there was a person locked in each one. There were old grandparents, young adults, and even kids. What I saw made me queasy and instantly made me ashamed for having anything to do with these people. Yeah, I was jumping the gun. Maybe, just maybe there was an explanation to explain it all away, but come on, there wasn't. Not for this. I was disgusted at myself for being all buddy-buddy with these people only a few hours ago and calling them "friends." They were criminals and I'd let myself forget what this really meant. And I admit, as a Shadow, I'm not necessarily the "good guy" since I'll pretty much destroy anyone I think is a threat to Ryo, but that doesn't mean I can't still be a *good* guy.

I heard men's voices somewhere behind me. They were down the hall and around the corner, but they were coming this way for sure. I had three options: go back the way I came, go into the room with the cages, or sneak through the door a few feet to my left and take a chance that whatever was in there wouldn't give me up. Since there was a possibility that the people in the cages would cry out for help if they saw me, or worse, recognized me, and going back the way I came would just be a waste of time, I chose the door to my left.

A long time ago the room had probably been a storage

closet for whatever business had been here, but now it was a junk room full of busted boxes and moldy crap. I ducked inside with only seconds to spare before three men, who I watched through the crack in the door, walked by and directly into the room of cages.

There was screaming before the men reappeared, dragging a fifty-something-year-old woman down the hallway. She was begging them to stop, for mercy, but all she got in response was a, "Shut up, dog," and a whack to the face by one of the men.

This has nothing to do with you. It has nothing to do with Ryo. Let it go, I tried to tell myself, but I wasn't listening. There was no way I could let this go. Not now. Not *ever.*

I crept out of my hiding spot and followed the men along the hallway, around a corner, down some stairs, and into a large boiler room. I didn't follow them down but stayed by the door at the top step to spy. At the bottom of a rickety flight of metal stairs sat an old industrial boiler that had a large trap door on the side that you could toss trash into. The flames inside were roaring. Even from up here I could feel the heat. I had a bad feeling about this as I watched them drag the woman down the stairs and next to the trap door. One of the men, a young man with shoulder-length black hair, took out his phone, and pointed it at her.

"Any last words for your husband, who was too cheap to pay your ransom?" he sneered.

The tears were still flowing from her eyes as she stood up straight and strong, and said, "I love you."

"Did you know your life isn't worth a million yen to him?" the other young man jeered. He was wearing sunglasses and looked as stupid as he sounded.

"Barely a car. You're not worth a car to him," the one holding the phone mocked, trying to get a response from her.

"You have my final words," she told them as strongly as she could, but her voice was quivering.

My blood was boiling. Having seen or heard enough, the eldest of the group, a man with short, business-cut hair that had gone gray at the temples, lit a cigarette and ordered, "Throw her in, then." He took a long pull on the cigarette before adding, "Let's be done with her."

She screamed as the other two men grabbed her and began to force her toward the open door of the roaring boiler. She fought, but she was weak from captivity and the two men were younger and stronger. In a few seconds it would be over. I knew I should let it be over, let it happen, but knowing and doing are not the same.

"I think I'm lost," I said loudly and in English as I stood up in the doorway so they could see me.

It worked. The men stopped as their leader held up his hand for them to pause. They let go of the lady and silently warned her to stay quiet.

"You should not be here," the eldest said to me. He spoke in pretty good English, I had to admit.

"I am aware. I'm sorry. I was walking, took a left, another left, and got totally turned around." I was lying and trying to sound as stupid as I could—always an easy combination. "Crazy bad with directions," I added and then winked and side-mouthed to him, "and I'm a little drunk too. That stuff Takashi brought was strong." The reaction I got from name-dropping the higher-up who'd hung out with us earlier worked. The man knew he had to show a bit of restraint.

I started walking down the metal stairs toward them, making sure I swayed a bit.

"Stay up there," the leader said, trying to stop me from coming down, but I ignored him. I'd use his fear of his boss against him as long as I could. He'd say, "The hell with it!" soon enough. I just needed to be in position when he did.

"So what's going on here?" I asked, acting as curious as I could. "Is she okay?"

"She is none of your concern," he threatened.

He met me where the stairs hit the concrete floor of the room and blocked me from stepping down.

"You must leave now," he said, and pulled back his coat to show me his gun. He'd reached "the hell with it" status right where I wanted him to. Attaboy.

"Is that real? Can I touch it?" I said excitedly, reaching out for the gun.

My excited, not-scared-for-a-second reaction wasn't what he'd hoped for, but his reaction to me was exactly what *I'd* hoped for. People can be way too predictable sometimes.

"No," he said as he pulled the weapon out and pointed it at me. "Go! Now!"

It was a move I'd practiced fifty gabillion times in training, but one I doubt anyone had ever tried on him. We'd had it busted into our minds through so much countless repetition that it was as instinctive and reflexive as breathing. Slick as you like, I twisted the gun out of his hands and popped off three lightning-quick rounds. The three men all fell to the ground dead practically at once. Smoke still streamed out of the cigarette that was gripped tightly in the eldest man's lips.

The gunshots had been so deafening that I had to yell at the woman for her to hear me over the ringing in our ears. She was wide-eyed and still in shock from it all.

"Are you okay?" I asked three times until finally she nodded.

The way she was looking at me told me she wasn't sure if she could trust me or not. I couldn't blame her. I could only imagine what she'd been through in here.

"I'm not going to hurt you," I promised, tucking the gun into my belt and holding up my hands. "You're safe now, okay?"

She nodded and seemed to relax a bit more. I had no clue if anyone had heard the gunshots or not, as we were pretty deep in the bowels of this place, but I couldn't risk it and had to move fast. Quickly as I could, I dragged each man over to the boiler and shoved them into the flames. The blood on the floor was an issue I didn't have time to deal with. I had to hope if anyone saw it, they'd assume it was from the victims. And it's not like there was a mop to clean it up with anyway, so what choice did I have but to leave it?

"Thank you," the woman said, finally finding her voice after I slammed the door to the boiler, closing it.

"Of course," I said automatically, my mind still busy trying to figure out what to do and what I'd gotten myself into by doing the stupid, right thing. What the heck was I supposed to do with this lady now? What had I done? I had to see this out now, consequences be damned. I had to get these people out and back to their families. I'd started down a path but had tripped and fallen, and was now cartwheeling down the mountain toward the bottom, which was coming one way or another. "How many of you are there?"

"Being held for ransom?" she asked before guessing a pretty precise, "Thirty-six?"

I nodded as I took in the information. Crap, that was a lot. Now what? I couldn't leave them here. I mean, I could, but I couldn't. And there was no way I could sneak them out of here either, without being caught. I could try a few at a time, but that would take forever, and every trip could be the one that would get us caught. Now, if it was only me, I'd maybe risk doing it, but it wasn't only me. If they caught me, who knows what they'd do to Ryo. Now, *that* was something I couldn't ignore.

I looked at the woman. She had old bruises. Old, infected cuts. She'd been abused, neglected, humiliated.

I had to make these men pay for what they'd done. I needed help, though. I needed a group of stone-cold killers to come wipe all traces of this filth off the planet. And I knew a bunch of them who'd do it, gladly, if they knew what was going on, but the problem was, this group wanted to wipe all traces of me off the face of the planet, too.

Uh-oh. Am I having a . . . yep, it's happening.

Idea time.

Terrible, horrible, stupid idea time . . . a Hutch staple.

But . . . yeah, I was going for it.

Chapter 25

Hook, Line, and . . . Huh?

I tucked the woman into a sweet hiding space in the back of the boiler room and promised I'd be back. She wasn't too happy about being alone, but I convinced her it was her only choice. Had she thrown a fit I don't know what I'd have done. With her safely hidden away, I raced back to the safe side of the compound, where, thankfully, Akiko was still awake.

"Didn't get caught, I see," she said without looking up.

"Tell me you know nothing about what's going on over there?" I said a bit more forcefully than I'd meant to.

For a second I regretted it, but then I didn't. If she knew anything about it, my tone was the least of her worries. She would be my enemy. It took her by surprise, so she didn't answer.

"Tell me," I repeated seriously. I had to know. I had to know if she knew. It mattered.

"No, I-I don't," she stammered.

"Good. Sorry, I had to make sure."

"What is going on over there?" she asked. She sounded scared. "Why do you have blood on you? Are you hurt?"

"Bad things, not important right now, and no," I answered in the order of her questions. "We'll talk about it later. Do you know anywhere else we can hide?"

"Why?" she asked, looking up and pursing her lips.

"I maaaay have done something stupid. Scratch that. I *did* do something stupid. More than one thing, actually. And I have to do more."

"Why?" she repeated, frustrated.

"Because it's what I do and it was the right thing to do."

"Noble but stupid," she muttered.

I almost laughed. "Yep, it's what I'm best at. Look, yes or no. Do you know of anywhere else we can hide? I can explain later."

She looked at me for a few seconds before smirking and pulling out her laptop.

"Let me see," she said as she began to hack away. "When I set up their looking glass into the school computers, they had to give me access to their own system. I set up some looking glasses of my own."

After about thirty or so seconds of her fingers whizzing away on the keyboard, she smiled and spun the screen around as she said, "Where do you want to hide?"

On the screen was a long list of addresses for other safe houses.

"Any way to tell if they're being used?" I asked.

"I don't know how accurate the list is, but these," she said, pointing at a box with an asterisk, "I believe indicate if it is occupied or not."

"Any of these super secluded, off-the-grid-type places?"

She pulled the screen back toward her and went at it on the keyboard again.

"Throwing all the addresses into a map," she muttered for my benefit. "This one."

She showed me the map of somewhere in northern Japan.

"Hokkaido. Small cabin in the mountains. It's rural and even if your people somehow track us to the city using the city cameras, those don't exist out in the mountains. It's blanketed in snow and truly off the map. It looks to be only accessible by snowmobile."

Perfect, I thought. As we sat staring at the map on her computer screen, our faces were inches away from each other, and I couldn't help but sneak a sideways glance at her. Her dark eyes were glued to the screen, and her short, steady breaths were intoxicating. My mind began to wonder if her skin was as soft and smooth as I remembered. What would she do if I tried to kiss her? Totally inappropriate in the moment, but this girl was awesome and good at making out so . . . Fifty-fifty chance she either kissed back or beat the hell out of me. Both sorta turned me on.

"Can we make out again?" I only half joked.

She smirked. "Later. Now tell me why we have to leave."

I filled her in on what I'd seen. Like me, the guns, cash, and drugs were whatever, but when her mouth dropped open as I got to the part with the old woman and the boiler, I knew she was on board.

"We have to get them out, and the only way to do it is with help," I finished.

"I agree, but who can we call? They control the police and most of the politicians. By the time anyone could help, the hostages would all be moved or killed."

"I know. Which is why I called in the cavalry, *my* cavalry."

"Cavalry?"

"My people. The ones hunting us," I clarified, always forgetting that normal American sayings are often lost in translation. "There were wireless cameras monitoring the cages. I waited for a camera to sweep by the door and made sure my face was in the window when it passed. It was too small and fast for the guards to see it in their video stream, but my people's facial recognition will find it. It may only take minutes, or it may take a few hours, but they will find it and when they do, they'll come. But don't worry," I said, then paused before adding totally unconvincingly, "I think I have a plan."

I quickly explained my plan to her.

"It's practically suicide. You honestly think that will work?"

"Fifty-fifty?" I said, cringing, knowing full well the odds were a lot lower. "Twenty-eighty . . . maybe?"

"My job seems relatively easy in comparison," she said.

"But it's the most important," I reminded her.

"I will not fail you."

"I don't care about me. Don't fail *him*," I said, pointing toward the room Ryo was sleeping in.

"Never," she said absolutely.

"Good. Gotta get moving, then. We should have a few hours, but that's a guess. If they already tracked us to Japan, they could be here any minute now, which is why you and Ryo need to get out of here. Once you're gone, I can make sure the hostages get out safely and then start on getting to the bottom of all this. I can't do either of them if I have to worry about Ryo."

"You're not worried about me?" she asked, joking.

"I'm pretty sure you can handle yourself."

"How will you know if *we're* even still alive?" she asked. "Ryo and me?"

"Trust me, I'll know. If he dies while I'm still linked to him, I'll go out of my mind and be kill-everyone-around-me nuts."

"Linked?" she asked as I realized I'd finally let something slip about the world she was now involved in. "What are you?"

My breath caught in my throat. "You'd never believe me if I told you. Stick with believing it's the CIA, trust me. All you need to know is I won't rest until he is safe and I'll die to protect him," I added, pointing at the room where Ryo slept. "Now go wake him up. You're a much prettier face to wake up to than me."

"I wouldn't mind," she said.

I could feel my face flush. Not the time or place, hormones.

She stared at me for a moment and I knew there were a thousand questions bouncing around in her head. I was super glad she didn't ask any.

A FEW MINUTES LATER, Ryo stumbled out of his room still half asleep, with Akiko poking him to hurry.

"Okay, okay," he yawned out. When he saw me, he asked, "What's going on?"

"The Yakuza sold us out," I lied. "My people are coming. We have to go."

Nothing like a death squad heading right at you to kick-start the morning. The sleep disappeared from his face as terror took over. It pained me a bit to have caused him that, but if it got him moving, so be it.

"Follow me," I told them as I headed for the door.

Dawn was still a few hours away, so the dark was on our side. I guided them along the edges of the complex until I found a weak spot in the metal fencing. With a few quick tugs I was able to pull a corner out far enough for Akiko and Ryo to squeeze through. Ryo immediately noticed when I didn't follow.

"What are you doing?" he whispered to me.

"I'm staying," I told him.

"You can't. Come with us," he pleaded, and it took every bit of willpower to not obey.

I shook my head. "I have to figure out what's going on. I have to fix this." It was now my turn to plead. "Go, please."

"You'll find us?" he asked.

"You'll see me again one way or another. I promise," I told him.

I locked eyes with Akiko.

She nodded in understanding. She knew the plan. She'd be ready. I shoved the piece of metal back into place. My heart sank. This was the most difficult moment of my life. Every piece of me was telling me to go after Ryo, but I fought it. I had to.

THE OLD WOMAN IN the boiler room was glad to see me again. I pretended to listen as I made small talk with her. She told me about her family, and how excited she was to see them again, but I only half listened. I felt empty. Ryo was gone and I had no way of knowing if he was okay. Alive? Yes, I knew that, but in danger? Hurt? No clue. Could I count on the link to let me know? I didn't know. There was a hole inside me that was getting bigger and bigger with every second of uncertainty.

The distant *Pop! Pop!* of gunfire was the most welcome sound in the world. It was like Mozart to me as it started off soft and slow before picking up until it was an all-out war raging out there. Just beautiful. Hot lead for breakfast, anyone? My love affair with the Yakuza had ended in the boiler room. FATE had taken the bait, and now these gangsters were getting theirs. The plan was working. I would make my next move under the cover of chaos.

With everyone busy fighting, the old woman and I made our way to the cages without running into anyone. Together, we quickly freed the prisoners. I'd been worried, but getting everyone out of here turned out to be pretty simple, really. Whichever way the fighting seemed heaviest, we went in the opposite direction. It wasn't until we reached the "safe" side of the compound that we even saw another soul. Peeking out a window I saw three fully armed Yakuza charging down the sidewalk in the morning light toward something or someone. Didn't know. Didn't care.

With the coast as clear as it got, I hurried the stream of people toward the same loose fence piece I'd shoved Ryo and Akiko through earlier. One by one they shimmied through the space until it was only me and the old woman. She thanked me, hugged me, and whispered into my ear, "Your secret's safe with me."

"Huh?" I questioned.

"My daughter's a big fan . . . Bobby Sky. Though Ryo is her favorite."

I watched her leave. "I'm not . . ." I started—but before I could get the rest out, a stream of bullets raked across the metal wall behind me.

I let go of the fence piece, rolled, and blindly opened fire in the direction of whoever was shooting me. It was two of the three Yakuza who'd run past earlier. I emptied the rest of my clip at them, killing both. I took their weapons and listened. The explosions and gunfire were dying down as the battle was beginning to end. My people simply don't lose, especially not to gangsters. I could hear some heavy fire being exchanged way off somewhere to my left, a holdout of the last Yakuza, I could only guess. I went right instead, where there were only some sporadic shots and the occasional yell. Yes, I'm fearless, but I still don't want to die.

In a large open space that was once a garden but was now overgrown with grass and weeds, a large group of Yakuza, fifteen or so, had circled up around someone on the ground. That *someone* became *something* real quick when the group of Yakuza opened fire all at once. Within seconds the body, even with all the armor it was wearing, was nothing more than a mass of torn-up meat. A cold way to go. And a waste of bullets, too. One well-placed shot would have done the job. Emotions make you do stupid things, like waste ammo. Whoever it was they'd killed had definitely been FATE, though. I'd recognize that specific state-of-the-art body armor anywhere. I wondered if I knew them.

With the group preoccupied, I saw movement from behind an old storage shed. A person burst from behind it, trying to get away. Her plain brown hair, in a tight French braid, was tucked into her body armor to keep from whipping around. If that had been all I could see, I'd have thought she was just another soldier of FATE, but I knew that run. It was a half-sprinting, half-prancing stride I'd mocked relentlessly. When she turned around to look at her pursuers, I didn't need to see those green eyes behind a face dusted with tiny freckles to know . . .

"Sam?" I whispered to myself.

SHE DIDN'T GET FAR before she was spotted and the group chased after her. My path was clear now, but . . . well, great. I knew better, but did I? Did I? She wasn't the mission. She wasn't the priority. But she was my Sam.

They trapped her in a run-down single-story pagoda and circled around her like a pack of wild dogs. Great. How many could I realistically kill before they turned on me? Five? If only I could curl bullets in circles like in the movies—that would be convenient right about now. Come on, FATE, let's make that happen. I'll drop it in the comment box next time I'm there.

In unison they opened fire on the pagoda, a couple hundred yards away, spraying it with bullets. My stomach was in my throat. Had they . . . nope. Sam popped up from a window, fired off a burst that took out three of them, and dropped back down. They opened fire again, and like before, the moment they paused she burst back up, only from a new spot this time, killing another two.

I took a deep breath before running out of my hiding place and opening fire.

One down. Two. Three. Four. Five. Six.

All dead before they could do anything.

Seven, eight, nine, and ten, though, had time to react and opened fire at me.

They tagged me in my left arm, chest, hip, and leg.

Back at FATE we called that "hitting for cycle"—which any of your baseball-obsessed friends can explain to you if you don't know what it means. Being shot as a normal person probably sucks, but since I couldn't feel any pain it wasn't that big of a deal (as long as no major players were hit—head, heart, man parts, etc.). All that really happened was that the momentum of the bullets, when they hit me, knocked me off balance. Oh, and yeah, there was blood, but whatever.

The point was, it worked. While they shot at me, Sam popped up and dropped them easily.

Now that everyone was dead, Sam and I were stuck in an old-fashioned standoff.

I kept my gun on her and she did the same. She'd been hit, too, from the looks of it.

"Don't we make the pair," she said dryly.

"You okay?" I asked.

"Right as rain. You?"

She kicked through what was left of the pagoda door and stepped out into the open.

"Nothing's falling out so, yeah, I think so. That's twice now, by the way, that I've saved you."

"Didn't do much math back at FATE, but I can count to two," she said with a smirk. "Doesn't matter, though. Can't let you go, not this time."

"I know."

"Then why'd you do this?" she asked. She slowly walked toward me.

"I thought there was a puppy in there. I didn't know it was you. This was totally an accident."

She laughed.

"Thought your leg was broken. Figured you'd be out of action for a while," I went on, remembering how mangled it looked after the Polaris crash at the ranch.

"Twisted," she admitted. "Still works."

I lowered my gun.

"What are you doing?" she asked as she kept her gun on me.

"What does it look like?" I dropped the gun to the ground.

"Why?"

"I have a plan?" I joked, before adding seriously: "This is the only way I thought I could get some answers."

"Our order is to kill on sight." There was a touch of sadness in her voice. Maybe I was just imagining it. But she hesitated, her finger hovering over the trigger.

"No doubt, but that would be a mistake," I warned. "I told Ryo everything. Like *everything. What* we are. *Where* we are. *Who* we are. He doesn't hear from me in three days and he goes public. You call home and tell them all of that. If he still says kill on sight, then that's what you do."

Her eyes narrowed. With the gun still pointed at me, she took out a small, practically invisible piece of square glass from her front vest pocket. After thumbing some messages into it, staring at it, and sighing, she smiled.

"Okay," she said as she tucked the device back into her pocket. "Kill order's been canceled. Order is to bring you in now."

She took out a pair of zip tie handcuffs.

"Really?" I asked.

She hesitated.

"This was my idea, remember?" I practically shouted.

"Yeah, I guess," she said, tucking them back where she'd pulled them from. "Come on," she grumbled as she guided me away.

"I'm really glad you didn't have to kill me," I told her as we both limped toward what sounded like the last of the fighting. "I wasn't a hundred percent sure if they would have let you do it anyway."

"I'm glad, too. But I still don't see the point of all this. I assume there is one, right?"

"Oh, definitely," I teased.

"And?" she asked.

"Well, there has to be a way to fix all this. Y'know, make it right. There's gotta be something I can do to get Ryo off whatever hit list he's on."

"You honestly believe that?" she said as she gave me a knowing look.

"I have to try, don't I? Can't run forever."

"You were off our radar," she admitted. "We'd lost you."

"Really?"

She nodded.

"You think we coulda stayed lost, though?" I asked, and we both knew the answer.

"A lot of us stopped doubting what you could or couldn't do a long time ago," she said with that same sad smile. "If I had to put money on anyone being able to, it would have been you."

"Makin' me blush," I said playfully. "But come on, seriously, you think I coulda done it? Hidden from FATE forever?"

Her smile brightened. "No. We'd have caught you eventually."

"Exactly. So why wait? Let's get it over with."

chapter 26

THE HOMECOMING KING

So good being home!

I can't believe I actually missed this place. Even the smell, the super clean, bleachy smell makes me smile. Am I insane? I mean, well, all Shadows are to some point, but to miss this place? This torturing, child-killing, stealing-your-soul, and wrecking-your-childhood place? Even with all that, I was still sorta excited to be back.

And to top it all off, Claire was waiting for me in the arrival bay.

"Claire?!" I called out, hopping out of the transport. They'd patched me up on the plane so I was all good again.

"Ah, the world-famous Bobby Sky," she said, waving politely before going full businesslike on me. "This way. He's waiting for you."

I turned back to the transport. Sam had hopped off as well, walking away without even a goodbye or anything. Not cool. I dashed after her and grabbed her arm.

"Hey," I said as she turned.

She raised her eyebrows as if to ask, *what?* I knew why she was being distant. Chances were Blake was still going to kill me, so rekindling anything from our past was stupid and would only bring a hurt even fire couldn't numb. I didn't care, though. I'd missed her and selfishly

I'd be the one dying, so I didn't have to worry about the hurt part.

"I'm gonna be fine. Bet you a loonie we hang out later?"

She allowed me a tiny *fine, I give up* smile and nodded.

"Drink it in," I joked, holding out my arms to show her my whole body as I walked backward away from her, "Drink it in. Last time you might get to see old Hutch here in one piece."

She shook her head disapprovingly, but the smile was still there. "Not funny."

"It sorta is," I teased. "Kinda morbid, but still funny."

She lowered her eyes. "Take care of yourself, Hutch," she said.

"Young love," Claire teased as I walked over to her.

"Shut up," I joked. I gave her a playful elbow. "Did you like that signed, shirtless calendar I sent you?"

"I opened that in front of Blake, by the by," she said, pretending to be angry.

"Ha!"

AS CLAIRE LED ME out of the bay and into the hallways of FATE, I told her about my life as a pop star. I had no idea if she heard a word, or cared. We eventually ended up in a small room overlooking a series of war games taking place in a hyper-real jungle room. Two teams were slowly stalking one person who was protecting another. Real-world Shadow and FIP practice. I vaguely remembered doing the same. I'd totally gone Rambo, covering myself and my pretend FIP in mud, burying us to stay hidden. I'd pop out whenever anyone was near us and "kill them." I won the game, which I felt once again proved my point that you can learn everything you need to know from movies.

Blake and two other military-looking men were in there,

chatting and watching the games below. They broke off when Claire cleared her throat. Since last I'd seen him, Blake had gone totally salt-and-pepper gray and had cut his hair. It now sat short on the sides, loosely parted on the top. He still dressed like he was living in an L.L.Bean catalog in his faded jeans, navy flannel shirt, and a light blue fleece vest.

"Bobby!" Blake exclaimed, his big smile extending to his sparkling eyes.

"Hey," I said, not returning it.

"It's good to see you," he said as he offered me his hand to shake.

I shook it. Might as well. Why was he being so nice?

"So, did you really give us all up to uh, oh what's his name, Rino?"

"Ryo," I corrected. He definitely knew my FIP's name. He had done that on purpose to get a rise out of me. It had worked.

Score one for Blake. It would be the last point he'd get.

"Right. Ryo Enomoto," he said. "So? Did you?"

"I did," I lied.

"You betrayed us?" Blake said, sounding seriously hurt.

"It seemed like the right thing to do after I figured out that you were trying to kill us both," I said evenly.

He nodded. "So you risked exposing and destroying us all, your family, so Mr. Enomoto could feel better?"

"Yep." *Nice try, Blake, but I'm not gonna fall for your smooth talk.* I'd been ready for this and had practiced my responses. "You did this to me, remember?"

"Fair enough." He put his arm over my shoulder like a buddy as he said, "Come on."

"Where?"

"To show you why Ryo Enomoto and Bobby Sky have to die."

HE LED ME TOWARD a part of FATE I'd never been before. A part that was totally off-limits to Shadows. I remembered passing the area and seeing the two armed guards standing on either side of the door and wondering what was back there. Was I about to peek behind the curtain? Looked like it.

Even though it was Blake who ran this whole show, he still had to pass a retina scan and voice recognition test to get through the doors. The whole time the two guards were pointing their guns directly at his head, ready to kill him if he failed either test. He didn't and they lowered their guns. The guards stared at me as I passed and I'm sure their confusion about who I was equaled mine about where I was going.

"Took me a long time to get used to that," he said as we walked through the door. "The guns," he added in response to my confused look, "took a while to get used to—loaded guns being pointed at me."

"I can relate," I answered, remembering my first few days here and the number of guns that were pointed at me.

"I bet." He laughed.

The door we'd come through led into a plain, quiet hallway. At the end of the fifty-foot corridor was another door with two more guards. It looked exactly like the other one and for a second I had a *Matrix* déjà vu moment. We headed directly for the far door. It was quiet in this hallway and our footsteps echoed. The cough I heard somewhere off to my right behind a closed door was the only clue I had that other people were down here.

The guards stepped aside as we approached to let Blake pass the security system. Another retina scan, more voice recognition but with a new password, a palm scanner, and finally even a prick of the finger so that some blood could be used in a DNA check. Oh, and guns pointed at the head as usual.

Even nuclear arsenals aren't protected this much. What was back here?

I followed Blake into a totally dark room. Once the door closed behind us I could only hear him walking forward, so I followed blindly into the darkness. After five paces a dim light above us slowly brightened until the room was comfortably lit, sorta like a movie theater. We were standing in the middle of a plain square room with blank walls. Or so I thought. Suddenly an image appeared at the bottom left corner of the wall in front of us. Then another appeared next to it and another next to that. Once the bottom strip of the wall was filled with images, the pattern snaked back around the other way. Slowly, the snaking images worked their way across and up until the whole wall was filled and there was no space left. All in all, there were thirty images up there.

As the smaller images had appeared I'd gotten the feeling that they were the puzzle pieces of a much larger, fuller picture. I was right. Once the wall was full the smaller images unfocused, focused, and then began to slide around like tiles until all of them were in the right places.

It was a park. Not one I knew, but if you've seen one park . . . trees, grassy fields, a fountain, kids playing, you get it. Something about it felt off though, strange, but before I could figure it out, the picture faded away and the screen went blank again. Then, like it was a never-ending cycle, a new small image appeared on the bottom left and slowly the screen began to fill all over again. A new picture. I turned to Blake, who I only then realized had been watching me the whole time. *Creepy, bro.*

"Figure it out yet?" he asked.

"I . . . no," I admitted.

"Welcome to the Eye, Hutch," he said ominously. "Snapping and sending us a never-ending supply of new pictures to examine for FIPs to link to our Shadows."

This was the Eye?!?

"These are the pictures from the satellite?" I confirmed.

He nodded.

"The ones of the future?" I asked.

He nodded.

"Freeze," he said out loud to no one, but instantly the images on the screen froze. He walked over to one of the smaller pictures, tapped it, and said, "Focus." The image became razor-sharp. He pinched the screen and blew up a tiny, tiny speck until I could see it was a car of some kind. Even zoomed in the image was perfectly clear. "Ever see this car before?"

"No," I admitted.

"Of course you haven't. It's a"—he studied the picture for a second—"2047 Hondai, I think."

"You mean Honda," I corrected.

"No, Hondai. Honda and Hyundai merge in 2037. But we're not here for this. Just showing off." He swept the image off the screen and pulled out his own small glass tablet from his pocket. "We're here for this."

The image of a girl, eighteen if I had to guess, appeared on the screen. She had her fist raised and was giving a passionate speech in front of a thick crowd outside a temple. She looked strong, determined, and beautiful because of it.

"The missile that was fired at your plane was in fact from a terrorist group. It was not us. Did they know it was you when they fired? No, they simply wanted to take out a plane and yours happened to have the bad fortune of being the one they fired at. It was bad luck for you but good luck for the world in the end. This," he said, pointing at the woman on the screen, "is eighteen-year-old Inna Yagodina from Astana, Kazakhstan." A younger picture of Inna appears on the screen and she's wearing an International shirt. "And this is her now, at fourteen—around the same time that your plane was shot down. She's a huge fan and like many of your devotees is devastated that you all died. What makes her so important, though, is who her father is and what she ends up doing about it. Stas Yagodina is a back-channel financier of terrorism, and he is the man responsible for getting the money to the group that shot down your plane. In mourning, Inna will refuse to leave her room. Her father, assuming she's in school, gets careless and takes a phone call at the house. Inna will overhear a conversation she isn't supposed to and learns that her father is not the simple businessman she believes but a terrorist and the reason International is dead. She doesn't cry or indulge in woe-is-me; she gets angry and acts.

"Inna offers her services as an informant for the US and eventually becomes one of the greatest assets the US will have. She single-handedly causes the complete collapse of a dozen terrorist networks around the world by spying on her father. After that she will insist we make what she's done public to inspire others to do the same. And boy, do they. Information starts pouring in from all over and terrorist groups around the world fall like dominoes. She is the symbol and voice of her generation in the battle against terrorism and basically shows the world the true power youth can wield when they are organized and determined. Believe me, the results are astounding."

The picture of Inna on the podium appeared back on the screen.

"That's why it is so important that Bobby Sky and Ryo Enomoto of International die," Blake concluded.

I got it. I really did. It made sense, but . . .

"Okay, I get it. Then let us go. I can explain it to him and he'll understand. We'll disappear. No one will ever know we aren't dead."

"It's just not worth the risk, Hutch," Blake said with a

finality I recognized. "Bobby Sky has to die," Blake said in the silence. "Nonnegotiable. But he's an imaginary person, no? A figment of the imagination by the name of Bobby Sky must go, but Robert Hutchinson? One of the best that's ever passed through these halls? Well, I could use someone like him."

My head jerked up. "Are you really . . . ?"

He smiled. "I'm going to bring you home, Hutch. I have use for someone like you."

"My home is by Ryo's side. Death is worth keeping him safe. Why are we even having this conversation? You pumped me full of stuff that makes it impossible to choose anything *but* him. This is pointless."

I shook my head. I'd rolled the dice and come up empty. I'd come here hoping I could fix it. There was no way to fix this. No way to make it right. Nothing I could say to Blake would allow Ryo to live. It was in my DNA to die protecting him. I was ready to do that now. I had faith in Akiko that she'd keep Ryo safe.

"I'm not going to kill you," he went on. "I did all of this to you. That is correct, but then that means I also know that with the right incentives anything is possible. Hutch, I'm going to do some terrible, unforgivable things to you, but in the end they will allow you to lead us to Ryo. We will then unlink you before we kill him so that all the memories from the day you were linked until that moment are erased, this moment included. Witnessing his death will then feel like nothing more than that of a stranger's and it won't faze you in the least. Then you can come home."

I didn't like where this was going. What was about to happen?

A screen on the wall came to life. It was a video stream of Sam. She was sitting at a table cleaning her guns. A normal routine after being out on a mission.

"Tell me where Ryo is hiding or she dies," Blake said flatly.

What? Was he serious?

"You have until five, four, three, two, one." And when he hit one and I hadn't answered, he spoke into his comm device and said, "Proceed."

A man appeared from off-screen, walked up behind Sam, and killed her.

"No!" I yelled as she collapsed to the floor.

I grabbed Blake by the collar, lifted him up off the ground, and slammed him into the wall. I would kill him for this. There was the sound of automatic weapons being locked and loaded behind me. The two guards from outside had come in and were aiming their guns right at me. I slowly let him slide down the wall until his feet touched the ground. If he was scared, he didn't show it.

"Well," he started, "I believe I may have touched on something there. Are you ready to tell me now, or shall we continue?"

I took a step away but kept silent.

A new image appeared on the screen. Leggo. She was rehearsing in an empty studio.

"No," I said, so quietly I'm not even sure it counted as talking.

"Yes, unless of course you'd like to tell me where Ryo is. Is her life incentive enough to betray him?"

I had not expected this. I had not been prepared for this. This was a torture I never could have imagined. And yet, I still couldn't do it.

"You have until five, four, three . . . two . . . one—"

"Wait!" I yelled.

He looked at me, ready for me to speak. But the words wouldn't come. I couldn't do it. My mind wouldn't let me betray him.

When Blake realized I wasn't going to say anything else, he spoke into his comm device and said, "Proceed."

A woman in leggings and dance gear entered the room and they exchanged a few words before Leggo nodded and the woman thanked her. But as the woman walked behind Leggo, she pulled out a wire and in a flash had it wrapped around Leggo's neck.

I wanted to turn away, but I forced myself to watch.

"Are you ready to tell me now, or shall we continue?" Blake asked.

I was numb. I was a mixture of fury, pain, and sadness. I didn't know what to feel or how to feel it. I wanted someone to come in, to stop this, to put an end to it. But I knew that nobody would.

"Please stop," I said. "It's not working. You're just killing innocent people. I can't betray him. It's not working," I repeated, begging him.

"Oh, but it is working. Each death is another chink in the armor. I told you this would be unpleasant, but know that it will continue until you find the power to overcome the link. For your sake, and for the next person who will appear on this screen, I hope it's soon." Blake sighed before he said, "It pains me we've made it this far, but I hope this shows you that I will take it as far as needed."

A new image appeared. It looked like the inside of some office or something. It took me a second to see it. Or, correction, to see *her*. How I'd missed her I couldn't say. She looked exactly the same—just tired—and was wearing her favorite green "work sweater," the one I'd bought for her when I was eleven. The color of her hair, like the sweater, was fading.

"Mom?"

"That is your mother," Blake confirmed. "Give a little wave to the camera please, Dwight."

A man sitting off to the right of my mother gave a tiny little wave.

"No," I started but couldn't finish. I stayed quiet for a long, long time. The first two murders had dented my armor. This had pierced it. He'd done it. He'd broken me.

"Hunter," I finally said.

"Excuse me?" Blake asked.

"Hunter. I want to be a Hunter."

"If you what?" Blake started. "You have to say it."

"I'll take you to him. You unlink me when we get there and let me be a Hunter after that and I'll do it."

Blake smiled and shook my hand. "Deal."

I know. I know. I'm a world-class a-hole. I get it and I agree. I'm not proud about it. Worst day of my life? Probably. But seeing my mother like that, in that situation, had somehow flipped the switch.

Before she appeared on the screen, betraying Ryo hadn't been an option. It hadn't even been on the radar. But that somehow did it.

I felt torn up about all of it, but, I mean, the man had a point. They'd find Ryo eventually. They would. And when they did, they'd kill him. So all my mom's death would do was delay the inevitable. I understood that, so when given the chance, yeah, I saved her.

The Hunter part? That was for me. Why not get something I want out of all this, too? I'd come in here and played my hand, but I'd been beaten by a better one. I had the chance to walk away with something, so I took it. You'd do the same in my shoes. It'd be a hard pill to swallow and you'd hate yourself, but you'd do it. You're not better than me and don't try to say you are. In the end, we are all selfish creatures.

chapter 27

INTERNATIONAL OFFICIALLY BREAKS UP . . . FOR GOOD

Blake was beyond giddy, while I was broken. I watched, defeated, as the kill team was assembled and they loaded up their gear into the jet that would take us across the ocean.

The few words I did say were to confirm where the cabin was on a map. Four Hunters would be more than enough to see the job through. I felt sick to my stomach, dreading what was coming as we boarded the plane, and the feeling only worsened the closer we got. We landed at the New Chitose Airport outside Hokkaido around nine hours later. The trip had gone way too fast. Betrayal makes time fly, I guess.

The wind was biting, but it was sunny as we got out of the plane. That always weirded me out. Sun meant hot to me, so whenever I happened to be in bright sunlight with subzero temperatures, I got thrown off. Made no sense to me. I watched as the kill team moved their gear into a fully decked-out Toyota 4Runner. I could have helped. I probably should have, since the deal was that I'd become a Hunter, one of them, when this was over, but I let them do it all. I'd done enough. *Was* doing enough. I wasn't about to help load up the gear that would finish the job. That seemed a step too far.

AFTER A COUPLE HOURS we turned off the last of the paved roads and hit the snowy back trails. The 4Runner tore through them like they were nothing at first, but eventually the snow deepened and the incline steepened. The SUV was about to be bested. No sooner had I prepared myself for a fun hike in deep snow than the 4Runner, with one last push, climbed over a ledge and came to rest where four snowmobiles sat waiting. Four, huh? There were five of us. Message received loud and clear. They still didn't trust me. I couldn't blame them. I wouldn't have trusted me either.

We drove the snowmobiles, or I guess they drove them and I sat behind a guy named Bale, arms wrapped around him like he was my boy. The trip took about thirty minutes before we parked about a mile away from the cabin. If you've never been on a snowmobile, one thing you should know is that they're loud. Like chain-saw loud. So while they're great for tearing through the backwoods, they're terrible for sneaking up on people. It was better to shut down the roar of the screaming engines way out so that if Ryo and Akiko heard them, they would just think we were joyriders off somewhere far away.

They cut and tore off branches from nearby pine trees and tossed them over the vehicles for a quick bit of camouflage. Once we were loaded and ready, it was time to head out. But before we started, Bale took out a pair of handcuffs and quickly latched himself to me.

"Really?" I asked, annoyed.

"Can't risk you running off to warn them."

"Nobody's running off in this," I said, pointing down at the snow that was up to our knees.

He just shrugged. "Orders. You're really not gonna like this, then," he said, taking out a Muter—a strap of synthetic material you wrap around someone's throat that disables their voice box.

"Seriously? I'm here. I'm doing this," I said angrily.

"Could get cold feet. Just a precaution."

"If I'd wanted to sabotage this whole thing, I'd have crashed the plane or found some way to warn them earlier. I wouldn't be here and, especially, I wouldn't be letting you cuff me."

"You done?" he asked flatly as he stared at me.

"Yeah," I admitted, defeated. This was happening one way or another.

I ducked my head so that he could reach around my neck and strap on the Muter. I'd never worn one before, so I immediately tried to talk. It was weird. My mouth moved and air hissed out of it, but there were no words. Very strange sensation. My mind was saying, "Talk," and my body was responding, but there was no sound.

All of us were in good shape, but even that didn't stop us from getting winded hiking through knee-deep snow in ten thousand feet of elevation. No one wanted to be the one to cave and ask for a break, not that I could have with the Muter on, so we all trekked on. After forty-five minutes of hard going we were there.

After cresting one last hill, we dropped down behind a large snowdrift that gave us both a clear view of the cabin and some cover. The cabin sat in the middle of a wide clearing with nothing but open, snow-covered fields for a hundred yards in all directions. The isolation and the open space all around it was what made it such a great hiding spot. There was no sneaking up on it. This would be a full-charge assault.

Weapons were drawn and checked to make sure they were loaded. I pointed at my throat, asking for them to let me speak.

"You yell, you do anything other than whisper, you die," Sheila, the squad leader, said as she pointed her silenced pistol at me. I nodded.

Bale clicked the remote for the Muter so I could talk.

"Okay, I got you here," I said. "Unlink me. That's the deal."

"Change of plans," Bale said, and before I could react, he muted me again.

"You see," Sheila began, "You're the fail-safe. Let's say we shoot him, but he falls down a slope and we can't reach him? How do we know he's alive? Or the cabin collapses and we can't find the body. How do we know he's dead inside and not running away down some secret passage?" The way she was staring at me, like I was fresh steak, pissed me off.

Unable to talk, I shook my head angrily as I figured it out. It was cruel. It was not part of the deal. They'd screwed me.

"Yes," she admitted. "When he dies, your link, and your reaction will be all the confirmation of his death we need."

I shook my head again.

"Deals change," she said, reading my thoughts.

So I was getting nothing. I was being royally screwed. Ryo was dying and I wasn't going to be a Hunter either? Instead, they would kill him and when he died, my link to him would fry my brain and scramble it up like an egg, or so the rumors went. I'd be a crazy, kill-everything-I-see, wild terror. It was a fate worse than death. I can see you smirking right now. *What? You deserve it,* I can hear you thinking. And maybe you're right. I'd sold out Ryo to save my mom after letting Sam and Leggo die, so why should I get any sort of happy ending out of this? I'd double-crossed Ryo, so it's only fair FATE double-crosses me. There's an irony in that I can get behind and respect. I don't have to like it, though.

An instant later the group burst up from behind the crest and charged at the cabin. Bale jerked me along with him. This dude was strong, but I didn't fight him too hard. My legs were heavy, and my heart was broken, so what was the point of fighting now? This was the bed I'd chosen. I was going to force myself to watch and witness my own treachery. I was sorta looking forward to the impending insanity that was coming for me. It would be nice to finally be done with all this.

Halfway across the snow-covered field, an engine roared to life behind the cabin. We ran sideways to get a better angle. Ryo was streaking away from us on a snowmobile. *Well played, buddy.* Sheila and the other three Hunters opened fire, but by then Ryo had already ducked down the other side of the mountain and was safely out of their line of sight. Their bullets puffed into the snowbank right where he'd been.

We sprinted across the open space (the snow was hard and thin here) and past the cabin. I was sprinting along with them. Heck, I was pulling Bale along. I had to see. I had to know. Was he going to do it? Had Ryo escaped? I allowed my heart to hope. *Go, baby, go!*

By the time we reached the snowbank and got our visibility back, it had been a good fifteen or so seconds. We'd barely covered a hundred yards in that time, but Ryo, running that puppy full throttle and driving it like a boss, was no more than a speck zooming down the face of the mountain toward a deep bowl far below us. The Hunters popped off a few hopeful shots, but they knew it, too, we all did. He was out of range. I smiled. I couldn't help it.

I felt a tug on my wrist and looked down to see that Bale had uncuffed himself from me. Determined and focused, he flung off his backpack, unzipped it, and flipped it open. Inside were four pieces that when put together made a rocket launcher. Like he'd done it a thousand times, which he probably had, Bale slid all the pieces together in seconds, took a knee, and fired off a rocket. The smoke from the tail of the rocket trailed it as it flew toward Ryo. It slammed into the snow behind him with a massive explosion of fire and ice.

The *boom!* echoed all around. For a few seconds we all stood still, waiting for the smoke and ice dust to clear. Was Ryo hit? Sheila was watching me, waiting for my reaction to tell if he was dead. But when the smoke cleared, Ryo was now fifty yards farther still, zipping across the snow.

One of the other Hunters, Griesman, I think was his name, whispered something to Bale. Bale nodded, loaded up another rocket round, and fired. Once again we all watched in silence as the rocket soared toward the speck that was Ryo. He was too far away now. Hitting him would be luck, like winning the lottery three times in a row. The rocket missed him, as it should have. It went over Ryo and detonated about five hundred feet above and in front of him. Yeah, hitting him would have been pretty impossible, but to miss that bad? Embarrassing. It was a terrible shot, really awful. Or was it?

The snow where the rocket had hit cracked and then slid. They'd made an avalanche and it was heading right at Ryo. There was no hoping he could outrun it. No chance it'd miss him. I watched in horror as the wave of white ice slammed into him like a freight train.

Brain, prepare to melt down in five, four, three, two, one . . .

RAGE.

chapter 28

ALLOW ME TO RETORT

I was tackled to the ground and pumped full of some super-strong tranquilizer. I have no clue what happened after that, for real. No clue how long I was out. No clue about, well, anything.

All I know is that here I am, locked in a small cell, rocking the latest trend in straitjackets. They're still white, if you're curious. Where was I? No clue, really. How'd I get here? Somehow. How long had I been here? Days, weeks, years—I didn't know. How was I gonna get out of this one? I wasn't, but I'd known that going in. I had one purpose and one purpose only: to protect my FIP at all costs, my life included. So here I am.

Whoa, whoa, you're probably saying. How are *you* still *you*? Didn't you, like, lose your mind or something when Ryo died? Did I? Didn't I?

Oops, better let out a good scream or two for the camera up in the corner watching me. Gotta play my part. Confused yet? Allow me to explain.

Okay, so I really hope that by now you've figured out that I'm not a total idiot. I'm not smart, I'll give you that, but I'm not a total idiot either. When I was younger, I realized that when people think you're an idiot, they won't expect much out of you. The moment I realized that, I'd gone with it. Played my part, honed it to perfection—a big, dumb oaf from the wrong side of town who surprised you sometimes. So, I'm not stupid. That's really all I was going for here. Now that you believe that, hopefully, we can move on.

Look, I knew from the moment the squad hit us in Wyoming that FATE wouldn't stop until both Ryo and I were dead. There was no way around it. They *always* had their reasons and those reasons never changed. The moment we were marked for death, that was it. We had to die. That was the only way it ended. Period. End of story. But knowing your opponent's hand can come in real handy, so I came up with a plan and it's what I told Akiko back at the Yakuza compound. I also spilled the beans on FATE, Shadows, everything to her. She deserved to know, but more importantly she needed to be able to tell Ryo when the time was right so that he would know who he was up against and why he had to stick to the plan, forever. I wanted to tell him myself, but there was no way he'd have gone along with it. Once they were safely in the cabin in the mountains, she'd let him know what was really going on and get the plan moving.

So yeah, from the moment I found the kidnapped lady and called in the hounds, so to speak, everything that happened after that was planned out. While I was back home dealing with Blake and learning why all of this was happening, Akiko was filling Ryo in and explaining his part in the plan. My part wasn't as simple as his, and it shouldn't have been.

The best lie is the one you believe. It's not a lie then. You'd call someone stupid for saying the world is flat, but if they believe it, actually believe it, you can't call them a liar. They're wrong, but not lying. That's what I had to do with Blake. Actors call it method acting. It's where you become the character you're playing. You live them. You breathe them. Daniel Day-Lewis is famous for it. He takes it so seriously that I heard in one of his movies, he actually built the hut his character lived in using only the super old-school tools his character would have had access to. It's a true commitment to the role down to your soul. That's what I had to do. I had to believe I was really betraying Ryo. That I was selling him out. Blake would have seen right through my lie had it been one. I had to believe for him. To convince Blake I was really doing this. I had to commit to the role. I was the betrayer. The destroyer of trust. And I knew I'd have to fall painfully deep into the lie to make Blake believe, but even I hadn't been ready for what he had in store for me. I will forever have the blood of Sam and Leggo on my hands. I'd allowed them to be sacrificed like pawns in a game of chess. I'll forever be haunted by that decision. But I would do it all over again if I had to. Ryo is what matters; everything else is inconsequential, even them.

WHEN I SHOWED UP with Bale and the others at the cabin, Ryo knew what he had to do and took off across the snowy mountain on the snowmobile exactly like we'd planned. You have to remember that I've been through the same training as the Hunters, and we're taught to immediately recognize how to use the land to our advantage in all situations. Causing an avalanche to wipe out an enemy was year-one-type stuff. And since I also knew that the standard gear for a snow operation like this would include a rocket launcher, well, it was almost too easy to set them up.

That part was a piece of cake. The harder part was figuring out how to make sure Ryo actually survived the avalanche, which was where having been trapped in hotel rooms for hours on end finally paid off. You see, I'd read about these avalanche survival kits in a random magazine at a hotel once. The moment an avalanche hits someone, if they have one of these kits, a protective bubble forms around them and saves their life. They were still prototypes—really expensive and not available to the general public—but I figured if there was anyone who could get her hands on one, it was Akiko. While I'd been captured by FATE, her job had been to track a kit down. So the moment the avalanche hit Ryo, the backpack he was wearing popped open and saved him. Twenty-four hours later, well past when anyone could have survived under an avalanche in case someone from FATE had stuck around to check, Akiko would use the beacon we'd placed on Ryo to find him and dig him out. Where they went after that is a mystery to even me, truly. But since Ryo now knows the truth, I trust he'll understand that keeping his head down isn't such a hard pill to swallow when the alternative is "or death."

Ryo is safe for now, so all I have to do is pretend to be crazy until I figure out a way to escape. Easy peas and string cheese.

My dear friend Blake won't be so happy to see me when we meet again—that much I promise.

I should probably let out another good holler. Maybe some mouth drool, too? On it!

Epilogue

The next phase in my life was not pleasant. Every day was filled with daily beatings, drownings, starvation, psychological torture, and tons more stuff like that. Lots of fun. A summer camp for crazy people. It was all done by the same man, who introduced himself as "The Professor." He had gray, shoulder-length hair and a beard to match. He could be vicious one meeting, friendly the next. You never knew which was coming. He had a real Jekyll and Hyde thing going.

I understood it. It was the technique you'd use to break a wild animal and show them who's Alpha. Totally made sense, too. When fire took a recruit's mind or a Shadow's FIP was killed, they basically became no different than a wild, rabid, crazy animal. Breaking them down and building them back up into something useful would have, in theory, worked. Problem with me was I still had my wits about me. I wasn't an animal that was so easily broken. Luckily, I caught onto the game early and played along. It wasn't easy and I almost slipped up a few times, but eventually he believed I'd been broken and rebuilt and released me into the general population with the others.

Gen pop was a bit surreal. The building was the exact same design, down to the paint color that FATE had been. All the rooms were in the same places, labeled the same, and even had the same stuff in them. I'd never been here before, but I had, you know? The only real difference, though, was that instead of being surrounded by future Shadows, I was surrounded by a thousand or so deadly, highly trained killing machines all teetering on the brink of a total mental breakdown. No one really spoke. It was mostly snarls and growls with a random word tossed in. Like a new caveman language. Talk about nuts. Holy heck.

We were all part of different platoons, but command was decided in a pack-like fashion. Didn't like where you stood in the hierarchy of the pack? Beat the man or woman above you and take their place. Fighting and moving up or down the ladder was a constant, but given how super violent we all were, it was surprising that no one ever died. The reason? The Professor, who ruled over all, had forbidden it. As the true Alpha, his word was that of God and no one dared disobey him. No killing each other was a rule and you'd have had a better chance turning off gravity than finding anyone who'd purposefully break the Professor's rules.

Funny thing was, he was an old string bean of a guy. Any one of us could have broken him in half, but that's the genius, if you want to call it that, of him breaking us and building us back up. He owned you when it was over. Or owned them. I only played along.

It was also a bittersweet time because I got to see classmates I'd thought were dead. When a Shadow in training succumbed to fire, we assumed they were "put out of their misery," so to speak, but apparently they were brought here. I remember running into Sissoko, who I'd been decent friends with. He looked at me and I could tell he recognized me and was trying to remember who I was. His jumbled-up mess of a mind couldn't connect the dots, though. Instead, he got frustrated, growly, and mad and then stabbed me in the side with a pencil. I stopped trying to find my old friends or make new ones after that.

When we weren't fighting amongst ourselves for rank, we were either doing elaborate combat training missions as packs or were left to our own devices to work on weaknesses. Again, crazy, totally unhinged man-animals with access to weapons. Great idea, guys, brilliant. But it worked somehow. This was a very odd place.

The training was so specific I knew it wasn't just "training," but that there was a plan. A reason for it all. We hadn't been rehabilitated out of kindness. We were going to be used for something, something big. There was too much repetition of the same missions for it to be meaningless. I wasn't sure I wanted to know what it was for or to be here when it happened. Or did I? Maybe I could stop it.

I missed Ryo terribly. He was the beginning, middle, and end of my thoughts like that song you can't stop humming. Ha, songs. I used to get paid to sing them. Seemed like a lifetime ago.

I HAVE NO IDEA how long I'd been here. Could have been three months, could have been three years. Time was irrelevant now. I was in the gym on the treadmill. No one really used the gym; they ran around in the woods like animals, so it was one of the few places where you could be alone, or at least be around only a couple of others, for a bit. The Nest was a cramped place, so anywhere I could find to be away from the constant fighting, I went. The weather outside was also beyond perfect today, so I was actually alone in here. I was going to soak it in while I could. I was sixteen miles into my run (and I didn't know how far I'd go since what else was I going to do today?) when the alarms went off. I'd never heard them go off before, so I didn't know what it was for.

Fire? Bad weather? Were we under attack? What idiot would attack us? I stopped the treadmill and looked around, confused. We don't act without an order from the Alpha. Alpha?

On the wall a comm screen came to life and on it was the cheery, bearded face of the Professor.

"Good afternoon, family," he said, sounding happy.

He called us his family. He clearly has a very peculiar sense of family.

"We have a trespasser in our midst who must be located. She recently infiltrated and carried out an attack on our sister facility that killed many of our friends."

What? No one attacked FATE. it would be the stupidest thing in the world. Oh yeah, let me attack a facility that is filled with trained killers training other people to be trained killers. The only place dumber to attack would be this place. Neither option was a smart move. But this girl had done it. Heck, apparently she'd done it, taken out some people, and lived. Yeah, I wondered why she'd tried something so suicidal, but mainly I couldn't stop wondering how good she must be to have survived.

"She has threatened to destroy *us* now and we cannot allow that. She must be stopped, so as a special treat," he said, smiling extra wide, "whoever finds her gets to kill her. I only ask that you please bring me her head when you're done. Happy hunting."

Even all alone down here I could hear distant wails of excitement. I could feel the ripple of energy. He'd lifted the killing ban. Everyone would be in a frenzy to find this person and finally scratch that killing itch. I had no interest in killing anyone, but maybe if I caught them alive, the Professor would make me his Beta or something. Yeah, I get that sounds a little weird, ah, whatever.

Then what he'd said sank in. If this person was out to

destroy him and FATE, then had I just found an ally? Trying to escape out of this place alone was impossible, which is why I was still here, but with a partner and chaos all around? That could work.

Telling us we could kill had gotten the blood pumping, all right, but it would also make us, them, go into total frenzy mode. Focus will be lost as everyone goes into a sort of berserker rage to be the one to find her. There'd probably be more fighting amongst ourselves for prime ambush spots than actual hunting. The Professor, a genius by all counts, had finally made a mistake. He'd given me an opening.

After the message ended, the picture of the trespasser popped up. It was a girl with short black hair and freckles. She was older, but I had always been good with faces and recognized her instantly. I'd helped beat the hell out of her a long time ago at the driving range. She was a Shadow like me. And black hair and freckles isn't a combo you forget.

I smiled. I'd just found my ticket out of here. Her name was . . .

"Ren Sharpe," I said to myself.

My family rules! I have to say it. My wife is the tits, my mom and dad are aces, and my sister is dynamite. Oh, and my kids are pretty cool too, I guess. You are bounce boards, welcome distractions, cheerleaders, and cut-to-the-chase, no BS note givers. If it sucks, you cut deep and true and I wouldn't want it any other way.

Remember that time you did something awesome and then thought, "Well that will never happen again." That's how I felt after *I Become Shadow* came out. No way I was going to get to do another one. No one's that lucky. So thank you to Faye for pushing for *Bobby*, Dan for championing him, and Bronwen for green-lighting this spectacle. While I'm at it, thanks to Abby, Monica, Rachel, and everyone else at Soho Teen for everything you have or will do for this book. Like a good manager, I may not know exactly what you do for me, but dammit if I don't appreciate the hard work.

Music is awesome. Don't ever be ashamed of what tunes you dig no matter how weird. So with that in mind, special thanks to Conner and Poss for showing me that a secret love of boy band music doesn't have to be a secret. And thanks to the rest of The Family for unknowingly being at the core of every character I write.

As usual, Gig 'em Aggies! and Fight On!